Seabreeze Sunset

A Summer Beach Novel, Book Three

by

Jan Moran

SUNNY PALMS

P R E S S

Library of Congress Cataloging-in-Publication Data
Moran, Jan.
/ by Jan Moran

ISBN 978-1-951314-01-9 (softcover)

Cover design by Silver Starlight Designs
Cover images copyright Deposit Photos

Sunny Palms Press
9663 Santa Monica Blvd STE 1158
Beverly Hills, CA, USA
www.sunnypalmspress.com
www.JanMoran.com

Dedication

For all my beach-loving readers.

Chapter 1

Summer Beach, California

IVY BOLTED AWAKE AT A crack of thunder, her heart racing at the late summer storm's intensity, while the sprawling old house shuddered at nature's wrath. She sat up, bracing herself against the onslaught. A few seconds later, a jagged shard of lightning flared outside her window, illuminating her room—and a shadowy reflection in the antique vanity mirror.

Blinking, Ivy drew back against her pillows, her throat constricting in alarm. *Am I dreaming?*

Within a few seconds, another clap of thunder shook the house. Fat raindrops splashed against vintage, wavy glass panes and obscured the outside world. Unnerved, she squinted at the mirror, but the vision had vanished.

Ivy snatched her robe and flung it on, and she was at her bedroom door before she remembered.

Shelly is gone.

Gripping the knob, Ivy leaned against the door. It had been weeks since her sister had left, heartbroken over her relationship with Mitch, the owner of Java Beach.

Ivy still couldn't believe that Shelly meant to stay in New York, even though she had texted to say her former boss had rehired her. But then, Shelly had always been more adventurous, given to quick decisions.

Leaning her head against the door, Ivy breathed in the fresh scent of rain and the earthy aroma it unleashed from the surrounding gardens and warm sand on the beach. She didn't understand her sister. Hadn't Shelly been anxious to change her life? Hadn't *she* insisted that they check out the old house Ivy had inherited in Summer Beach? Ivy had wanted nothing to do with this house at the time—except to sell it as quickly as she could.

Change wasn't easy, even when life forced change upon you.

Ivy drew her robe sash around her waist and tied it. When her husband had died—now more than a year ago— he'd left this historic old beach house to her. He'd spent every penny of their retirement savings on it.

Without her knowledge.

Another burst of lightning, bright as the flashbulb pop of an old camera, lit the room. And again, Ivy glimpsed the shadowy silhouette, now suspended in the corner.

A woman, gazing upward.

Amelia?

Ivy drew flat against the wall, but in an instant, the hazy figure vanished. She wagged her head. The light *had* to be playing tricks on her to make her imagine the former owner.

Before she could collect herself again, thunder ripped open the sky, gripping the house in its angry clutch as rain pounded the terra cotta, barrel-tiled roof overhead.

As thunder rumbled through the old structure, Ivy pressed her hands against the solid wood door. This house had stood for decades. Surely it would withstand nature's latest assault.

Poppy. Ivy flung open the door and rushed through the hallway to check on her niece. After Shelly left, Poppy moved back into Shelly's room. She'd been staying in the maid's quarters behind the house that Jamir had helped renovate before he started his pre-med summer school studies at the university. Now, one family occupied those rooms, which they called the sunset suites. The parents had two rowdy teenagers, a baby, and a nanny in tow. Poppy was happy to move into the main house for two weeks.

As Ivy turned a corner in the hall, she collided with Poppy, whose eyes were round as lollipops with fright. Her niece's honey-blond hair stuck out of a messy topknot.

"Did that wake you, too?" Ivy whispered, sliding her arms around Poppy's slender, shivering shoulders. The soft, midnight rain must have been the leading edge of the rapacious storm.

"And our guests." Poppy nodded toward a glimmer of light under a nearby door to a guestroom. "Gilda's awake."

"Pixie must be a nervous wreck. Fairly early for them." Gilda's Chihuahua often suffered from anxiety. Gilda, who wrote articles for magazines, usually worked late into the night. The Ridgetop Fire had demolished her house, which would take months to rebuild.

Ivy rubbed the back of her neck. She still had an odd, prickly sensation she couldn't explain. The sound of the rain intensified, and Ivy gazed up at the ceiling. "We should watch for leaks. This is the first torrential downpour we've had."

Summer Beach rarely had rain in the summer, so sunshine was practically a guarantee for their guests. Yet, Ivy recalled from her childhood that late August rains weren't unusual in Southern California. Heavy summer rain often spurred flocks of doves and ducks and other migratory birds toward Mexico for winter. Nature, like life, had its seasons.

"We should have umbrellas for guests," Poppy said. "May I spend petty cash today? I can get a few cheap ones."

"No need to skimp," Ivy replied. "Get good quality." Poppy knew their budget constraints, but the cost of a few umbrellas wouldn't sink them. She glanced up again. "Considering this old structure, we'd better get buckets and towels ready."

Ivy hurried to her room to change clothes. After flinging off her short summer gown, she shimmied into a loose, cotton beach dress. With the rain, the muggy air felt damp on her neck. This weather was more like the east coast summers that she'd grown accustomed to these last few decades.

Glancing from her window, she saw a light flick on in Bennett's apartment over the garage. She exhaled a sigh of relief. Just knowing he was awake and nearby was comforting. Bennett was always up early for a run on the beach before reporting in at City Hall. She glanced at the clock. *Six a.m.* Guests would be up early today.

As Ivy pulled her hair into a ponytail, thunder rolled across the beach, and lightning exploded almost instantaneously. Overhead, the lights blinked.

Once, twice, three times.

Ivy paused, holding her breath. The storm was right upon them, carrying with it even more subtropical humidity from Mexico. She slid her feet in flip-flops and grabbed a flashlight she kept by the bed.

Before Shelly left, they had purchased flashlights for every guest room in case of emergencies. Poppy had created a fire-and-earthquake exit plan and laminated it to hang on the back of each door. Though she hoped guests wouldn't need to follow the precautions, Ivy was glad they'd provided them.

Hesitating, she raised her eyes to the spot near the ceiling where some sort of shadow—not that she believed in spirits—

had appeared. She flipped her ponytail to one side. *Merely a trick of the light.* Shelly might believe in ghosts, but Ivy certainly did not.

She paused, listening.

The steady *drip, drip, drip* was not her imagination. There in the corner near the window, water splashed onto the intricate, parquet wood floor.

Ivy lifted a large antique water basin from a dresser and placed it under the leak. Drops tinkled against the white porcelain festooned with delicate pink roses.

"That will have to do for now," Ivy said to herself, craning her neck toward the ceiling. Her heart sank as she stared above. Repairing a roof of this size wouldn't be cheap.

Considering that reservations for the autumn season were already slacking off, she worried about paying the overdue tax bill that Jeremy had let lapse. Unless she paid it soon, authorities would auction the house for back taxes. From her careful calculations, she'd figured she could scrape together the money, but just barely. Less the cost of a few umbrellas to keep the paying guests dry.

How she missed Shelly. Her sister would have laughed and dreamed up another idea to bring in funds.

And now, Ivy could hardly get through to her.

Kneeling, she mopped up water splashes around the porcelain bowl with an old white towel before tucking it around the perimeter. Taking the flashlight, she padded through the upstairs hallway, checking for leaks. Most guests were still resting—or trying to. She heard an occasional murmur float from the rooms that lined the hall.

Gilda cracked open her door. In one hand, she gripped the collar of a pink robe that matched her swirl of cotton-candy hair, and in the other, she held the quivering Pixie. "What a storm, huh?"

"We can always use the rain," Ivy said, trying to sound upbeat.

"Going to delay construction."

"Can't imagine it will last too long," Ivy said. Gilda was comfortable at the inn, but she'd told Ivy she was eager to get her high-strung Chihuahua back in familiar surroundings. The fire that raced along the ridge overlooking the village of Summer Beach had damaged and destroyed many homes a few months ago. Along with Gilda, other ridgeline residents, including Bennett, Imani, and Jamir, had taken rooms at the inn.

Ivy scratched Pixie behind the ears, and the little dog licked her hand. "A flashlight is in the nightstand drawer in case we lose power. Any leaks in there?"

"I'll check and let you know." Gilda stifled a yawn.

"Appreciate that." Ivy smiled. "Try to get some rest."

Ivy descended the stairs to the first level. Poppy was in the ballroom tucking towels against the base of a door that faced the south, where the strongest winds were pummeling the side of the house. Rainwater was pooling under the arched Palladian doors.

"Let me help you," Ivy said, sinking to her knees beside Poppy.

"Thanks, but I've got this, Aunt Ivy," Poppy said. "Maybe check the kitchen?"

Ivy hurried through the spacious ballroom where they'd hosted a celebrity-studded wedding last month. And last week she'd rented out the space for a beach-front fundraiser for the local children's hospital one afternoon and a lavish *quinceañera* for a teenaged girl and dozens of her friends and family the next evening.

A knot formed in Ivy's throat. She recalled the artistic floral arrangements Shelly had created for the wedding and thought how her sister would have loved decorating those last two events. As it was, Ivy had engaged one of Imani's acquaintances for floral designs. While the arrangements were pretty, they didn't have the memorable panache of Shelly's designs.

Shelly had even been absent from her video channel on gardening and design. She had repurposed video footage from the inn's garden, not that anyone but Ivy and Poppy would know.

As Ivy approached the kitchen, she heard a low hum. Pushing open the door to the 1950s vintage kitchen, she saw Bennett hosing up a puddle with a wet vacuum.

Glancing over his shoulder, he said, "Morning, Ivy. Figured you might need help. Seems water blew in under the door."

From the deep tenor of his slightly gravelly voice, Ivy could tell he'd just rolled out of bed. His voice sent a tremor through her.

A biological, physiological reaction. A little dopamine on the brain, that's all.

At the sight of Bennett working in the kitchen, memories of her late husband flashed through her mind. Jeremy would never stoop to manual labor—*his* words, not hers. Jeremy would have stepped over the puddle in his polished Gucci loafers and told her to call a handyman. As soon as Jeremy left for the office, Ivy would simply do what was needed if she could. After a while, she'd become quite proficient.

Watching Bennett, she thought how nice it was to have someone who took action without being asked.

Bennett didn't have an ego to stop him from helping. That's why he was an effective mayor. Summer Beach was lucky to have him.

So am I, she mused.

"How did you know to look for this leak?" she asked, skirting the damp floor.

"A real estate agent has to watch vacant properties. The property manager was good, though."

Bennett turned off the machine and swept a dry cloth across the tile floor. As he worked, Ivy could see his muscles through his thin T-shirt. He kept fit, and she liked that.

Not that it should matter to her, of course.

Still, she appreciated how he always thought ahead. "Is

your apartment leaking?" He was staying in the old chauffeur's quarters above the garages behind the main house.

"No, that roof is sound."

"Not in my room."

He jerked his head up and leaned back, putting his hands on his thighs. "You have a leak?"

"I put a big porcelain bowl under it."

"Something's not right," he said, rising. "We inspected this house before the transfer. Let's have a look." He wound the hose around the vacuum canister and rolled it to one side.

"I sure appreciate what you do around here," Ivy said. "With Shelly gone, there's so much more to take care of."

"Hey, it's what I do." Bennett put his hands on her shoulders and gazed at her, a half-smile tugging at his lips. "You're quite capable, Ivy. Everyone knows that. But it's okay to ask for help."

"I just miss Shelly," she said, sidestepping the topic. Heat from his hands coursed through her, his touch warming her, comforting her. She had to be careful not to shift her emotional dependence from Shelly to Bennett. *Because that's what this feeling is, right?*

Thunder cracked around them, splintering the pre-dawn sky with a flash of lightning. Ivy cried out, and Bennett slid his arms around her. Outside, the downpour sluiced across the glass panes and pelted the veranda.

Ivy shivered in Bennett's embrace. While the thunder and lightning didn't scare her, the feeling of his arms encircling her

she'd go back to work in New York." She hoped Shelly wasn't seeing her old boyfriend, Ezzra.

Gilda's door cracked open. "Everything okay?" she asked. Pixie was still shivering in her arms. "The lights are flickering."

"Everything looks good up here," Bennett said. "No sign of leaks." He stopped to scratch Pixie's head. "How's our little kleptomaniac doing?"

Pixie's tail wagged, and she licked Bennett's hand.

"The thunder scares her," Gilda said. "But she's doing well in her obedience training. They're teaching her to respect other people's things. And return what she *borrows*," she added, emphasizing the word to Pixie.

"I've noticed that," Ivy said, wondering if Pixie grasped the concept. She had seen an improvement in Pixie's behavior. At least they knew where to look for items that went missing now.

"Any water leaks in your room, Gilda?" Bennett asked.

"Nope. We're cozy and dry, but let me know if you need to inspect. I can move to the parlor. I'm working on an article on autumn feasts and new ways to prepare pumpkin, squash, and yams."

"Sounds yummy," Ivy said. "I'll ask the housekeeper to check your room." A woman who lived nearby helped tidy guestrooms and manage mountains of laundry. Without Shelly, Ivy had to redistribute her work, and she quickly found that she and Poppy alone couldn't handle it all. Besides, Poppy still had publicity clients in Los Angeles to serve.

"We have to go now," Gilda said, waving Pixie's paw. "Say goodbye to your friends."

Bennett grinned and turned back to Ivy. "Let's have a look at your room before I have to go to the office."

Ivy led the way and eased open her door, half expecting to find the shadowy apparition again.

Bennett frowned at the soggy ceiling. "Quite a leak you have going there."

"Thank you, Mr. Obvious," she said, chiding him.

Grinning back at her, he ran his hands across the walls. "Walls are dry, so the water is contained to the ceiling. There's a depression in that part of the ceiling, a low part where water has gathered. You might have a broken tile on the roof, or maybe rain is blowing into the attic area from an opening under the eaves."

"Hadn't thought of that." As Ivy put her hands on her hips, a thought struck her. "Is it much of an attic?"

"Never checked it out, though the inspector would have," Bennett said. "We can look for the access point later. I've got a city council meeting today, and I need to prepare an update on Darla's case."

Ivy sighed. "Don't remind me." Her neighbor was still pursuing a lawsuit against the inn. Even though Imani was handling the case for her at no cost for her time, Ivy still had deposition costs and other fees to pay.

"She's a stubborn one. Did her sister Debra give you any

guidance?"

"Not really." Debra had traveled to Summer Beach to settle the estate of their parents, but Darla protested that, too. When Debra was staying at the inn, she'd confided quite a lot in Shelly. Finally, Debra left town to let her sister cool down.

Ivy circled the steadily dripping leak. "I can ask Forrest to look at this." Her brother and his children—Poppy, of course, but also Reed, Rocky, Coral, and Summer, along with his twin Flint and his kids—had helped clean and paint the house before she and Shelly had opened for business.

Bennett put his hands on his hips, considering the job. "Not much to do until after the rain stops. In the meantime, monitor this pot." He lifted the porcelain bowl. "That'll be heavy when it's full of water. I can empty it for you."

"We can manage, I'm sure. You have a busy day." Still, she appreciated that he was thinking about her.

He peered at the ceiling. "If the wallboard gets soggy, you'll have to replace part of the ceiling. Forrest will be the best judge of that." He brushed a soft kiss on her forehead. "I have to go. Seriously, call me if that pot gets too full. Or ask Jamir to help. He's young and strong."

"Okay. Off with you then."

"See you later?" When Ivy nodded, he added, "Tacos on the beach tonight?"

"That would be great." They had an easy, no-pressure relationship, and she liked that.

After the Independence Day boat parade when Bennett

had held her hand in public, their relationship had shifted into the open. Summer Beach locals had become accustomed to seeing them together. Jen and George, her new friends who owned the hardware store, had asked them to a Saturday barbecue. Nan at Antique Times seemed delighted that she and Bennett were spending time together. In fact, Ivy suspected that when Bennett had asked Nan to find other lodging for him after the fire, Nan might have neglected her duty.

Ivy smiled as she thought of Nan. In retrospect, she was glad for Nan's part, although she wanted to take her relationship with Bennett slowly. There was still much Ivy didn't know about him. And she'd learned her lesson—the hard way. She thought she'd known everything about her husband, but she hadn't. This house alone was proof of that. And she figured rumors of Jeremy's affair still swirled in Summer Beach.

Could you ever know everything about a person? Probably not, she decided. But *when* in a relationship was time enough to entrust someone with a shared future?

Ivy pressed a hand against her temple, which always throbbed when she thought of Jeremy's actions. She had to let those thoughts go. Moving forward was the only way out of the mess he'd left.

Still, she doubted that she ever would have reconnected with Bennett after all these years had it not been for Jeremy's deceitful, irresponsible actions. Shelly would say it was cosmic revenge, or the universe trying to set the world back in order. Ivy wasn't so sure, but she'd spent many restless nights wrestling with her anger at Jeremy. Yet even she had to marvel at how popular the inn had become—though not without great effort.

Ivy would miss Bennett when he moved back into his house on the ridge. The construction work on his home was slow because many homes had suffered damage. Bennett was also waiting to use a local Summer Beach contractor and tradespeople.

Deciding to inspect the ceiling closer, Ivy brought out a stepstool and an old wooden measuring stick she'd found from her closet that had a slogan printed on it. *We measure up at First Summer Beach Bank.* She smiled at the nostalgia and recalled that when she was a little girl, banks often gave out measuring sticks or toasters for opening accounts. How times had changed.

Climbing up to get a better look, she gently poked the ceiling with the measuring stick. It felt like a soft-boiled egg ready to burst.

Just then, she heard Poppy's distinctive knock on the door. "Come in."

"Hey, Auntie. We've got a new—oops, watch out." Poppy ducked.

Pieces of paint fell from the ceiling, exposing faded patterned wallpaper. "Probably painted over with an oil-based paint. This is still holding a lot of water." Ivy poked it again, her spirits falling as she mentally calculated the cost of a roof repair.

"Wow, the roof is leaking a lot."

"Might be through the exterior eaves," Ivy said, trying to stay positive. She tapped the ceiling. "This is strange. Looks like an outline of something here." She drew the wooden measuring stick across the ceiling, tapping in a square pattern. "This could be an entry into the attic."

Poppy's eyes widened. "Oh, my gosh, I wonder what's up *there?* Let's look."

"Not today. We have a full house of guests." Ivy climbed down the stepstool, but it was all she could do not to launch into another investigation.

Poppy wriggled with excitement. "Maybe Amelia hid more things up there."

Ivy gazed up at the ceiling. "An attic opening would be obvious. Amelia liked more obscure spots."

"Could be why she sealed it."

Over the past few months, Ivy and Shelly had discovered several hiding places of the grand old home's former owner, Amelia Erickson. She had been an avid art collector but suffered from Alzheimer's in her later years.

Poppy twisted her lips in thought. "Maybe this wasn't the original opening. Who would put an attic entrance in a bedroom?"

Not the original... "Then, where *is* the attic entry?" Ivy stared at Poppy, wondering. Just then, her phone in her pocket buzzed with a text. She took out the phone and glanced at the screen. *Shelly.* Her heart skipped as she opened the notification. Shelly had sent a single heart emoji. Ivy smiled. At least Shelly was thinking of her.

Want to talk? Ivy tapped back.

Maybe later.

Suddenly, Poppy cried out, "Auntie, watch out!"

Chapter 2

WHEN POPPY CALLED OUT, IVY instinctively ducked. Still, she wasn't fast enough to avoid a piece of the ceiling that nicked her in the shoulder as it crashed down, narrowly missing the porcelain bowl in the corner of Ivy's bedroom.

Above them yawned a gaping hole, and brown water splashed into the porcelain bowl below. A damp, musty odor wafted from the opening.

"Guess I shouldn't have been poking around up there." Ivy knelt to lift the soggy piece of the ceiling and shifted it onto a towel. She wiped her forehead with the back of her hand.

"I'd love to see what's up there," Poppy said, stretching

on her tiptoes.

Ivy scrunched her nose at the odor. "Me, too, but we need to clean up this mess and check on our guests."

Poppy knelt gingerly beside her to help. "I sure wish Shelly would come back."

Ivy tossed debris onto a towel. "I know. We all miss her, but she has her life to live. If it's not here, we have to accept that."

"You two were always up for exploring this old place together. That was a lot of fun."

Ivy had to agree. Losing Shelly to New York was another painful loss. *Is it selfish to feel this way?* Ivy wanted the best for her sister. Given that Shelly wanted to start over and meet someone, Ivy thought Summer Beach might hold a happy future for her. And then there was Mitch, of course. A rumble of thunder drew her back, and she rubbed her arms.

Although Ivy was curious, she was uneasy over what they might find. They'd already uncovered priceless paintings and crown jewels. *Hot property,* according to Shelly. The rightful owners were thrilled, of course, but Ivy was tired of answering FBI questions and dodging media calls. Amelia's treasures often proved time-consuming, and Ivy's focus had to remain on doing whatever it took to pay off the tax bill.

However, Ivy suspected that Amelia might have tucked away more letters or journals in the house. She'd already found some evidence of that. And she would hate to find out that the woman was really an avaricious hoarder of illicit stolen goods. No telling what that attic might hold.

Maybe Shelly *was* right about Amelia.

A draft of cold air swept around Ivy, and she shivered, although the storm had ushered in warm subtropical air. And didn't heat rise? Realizing she was in the spot where she'd seen the strange shadow this morning, she stepped aside. *Pure coincidence.*

"I'll call Forrest right away," Ivy said. "Your father offered to help, so I'm going to take him up on the offer. Come on, help me with this basin. It's heavy, but together I think we can dump it in the tub."

"Yuck, this stinks," Poppy said, wrinkling her nose. "I'll make sure Dad gets out here right away."

"Try not to breathe through your nose." Ivy nearly gagged, then held her breath. The rainwater from the attic was brown with decades of attic dust. "On three. One, two, three."

Ivy and Poppy hefted the heavy porcelain bowl, around which swirled delicately painted roses and vines. For all she knew, this was a priceless piece. After lugging it to the bathroom, they poured the dirty water into the tub and ran steaming hot water after it.

"That's good," Ivy said, brushing her hair back from her face with her forearm. "I'll have to disinfect the tub." Her dress was drenched in the front, so she'd have to change again, too. She repositioned the porcelain bowl under the gaping hole in the ceiling while Poppy mopped up splashes on the floor.

Ivy winced against the strain the weight put on her back. "I'll watch this today, but I have to change and check the kitchen again. Jen probably has nice umbrellas in stock. You should go early."

"I have to replenish the breakfast fare," Poppy said, though she looked wistfully at the opening in the ceiling. "Oh, I almost forgot. I came to tell you a new guest arrived, so I told her we'd have a room shortly. I'll check on the sunset suites to make sure they're dry before I give her a key. She looked exhausted but said she'd wait at Java Beach. Guess she knows her way around town."

"Awfully early for check-in."

"Maybe she had an overnight flight."

"With this weather, that would've been a rough landing at the San Diego airport," Ivy said. "Even if planes were cleared to land, which was doubtful."

"Maybe she flew into L.A. Might be clear there. Or she drove in."

At the nape of her neck, Ivy felt a funny tickle, which her mother had always insisted was her intuitive alarm. "During a stormy night?" Something didn't register. Maybe the woman had left her husband or fled an abusive situation during the night.

Poppy raised her palms and shrugged. "Mystery woman, I guess. No reservation on iBnB either. But she asked if you were here."

"What was her name?"

"Paisley Forsythe."

The name didn't register. "Probably a referral. Would you make sure her room is extra comfortable?" They'd been welcoming a lot of referral guests now, especially after the big wedding that Carol Reston and Rowan Zachary put on when their respective children married.

"Will do," Poppy said as she hurried out.

And yet, thinking about what Poppy had said, Ivy paused.

She couldn't help herself.

Tapping the flashlight on her phone, she hiked her wet skirt and stepped onto the ladder. She flicked the beam toward the gaping hole and peered at it.

Rain was pelting onto the tile roof, and it sounded even louder in the attic. Peering up, she couldn't see anything except old wooden rafters. She wasn't quite level with the attic floor, but she could see enough. *And smell enough.* A musty stench assaulted her nose, and she hastily retreated.

She expelled a sigh of relief. *Nothing to see up there.* Tamping down her curiosity, she hurried to clean the tub, bathe, and change. She put on a peach seersucker sundress that brushed her calves and set off her eyes—or so Bennett had once told her. She added dangly coral earrings and a quick swipe of matching lipstick before fluffing her hair. The humidity brought out soft waves, which Shelly insisted were in style. Fortunately, beach causal was the Summer Beach vibe.

As Ivy passed a guestroom, Imani opened the door. Her

guest's vivid orange sundress was a shock of happy color. Imani had pulled a matching, broad-brimmed straw hat over fine sisterlocks that dusted her shoulders.

"Good morning," Ivy said. "I hope you managed some sleep through that storm."

Imani fell into step with Ivy as they made their way down the staircase. "Last night's sweet rain lulled me to sleep, but that crack of thunder this morning sounded like the devil shaking the house." She shook her head as they approached the dining room. "Wouldn't you know it? Nature gives me a day off but wakes me before sunrise."

"To fully enjoy it," Mitch said behind them.

Ivy turned around, surprised to see him. His spiky blond hair was damp, and he wore a retro-yellow rain slicker over a bright Hawaiian shirt.

"Thanks for braving the deluge," Ivy said.

"A little rain doesn't bother me." Mitch grinned, motioning to the large white box he carried. "Gotta make the donuts no matter what."

"Seriously?" Ivy lifted the lid of the box he carried. Inside, nestled among the usual pastries, were chocolate cake donuts with a light dusting of powdered sugar. "They smell heavenly. I'm sure our guests will love those."

"If Jamir doesn't see them first," Imani said, chuckling. "Luckily, he's still sleeping, so folks will have a shot at them, at least."

"If you run out, I've got more at the shop," Mitch said,

jerking a thumb over his shoulder. "It's a slow morning," he said. "With all the rain, I thought I'd make some comfort food. Most of my crowd won't come out until the sun does."

"Our guests will be slow to venture out, too." Ivy glanced over the gathering guests, who were ambling downstairs and filing into the dining room for breakfast. Poppy was arranging yogurt and cream she'd brought out from Gertie, the hard-working vintage refrigerator.

As Imani made her way toward the coffee, Mitch placed the pastry box on the serving table and turned to Ivy. "Hey, could I talk to you for a minute?"

"Sure, but I need some coffee, too," Ivy said. "And I have to check the kitchen. We had a mini-flood earlier."

Mitch trailed Ivy to the kitchen. There she saw that Bennett had wedged a towel against the door to keep rain from blowing in.

"Looks like a problem here." Mitch opened the door a crack to inspect the door jamb. "Weatherstripping is old. I can replace that for you."

Ivy inclined her head. "I'd like that, thanks. Jen and George opened a house account for me, so you can get anything you need at Nailed It."

His offer touched her. Even without Shelly around, Mitch was happy to lend a hand. That seemed to be the way of life in Summer Beach. Ivy was still getting used to accepting help, even though she freely gave it when she could. As a mother who'd cared for two active girls and wife to a husband who traveled for business, she wasn't used to having much help, so it still surprised her when people offered.

She poured a coffee for herself, though Mitch waved off her offer. Easing onto a stool, she asked, "What's on your mind?"

Mitch ran a hand through his sun-bleached hair. "Have you heard from Shelly?"

"Brief texts. She *hearted* me this morning. You?"

"About the same." He chewed on his lip in thought. "What do you think I should do?"

Sipping her coffee, Ivy pondered his question. If she knew the answer, she'd be talking to Shelly, but that's not what Mitch wanted to hear. Or what he was actually asking. She leaned forward, tracing the rim of her cup with a finger. "Do you really care for her?"

Mitch looked surprised. "I've never felt like this about anyone else."

Ivy lifted her coffee and studied him over the rim of her cup. This wasn't about getting Shelly back because she missed her. Ivy and her sister were adults, and they'd lived apart for years, but life was more fun with Shelly around. "That's not what I asked. Do you think you have a forever kind of feeling for her?"

Scrubbing his scruffy chin, Mitch blew out a breath. "Yeah, I think I do."

"You *think*? This is one area that you have to know for sure. I know it's only been a few months, but many people who fall in love know those feelings early in the relationship." She'd felt like that about Jeremy. *And maybe, if I'm honest with myself...* She blinked away the thought.

"This is new territory for me, but yeah, I'm sure." A flush spread across Mitch's face. "Love wasn't something my folks showed much. Definitely didn't talk about it. They were too busy screaming at each other." He shrugged. "Me and Shelly...we've talked, but I don't know how to tell her."

Ivy touched his hand. "But you know how to show it. And you did. Deep down, Shelly knows that." Ivy thought back to the countless ways Mitch had shown Shelly he cared. From helping her clear the yard and plant numerous flowers, shrubs, and trees...to making her favorite pastries and dishes with local, organic ingredients just the way she liked them. "It's time to be direct with her. Tell her what you feel."

"I don't get it." Mitch furrowed his brow. "Is that all I have to do? Tell her that I love her, and she'll come back?"

Oh, he's so young. Ivy curved up one side of her mouth. She felt like she was talking to one of her daughters. Still, he seemed so right for Shelly. "If that's what's in your heart. You two have to open up to each other. You can care a lot for someone, but it's often what *isn't* discussed that chips away at the relationship, so you need to talk. And you have to love the whole person, even though no one is perfect. That goes for both of you."

As Mitch mulled this over, Ivy thought of Jeremy. She had loved him, but he'd let her down in many ways that added up. Small things, mostly. Like taking for granted all the mundane things she did for him because he expected it. Or insisting he was too busy to take her calls when he was traveling. Not until after he'd died had she discovered his betrayal. *Right here. In Summer Beach.* Thinking about that, Ivy pressed her lips together in a firm line.

"Yeah, I'm far from perfect," Mitch said glumly. "I should have told her about my history. After I landed in Summer Beach, I decided to become a new person. The kind of person I knew I could be. So, I buried my past. Bennett knew about it—" He stopped and swallowed hard, then met her gaze and held it. "I'm talking about my prison record. I want you to know about that."

"I know," Ivy said gently. "Bennett and Shelly told me. In confidence, of course." Mitch's prison time had surfaced when the tiara had gone missing from a cache of royal jewelry. Ivy and Shelly had found the pieces stitched up inside a large doll in the trunk of the vintage Chevrolet. In the end, Pixie was to blame, but not before Chief Clarkson brought Mitch in for questioning. "I'm sure that experience changed you a lot."

"Made me wake up and grow up." Swiping the heel of his hand across his eyes, Mitch blinked back his emotion. "I need help," he choked out. "I know Shelly's the one for me, but I don't know how to say it. And I miss her so much."

Even though Mitch was mature for his age, he wasn't much older than her daughters. Ivy's maternal instinct was to take him in her arms and comfort him. But he was an adult, not a boy, even if his emotions were raw. Instead, she placed a hand on his shoulder. "Then you have to figure out how to reach her. Find out if you're truly compatible. You can love someone, but not have the same values or be able to live with them." She paused, then added, "For many reasons."

"This is complicated."

You have no idea. Ivy wagged her head. "Just talk to her. Ask what's important to her." She hesitated again. "And ask her about Ezzra."

"Who's Ezzra?"

"Old boyfriend in New York." Ivy had suspected that Shelly hadn't told Mitch about him. "That's why she came to Summer Beach with me. They had just broken up."

Mitch ran his hands through his hair again, leaving it disheveled, though that was his style. "I thought things were so good between us, but I guess I didn't have the whole picture."

"Now, you do." Ivy nodded outside. "Rain is subsiding." The fierce wind had ceased, and the thunderstorm had slowed to a patter. Just as Mrs. Reed had forecast.

Mitch pushed off the stool. "That means my customers will be out soon. Better get back." He paused by the kitchen door. "Bennett and I talk, but I like getting a woman's perspective."

She smiled at him. "All you have to do is ask."

Poppy pushed open the kitchen door just as Mitch was leaving. "See you tomorrow, Mitch?"

"Probably be Katie again in the morning." He glanced

pointedly at Ivy. "Something important just came up."

Ivy grinned. She had to hand it to Mitch. Not only was he a hard worker, but he was also the kind of guy who knew what he wanted and figured out a way to get it. Java Beach was proof of that. Whatever he was planning, she hoped Shelly would be receptive. In her heart, Ivy knew Shelly cared for him.

Ivy drained her coffee and motioned to Poppy. "I'll help you in the maid's quarters."

"You mean the sunset suites."

"I keep forgetting." That wasn't the only thing Ivy forgot. Without Shelly, her to-do lists had become even longer.

The rain was easing. Hurrying through the sprinkles, they crossed the terrace and raced past the pool toward the rear units that Jamir had helped renovate. They wound through a tropical paradise—sweet white plumeria blossoms, lush ferns, and pink ginger flowers—that Shelly had planted along the stone pathway. Ivy felt like she was entering another world. "Feels like a tropical getaway back here."

"Reminds me of Hawaii, especially in this weather," Poppy said. "Mom and Dad rented a house there last summer for all of us. We had a blast. Bet we could get a lot of families in these rear units."

"Great idea. Would you post that online for me?" Pausing at the door to an empty suite that a guest had vacated late yesterday, Ivy turned the key. She stepped inside. "Looks dry enough."

Poppy sniffed the air. "A little musty." She opened a window. "I'll clean the room and air it out. And bring in a couple of tuberose stalks from Imani's arrangement in the foyer. The scent's amazing."

"Most guests love the tuberose." Imani often brought blooms and greenery from her flower stand, Blossoms. Ivy tried to pay her for them, but Imani wouldn't hear of it, saying that before losing her home in the fire, she used to fill her rooms with flowers. The Seabreeze Inn was her home for now, Imani argued, so Ivy had given up. But she sent all their guests to Blossoms.

"I'll give you a hand with the room," Ivy said. "That woman sounded like she needs a rest."

Poppy beamed at her. "Thanks, Aunt Ivy."

After cleaning and tidying the room, Ivy and Poppy made their way back to the kitchen. Ivy spotted a cell phone on a stool.

Recognizing the surfing-themed case, Ivy said, "Looks like Mitch left his phone."

"Not the first time." Poppy laughed. "Want me to run it back to him?"

"No, I'll do it." The skies were clearing now, though more rain was forecast tonight. "While you're looking after the breakfast crowd, I can welcome our guest and pick up umbrellas on the way back." Ivy stretched her arms overhead. "Besides, I can use the walk." Poppy had taken over the yoga classes and often the beach walks while Ivy tended to guests or other business.

"There's a lone umbrella in the stand by the front door," Poppy said. "Oh, and Paisley is a slender blond, about 30. You can't miss her—she's pretty attractive. Could be an actress or a model. She's wearing a pink slip dress."

"I'll find her." Ivy started off. Once outside, she unfurled the red-and-white umbrella emblazoned with a Boston Red Sox logo. She hadn't used it since she'd moved from Boston.

As Ivy sidestepped puddles along the lane that led into the village, she drew in a deep breath. Salt air mixed with the rain's natural ozone scent, drenching the seaside town with a fresh aroma. Everything looked clean. It was as if Summer Beach had been power-washed in the downpour. The air was sweet, the ground moist, and the landscape rinsed of sand and dust.

Tourists were filling the town again, their sweatshirt hoods and sunhats warding off the sprinkles that persisted as the sun peeked through the clouds. Fluffy clouds parted overhead, though darker ones still gathered to the south.

After leaning her umbrella by the door, Ivy stepped inside Java Beach, where beach reggae was blasting. The rich aroma of coffee wafted through the cafe. Instantly, she recalled the day she and Shelly had arrived in Summer Beach. That was the first day they'd met Mitch.

Even then, Ivy had noticed the blisteringly fast attraction between them.

Ivy peered past the line that stretched to the door and

spied Mitch at the counter, waiting on customers. Wedging her way past a tiki torch and ducking under a nautical net, Ivy held his phone up like a trophy. "Look what I found," she called out.

When Mitch saw her, he lifted his hand and waved her around the line. "I'm forever losing that." He shot a glance toward the indoor tables. "Um, thanks. See you later."

"Actually, one of our guests is here."

Mitch arched a brow with practiced nonchalance. "Oh?"

Under a vintage Polynesian travel poster of grass-skirted hula dancers, a willowy blond woman sat at a table hunched over a tall cup of coffee, chewing a fingernail. She fit the description Poppy had given her.

Ivy lifted her chin toward the woman. "Bet that's her."

"I don't think so," Mitch blurted out. He sounded oddly worried.

"Really?" Ivy looked around at the tables, but that was the only woman who fit Poppy's description. "I'll see," Ivy said. Maybe their earlier conversation had disturbed Mitch.

"Ivy, no—" Mitch began, but a customer stepped up to order.

Ivy cut through the crowd.

At the first table sat Darla, her gaudy rhinestone sun visor and dyed royal-blue hair were hard to miss. She was in a heated discussion with two other local women. At the sight of Ivy, the older woman stopped in mid-sentence. The other women shifted their eyes in Ivy's direction.

Nan's husband, Arthur, sat at another table, having his morning coffee with his cronies. With a quick glance over his shoulder, he stood abruptly. In his clipped English accent, he said, "Ivy. What are you doing here?"

"Morning, Arthur," Ivy said brightly. "Returning Mitch's phone and looking for an early guest."

"Well, I, uh…" Arthur shifted on his feet in the narrow aisle between tables and smoothed a hand over his shiny bald head.

Ivy couldn't step past him. "Good to see you. Say hello to Nan, will you?"

Still, Arthur blocked her way. Was he trying to be funny?

"Excuse me, Arthur. I think I see our new guest." Ivy waggled her fingers at the blond woman.

"I don't think—"

"Hi, are you Paisley?" Ivy moved an empty chair and cut past Arthur.

The woman looked up and nodded. A taut expression drew her perfectly arched brows together. She had the air of a cornered cat about her.

"I'm Ivy from Seabreeze Inn." Ivy smiled and extended her hand. "We have a room ready for you now. Sorry to make you wait. All this rain."

"Ivy…Marin?" The woman stood, unsteady on her feet. Her wrinkled pink dress had thin spaghetti straps and was awfully short for her long tan legs. It didn't look much like a traveling outfit, but then, this was the beach. People wore what they felt like.

"That's right, but most people call me Ivy Bay. How'd you hear about the inn?" As the words left her lips, Ivy noticed that the noise level in the room subsided.

Paisley seemed to choose her words with care. "I read about it online. I mean, I've seen it before, but it's been more than…a year ago." Her last words were barely audible.

"Whenever you're ready, Poppy can show you to your room." Ivy handed Paisley a key to the sunset suite they'd cleaned. It wasn't any of her business, but Ivy couldn't help asking the question that nagged her. "You arrived awfully early. Red-eye flight?"

"I drove in from L.A."

"Through the storm?" But then Ivy remembered that the rain showers had come from the south—the opposite direction. "Guess it wasn't as bad driving from the north." Still, this was an odd time to arrive. The woman must have left Los Angeles at 4:00 a.m. And she had no reservation. Ivy was curious. Judging from the hushed tables around them, her neighbors were wondering about Paisley, too. Summer Beach residents were an inquisitive lot.

"It was a little scary," Paisley replied. Her slightly hoarse voice was low.

Someone coughed, and Ivy glanced behind her. Darla and Arthur and the others seemed to be surreptitiously listening. Ivy turned back to her guest. *What a nosy bunch.* She laughed to herself, her thoughts drawn again to the day she and Shelly had landed here, straight from the east coast.

Ivy slid the room key from her pocket and handed it to Paisley. "You're in one of our newly renovated suites behind the main house. The Seashell Suite on the lower level. You'll see it marked on the door and the key. Take your time and enjoy your coffee. I'll be back at the inn shortly, and if there's anything I can do, please let me know."

"Could we..." Paisley hesitated and shifted her gaze, then brought it back to rest on Ivy's face. She seemed to search for words again.

Or was she holding something back?

"Yes?" Ivy drew a hand across the tickling sensation on the back of her neck. The younger woman was clearly agitated. She'd chewed off much of her pink nail polish. *What's going on with her?*

Paisley only shook her head.

Drawing on her familiar cache of innkeeper pleasantries to ease the awkwardness, Ivy added, "After you've rested, please join us later in the afternoon for wine and cheese in the music room."

"I don't drink." Paisley drew the edge of her lip in.

Behind them, another cough erupted. Ivy turned in time to see Darla quickly glance away.

"Well, let me or Poppy know if you need anything," Ivy said. "I hope you enjoy your stay with us at the Seabreeze Inn." She turned to leave.

A strange sensation settled over Ivy. The tourists were

chattering with excitement, sharing opinions on the best tacos and margaritas, and the right SPF level for a partly overcast day like today. Yet, all the locals were staring at her. Arthur had compassion in his eyes, Darla looked strangely upset, Katie hovered behind the latte machine, and Mitch stood stoically behind the counter.

What strange beans were brewed in the coffee this morning? She nodded to the locals on her way out.

Outside, she picked up her umbrella, though she didn't need it anymore. As she continued toward the hardware store, she wondered about what had happened back there. It was as if people were listening...and waiting. For what?

For something to happen...

Who was Paisley Forsythe?

Was she a celebrity? Ivy didn't recognize many of them in Summer Beach. They kept low profiles and blended into the summer crowd with their jeans and sundresses. She hadn't known Carol Reston by anything other than her stage name, so maybe...

No. Not a celebrity, but someone they knew. She'd sat alone as if ostracized.

Ivy recalled the strained look on Mitch's face as she left. He'd looked almost...apologetic. Why?

Alone on the sidewalk outside of Java Beach, Ivy hurried toward Nailed It, intent on finding umbrellas for the guests before the next storm passed through. The scene at the coffee shop had been so surreal—as if an apology hung in the air.

She thought of Mitch's behavior and what Arthur had said. Even Darla's attitude had changed.

What was different about today?

Only the new guest at the inn. *Paisley Forsythe.* Young, beautiful…and deeply troubled about something. Not that her guest's business was any of hers.

Who *was* Paisley Forsythe?

Suddenly, a repulsive thought whipped through her mind like a tornado.

No. An appalling, nauseating thought. *No, no, no.*

Could it be? As Ivy reached for the entry door at Nailed It, a chill seized her limbs. Through the glass door of the hardware store, she saw Jen on the phone, her forehead scrunched into a sorrowful expression.

Suddenly, without a doubt, Ivy *knew.*

Leaning on the door, she blinked, her eyes blurring. She tried to take a step, but her legs gave way beneath her.

Jen whirled around. "Oh, my poor Ivy!" she cried, racing toward the door.

Ivy felt a chilly blackness draw over her eyes like a window shade.

Chapter 3

UNDER THE MARINE-BLUE AWNING at the entry to
City Hall, Bennett shrugged out of the hooded slicker he usually used on his boat. He hung it on a temporary rack Nan
always wheeled out by the door in inclement weather, which
was rare here. Beside the coatrack, a colorful array of umbrellas filled a stand, and a pair of yellow rain boots stood beside
it. He opened the door and went in.

"Morning, Nan."

"Hi, Mr. Mayor. Trouble this morning?" Nan gathered a
handful of pink message slips.

"Old house, heavy rain. Helped Ivy with a leak." Bennett
thumbed through the messages. "Busy morning here."

"Yours is. And you have an appointment with the city attorney on the mediation. Maeve is talking to Boz right now in the conference room. They just began."

"On my way." Bennett asked Nan to follow up on a couple of calls before stopping by his office to get his notes and files for the meeting. Since Summer Beach was a small town, the city attorney, Maeve Green, was a retired judge who handled the city's few legal matters on a part-time basis. That is, until Jeremy Marin had challenged the zoning on the old Erickson estate—*Seabreeze Inn*, he corrected himself. That's when the city had to hire an expensive team of San Diego attorneys to defend their village life.

He'd thought Summer Beach was back to business as usual until Darla's attorney had served a complaint on the city—and on Ivy.

In an attempt to reduce the number of cases on the docket, the judge had ordered mediation, so here they were, strategizing on how to defend the city's decision to grant a zoning variance to Ivy so she could operate as a bed-and-breakfast inn. As head of the zoning department, Boz had actually blessed and led that effort.

After retrieving his paperwork, Bennett joined Boz and Maeve in the conference room.

"Hi, folks." As Bennett took a seat, he glanced outside the glass windows. Rain sluiced across the window panes, making the usually sunny room as dreary as the issue they had to address. Beyond the village, charcoal clouds hung over the beach, and the iron-gray sea crashed to vacant shores. Every boat was tucked into the marina. Yet as dark as it was, sunshine would prevail.

"Boz was giving me the back story on Darla." Maeve adjusted her red-framed glasses, which contrasted with her short, steel-gray hair. "Do you think this is a personal vendetta, or do you think it is a valid concern for the community?"

Bennett turned the question over in his mind. "Couple of issues at play here," he replied, lacing his hands. "After the Jeremy debacle—and thank you very much for your service on that—his widow listed the property for sale."

Nan slipped inside and took a seat at the conference table. She plopped down a notebook printed with mermaids and sat next to Boz, ready to take notes.

Maeve looked down at her yellow legal pad. "That's Ivy, right? And you're living in the house, too?"

Across the conference table, Boz suppressed a small smile, and Bennett realized how that sounded, not that Maeve meant it that way, he was sure. But a mediator might not understand.

"I'm renting the former chauffeur's cottage above the garage. Others who sustained damage to their homes—or lost them entirely—in the Ridgetop Fire are also living in the main house."

"Right," Maeve said. "Didn't mean it the way it sounded. But you and Ivy are dating, yes?"

"I don't know if I'd describe it quite like that," Bennett said. Although he cared for her, the word *dating* sounded so…sophomoric. As if he didn't know what he wanted. Or it seemed like their relationship had progressed beyond what it had. Physically, that is. He drew a finger alongside his nose. What exactly *was* their relationship?

"The mediator will," Maeve said. "And Darla is charging that because of this relationship, Ivy received preference in the zoning change."

Boz laughed. "Quite the opposite. I don't think they liked each other very much at the time. Ivy came to me."

"In fact," Nan added, "Bennett asked me to find him another place to live."

"And did you?" Maeve asked.

Outside the window, lightning flashed, followed by a more distant roll of thunder.

Nan's face flushed. "Guess that's a signal to tell the truth." She glanced apologetically at Bennett. "I told him I was trying, but actually, I didn't try very hard. I was busy, but that's not why I didn't check." Her cheeks nearly matched her red curls now. "Arthur always warns me not to play matchmaker."

"That's okay, Nan." Bennett valued Nan and her work, and he'd suspected that she hadn't looked around much. "No harm done. Maeve, I can't deny that I was attracted to Ivy at the time, which is why I referred her to Boz to remove myself from the zoning consideration."

"And yet you voted for it." Maeve stared at him.

"I did." Bennett knew Maeve was being thorough in order to uncover all the pitfalls that could trip them up. "I voted for the new zoning because I believed Summer Beach needed another inn. Some of our residents had no other place to go after the fire. For many of them, it would have been a gross inconvenience."

"Like Imani," Nan added earnestly, spreading her hands to make her point. "She owns the flower stand in town, and her son Jamir is starting at the university next month. To have lived with her sister in Los Angeles wasn't an option. The commute would have been four hours in traffic each way."

Maeve nodded and made a note. "Had you not voted, what would the vote have been?"

"Tied," Boz said. "Summer Beach has one other inn. That's not enough for a town this size, especially for residents with extended family, or for those who want to hold parties at a larger venue. The city gains taxes and events bring in business to local shops. It's a win-win for everyone."

"Except for the next-door neighbor." Maeve tapped her pen.

Nan crossed her arms and huffed. "Well, Darla doesn't have to call the city to complain about vagrants breaking into that old house anymore."

Maeve's interest was piqued, and she looked between them. "Was that a problem?"

"Increasingly so," Boz said. "You know how cold winter nights can get. People were breaking in and starting fires. Burning furniture in the fireplaces, which hadn't been properly cleaned in years. I feel bad for folks, but that's a fire hazard that could affect the entire city. Our fire captain, Paula Stark, was quite concerned."

Maeve nodded and made a note before turning her attention back to Bennett. "You had the house listed for sale?"

"I did, but the only interest was from developers who wanted to raze it to build a multifamily tower or a giant resort." Bennett turned up his palms. "Either option would have destroyed views, limited beach access, caused parking issues, and generally destroyed the neighborhood character. And I have the email inquiries and other documentation to prove that."

"What about individuals?" Maeve folded her arms on the conference table.

"I'll share the inquiry records with you, but there weren't many." Bennett was having a hard time reading Maeve.

"The house was a real white elephant," Nan said.

"That's true," Bennett said. "Excellent location, but the layout is kind of old-fashioned for the way people want to live today. The house also needed a lot of upgrades. If people want to spend that kind of money on a home, they generally prefer ritzier La Jolla or Del Mar."

"Hmm," Maeve said. "And were you dating Ivy at the time?"

"Hadn't met her. She was in Boston." Bennett stopped. "Wait, that's not quite right. I had met her years ago when we were teenagers. I didn't know her well, she had a different last name, and she looked a lot…different. I didn't make the connection until after she'd moved here."

"Okay, here's where we are." Maeve laced her fingers. "You all make some good points, but the relationship between Bennett and Ivy is questionable as to how it might have influenced Bennett's vote." She held up a hand to Bennett. "I know you're a by-the-book kind of guy, but I'm just telling you how it looks. And Darla's attorney is seizing on that."

Boz splayed his hands on the table. "In my opinion, the inn has added to the value of the neighborhood without detracting from it any more than a single-family use would have. Anyone who bought it would have had a large family or parties. And Ivy added a parking area in the rear of the house, so there's no impact to on-street parking."

"And the events Ivy holds benefit the community," Nan said. "Kids practice in the music room, and Ivy offers art and yoga classes to guests and residents. And it's a venue for weddings and parties."

"So noted," Maeve said.

"What happens if the mediation is settled in Darla's favor?" Bennett asked. He had to know what options Ivy would have.

Maeve shook her head. "Ivy would lose the license."

"But she could offer rooms by iBnB, right?" Nan asked.

"That's in the complaint, too," Maeve said. "Darla is trying to block that, which would impact other Summer Beach residents who rent out extra rooms, especially in season."

"And that would hurt our residents and visitors," Boz said.

"And spell disaster for Ivy." While Bennett was grateful to his team for standing up for their residents, Darla was a Summer Beach resident, too. But then, so was Ivy.

"I'm afraid so," Maeve said. "But this complaint is about Summer Beach, not Ivy. She has her own to deal with, I understand."

"Imani is representing her," Bennett said. He knew the case was weighing heavily on Ivy, especially since Shelly had left.

Maeve made a few notes and then took off her glasses. Leaning forward, she asked, "To help with the mediation, what do you think really drove Darla to file these complaints?"

Bennett rubbed his forehead. Outside, the rain was subsiding, and in the distance, he could see the sun's insistent rays breaking through the storm clouds. If only he could illuminate the truth behind Darla's actions, he was confident they could avoid this legal storm, too.

"Jealousy," Nan said.

"Inconvenience," Boz ventured.

Bennett stroked his chin. "Maybe a feeling of being left out."

Maeve put her glasses back on. "Or an addiction to drama." She picked up her pen again. "Perhaps simply greed."

"She has a substantial inheritance coming," Nan said.

Bennett and Boz turned to her in surprise.

"How do you know that?" Bennett asked. Nan's ability to ferret out information from people amazed him.

"Her sister Debra came into our antique shop," Nan said. "I sort of overheard a phone call she took. I couldn't help it, really."

Maeve chuckled. "You'd make a good private investigator."

"Or *instigator*," Boz said, grinning.

"These details are helpful," Maeve said. She made another note and crossed a letter with a flourish. "This kind of information helps us know how to negotiate in the mediation. If we can't reach an agreement, we'll have to go to trial. And you know the time and cost associated with that."

Bennett nodded. *Indeed he did.* "Nan, please share whatever you know with Maeve." What did Darla want, he wondered? He knew what her friend Matthew, the attorney representing her, wanted. Old Matthew was always out for a buck. He was the kind of guy who hoarded every dime and seldom spent a penny. He was wealthy, but you wouldn't know it.

Narrowing his eyes, Bennett asked, "Think it has more to do with Matthew?"

Maeve shook her head. "He's tough to read."

They spoke a few more minutes about how to prepare for the mediation, which would take place at the office of the mediator—another attorney. While they talked, the rain let up, and the sun shone through.

Bennett hoped this was the worst of his day.

Maeve slid her notes into her briefcase. "Let me know if there is anything else you can think of. I'll go to work on this right after my walk on the beach. I think I'll have time to get that in before the next storm passes through."

As Bennett was walking Maeve out, his phone buzzed in his pocket. After saying goodbye to the attorney, he checked his phone.

"Hey, Mitch. What's up?"

"Thought you should know we've got trouble." Mitch's voice dropped a notch. "Paisley is back in town."

"Oh?"

"And you'll never guess where she's staying."

"Please don't make me. It's been a tedious morning."

"She checked into the Seabreeze Inn. She was in here having coffee when Ivy delivered the key. Seems Paisley had arrived early, and Poppy checked her in."

Bennett didn't like the sound of this. Whatever Paisley was up to couldn't be good. "Wish I'd seen her first."

"Want me to say something to her?"

"I'll talk to her." Bennett thought he could get Paisley's number from the owner of a boutique on Main Street that Paisley used to frequent. "I don't know what she's doing here, but I hope Ivy doesn't find out who she is. No one said anything at Java Beach, did they?"

"They didn't say *anything*. That's what tipped Ivy off, I think. I couldn't decide whether or not to warn her, but then I saw her stumble into Nailed it. Jen's with her. I called Jen to warn her that Paisley was back, so she knows."

Bennett checked the time. He had another meeting he could push to the afternoon. "I'll see what I can do. Thanks, Mitch."

After hanging up, he turned to Nan, who clearly overheard his side of the conversation. He drew a deep breath. "You might as well hear it from me first."

"Arthur already texted me," Nan said, shaking her head. "Go. I'll cover for you."

Chapter 4

WHEN IVY REGAINED HER EQUILIBRIUM, Jen was kneeling beside her, helping her sit up. "What happened?" She was at Nailed It, and just minutes ago, she'd been at Java Beach. What was she doing on the floor?

"You fell and almost hit your head," Jen said with compassion. "Come into the office. I'll get you some water."

Ivy squeezed her eyes shut as the memory flooded back. *The woman in the pink dress.* Blinking, Ivy rose and followed Jen on wobbly legs. Blood roared through her brain, and she pressed a hand to her pounding forehead. "That woman…"

Jen sighed and handed Ivy a bottle of water from a small

refrigerator in the office. She leaned against a desk and peered at Ivy. "Are you sure you're okay?"

Ivy nodded. In Jen's small shared office, she eased into a chair and clutched the water bottle. On one desk were framed pictures of Jen with her sisters on the beach, and on the other desk were photos of George's prize fish. Smiling faces surrounded her, but she was so angry and hurt that she felt like smashing something.

Ivy pressed her fingers against her temple, which was throbbing as much from her revelation as her momentary blackout. "That's *her*, isn't it?" she urged, spitting out the words. "The woman Jeremy was seeing." *Paisley Forsythe.*

Jen nodded. "I can't imagine what she's doing back here," she said, flexing her jaw. "What nerve."

"It was so surreal." Ivy spread her hands as she told Jen what had happened. "All the locals grew so quiet when I walked into Java Beach. Now I know what everyone was thinking."

"They were probably bracing themselves for a blow-up. But you didn't give them the satisfaction." Jen grinned. "Good for you."

"That's because I had no idea who she was. Arthur seemed at a loss for words, and even Darla was speechless. Stupid me, I should've known right away."

"Don't deride yourself. You didn't know because your husband hid his affair." Jen pressed her lips together. "And none of us knew what to say when you arrived in town."

"He put you all in an awkward position, too." Ivy could understand their reticence. "But why on earth would she want to stay at the inn? Surely she knows who I am."

"I'm sure she does." Jen began to say something before stopping to shake her head. "You know, Paisley fancies herself a designer. She used to talk about how she was going to do all the decorating for whatever your husband was going to build there. Maybe the curiosity of what you'd done with the old house was killing her. And it looks great, by the way."

Ivy couldn't help but smirk a little. She took a swig of cool water and held the bottle against a pulsing vein above her eye. She thought about all the work that she, Shelly, and Poppy had done on the house. Maybe Paisley had seen Shelly's videos where she'd chronicled the renovations. Ivy curved up her mouth in a half-grin. "We did a pretty good job, didn't we?"

"Yes, you did," Jen said forcefully. "And that husband of yours should have known better than to take up with that woman."

"Seems no one in Summer Beach liked Jeremy very much either, but he did have a good side to him," Ivy said thoughtfully. She had plenty to be furious with him about, but he was gone. What good would it do? She was trying to let her anger go and recall only the good times. But it wasn't easy. Hurt still lined the walls of her heart.

Jen was staring at her, waiting.

"He was good with our girls," Ivy said, blinking back the

fury that seized her chest. *Actually, he'd spoiled them.* Even so, Misty had a proper perspective on life, but Sunny had developed an unfortunate entitlement problem that she'd have to resolve.

"I'm sure he used to have some good points if he attracted you." Jen sat in a chair across from her. She tucked her long, highlighted hair behind her ears and rested her elbows on her faded blue jeans. "Now, what are you going to do about that woman?"

Ivy expressed a puff of air between her lips. "First, I'd like to strangle her. I'll tell her she can't stay at the inn. But I'm also curious about what she wants. And I need to talk to her."

"You can do all that, except for the strangling part," Jen said. "Have it out with her, and then show her the door. Which you painted a very nice shade of carnelian red, by the way."

"Thanks to your recommendation."

"You're the one with the good eye for color." Just then, the bell on the front door jingled, and Jen leaned out of the open office door. "It's Bennett. Want to see him?"

Ivy wiped wayward tears from her cheeks. "I'd like that." Had he heard what happened?

Jen gave her an encouraging smile. "I have a customer, but I'll be right back."

"Hey, are you okay?" Bennett came into the office and sat beside her, sliding his arm around her.

"So, you heard," Ivy said, leaning into him, though she

couldn't help feeling perturbed over how fast word traveled in Summer Beach. That was the downside to life in a small town. She was here to earn a living and create a home, not be the topic of conversation at Java Beach. "Which arrow of gossip sailed your way?" she asked sharply.

"It's not just gossip. People are genuinely concerned about you." Bennett smoothed a hand over her arm in comfort. "Mitch called me. He didn't know how to tell you, and while he was trying to figure it out, he stuck his head out the door and saw you come in here—in obvious distress." Bennett jerked his thumb toward the front door. "I'm glad Jen was here."

How many other people had witnessed her meltdown? "So, were Jeremy and—" She stopped to force the woman's name from her throat. "...*Paisley* together a lot here?"

She watched Bennett sigh and shake his head. Obviously, he hated to tell her, but to his credit, he went on. She took another drink of water and lifted her chin.

"They went to a lot of restaurants here, and Paisley holds a black belt in shopping. All the shop owners knew her. She always carried a wad of cash."

Ivy crossed her arms. "Bet that's what happened to our emergency funds. After he died, I discovered a lot of cash withdrawals in California." By managing all their accounts, except for the household account, Jeremy had been careful not to alert her.

"I'm really sorry you have to go through this," Bennett

said, his voice full of compassion. "If you'd like, I can talk to her."

"This is my problem. And I need to know certain things." Ivy curled her fingers into a tight ball. "I'll confront her when she returns to the inn."

"You can reach me anytime," Bennett said, gently taking her hand and folding it in his against his heart. "Poppy is there with you, or call Imani or Jen or Nan. You're not in this alone."

Not alone. Ivy sucked in a breath. Bennett's words were a salve to her soul.

"You're part of Summer Beach now," Bennett said. "And we protect our own."

Ivy quirked her mouth to one side. She appreciated Bennett's words. In her heart, she knew them to be true. Misfortune often united communities—and her misfortune was Paisley, whom no one seemed to care for anyway. Ivy had only been here a few months, yet this little community had embraced her as one of their own.

Except, of course, for Darla and her instigator attorney, Matthew.

Jen slipped back inside the office. "Is there anything else I can get you? Cup of coffee, more water, a baseball bat?" She put her hands on her hips and threw a swift look at Bennett. "That last bit's a joke, Mr. Mayor. I'm not advocating violence."

"Actually, I came here to get umbrellas for our guests,"

Ivy said.

"Come on, you," Bennett said, kissing her cheek. "Get your umbrellas, and I'll drop you off at the house."

Jen quickly showed Ivy a selection of umbrellas, and she chose their best ones. Large, marine-blue with white trim and sturdy wooden handles. Jen put the umbrellas on Ivy's house account with a generous discount.

"Thank, Jen," Ivy said. "For everything."

Jen hugged her. "You've got this."

Did she? For all her outward bravado, Ivy was still uncertain. She imagined how Shelly would react in this situation, recalling how she'd gone after Darla when their crotchety neighbor threatened them with derogatory front-yard signage.

Ivy managed a wry laugh. "I'll channel Shelly's belligerent New York attitude." Anger would see her through, even when she didn't trust her words.

"That I'd like to see," Bennett said as he walked her to his SUV that was parked in front of Nailed It.

Ivy glanced around as she stepped up into his vehicle. People were emerging onto the rain-dampened streets. Fortunately, there was no sign of Paisley.

After Bennett got into the car, he rested his hands on the steering wheel. "Mitch said Paisley looked pretty upset. She might feel guilty and want to apologize."

Ivy puffed out a breath of disgust. "*I'm* the injured party, not her. If that woman is here to confess, it's not my place to absolve her of guilt and make her feel better."

She fastened her seatbelt with a resounding click and faced forward. After Jeremy's death, when she'd discovered he'd cheated on her, she had trudged through the mud of an abominable emotional abyss.

"I have a right to my anger." From the side of her eye, she could see Bennett studying her.

"Not arguing with that," he said, turning the ignition.

Ivy folded her arms. Was Paisley like the man who confesses his affair to his partner for the selfish reason of easing his conscience—without thought to the potential of irreparable harm to his wife? And then refuses to seek counseling as the wife is left sorting through the rubble of the relationship?

Quite possibly.

After the short drive, Ivy grabbed the umbrellas and hopped from the car. She deposited the umbrellas by the front door and then sat at the reception desk to one side of the grand foyer.

Poppy hurried to meet her. "Mitch called and told me everything."

At least Ivy didn't have to repeat the story to Poppy. "And has our new guest returned?" She hated the taste of that woman's name on her tongue.

"No sign of her."

"When she returns, I'll take her to the library for a private discussion." Ivy pressed her lips in a grim line. As the anticipation unleashed acid in her stomach, she made a few notes, though she hardly needed to. The questions had been seared into her brain during months of sleepless nights.

Poppy drew her brow up in concern. "Are you sure you don't want me to stay with you?"

"I've got this," Ivy said, resolute.

Poppy cocked her head. "You sounded just like Shelly when you said that. Bet she'll be sorry she missed this."

"It's not a performance," Ivy said. "But that odious woman will not leave here lightened of her guilty burden at my expense."

"She doesn't have to stay here," Poppy said. "I can reverse the credit card charge."

Ivy considered this. "Wait before you do that." She wanted Paisley's explanation first.

Poppy gave her a sympathetic glance. "I'll go check on the leak in your room. But I'll be around if you need me."

After Poppy disappeared upstairs, Ivy heard a buzz on her phone. She checked the incoming message.

Sunny.

Ivy thumbed through the text.

Mom, I'm working as a nanny. Misty probably told you.

Work was good for her. Ivy's fingers flew over the tiny keyboard on her phone. *That's good, darling.*

No it isn't! Hours are tooooo long and the pay sucks.

Ivy sank her face in her hands. Though she loved her daughter, she wasn't in the mood to deal with Sunny's histrionics. What sort of work did she expect to find without a work permit or a degree in a foreign country where she barely spoke the language?

Separating her anger at Paisley from her frustration with Sunny, Ivy tried to contain her emotions. Lashing out at Sunny wouldn't help either one of them. She tapped out a message. *With some experience, you can find something else after a while.* Ivy paused. *Proud of you for hanging in there.*

After sending it, Ivy stared at the rotating dots. Sunny was texting more.

Nooooo! Going to quit, but I need to go to Ibiza for the summer parties. Can you pleeeeze help? Need $$$.

Ivy would barely have enough for the pending tax payment. *Thank you, Jeremy, for spending money on Paisley Puss instead of paying the taxes on your secret house adventure.* Sunny didn't *need* more parties; she needed to work or return to school. And Ivy had to save her livelihood. Time for tough love.

Sorry, no.

Whyyyyyy not?

"Because you need to grow up and accept responsibility," Ivy mumbled. Footsteps sounded on the hardwood floor. "One moment," she said.

You made your decision. Now you have to work for what you want to do. Have to go. Love you. Call if you really need me.

Ivy tapped *send* and looked up.

Right into Paisley's cowardly, pale-blue eyes.

Chapter 5

IVY CLOSED THE LIBRARY DOOR and turned to Paisley. Composing herself, she folded her arms. "We need to talk, don't we?"

Paisley's slender shoulders quivered, despite the warm, tropical-level humidity. "You know."

"I figured it out pretty quickly," Ivy said as evenly as she could. "All the locals in Java Beach were giving you the evil eye."

"I used to go there with…" She raised her eyes to Ivy and croaked out a name. "Jeremy."

Hearing her husband's name on this woman's lips felt like a hot poker through the heart, although Ivy tried not to let it show. "Clearly, they remembered."

Nervously, Paisley licked her lips. "Could I have some water?"

Heaving an audible sigh, Ivy pulled her phone from her pocket and texted Poppy. She didn't want to leave Paisley alone, even though she couldn't wait to get rid of her. Ivy waited for the woman to begin, but she seemed…scared. Not the gloating type she'd imagined. Or was she? Was this an act?

Ivy shoved her phone into her pocket. "You didn't arrive here by accident. What do you want?"

"Can we sit down?"

Ivy nodded toward the table where she and Poppy usually sat to review the reservations and draw up plans. "There," she said, motioning to an extra chair.

Paisley stretched out a quivering hand and eased into the chair. "The house turned out really nice."

"We're not here to discuss the décor, are we?" It was all Ivy could do to keep her anger in check.

"No."

An antique clock Ivy and Shelly had discovered on the lower level ticked loudly in the silence between them.

Just then, Poppy came in with two glasses of water. She placed them on the table over a pair of coasters. "Call me if you need anything else." Casting a sharp look toward Paisley, she turned and left.

Paisley pressed the glass to her lips, which were full and puffy and looked like they'd been stung by a bee. Her hand was shaking, and a little water dribbled down her chin. She wiped it away with her finger. Her bitten-to-the-quick nails looked inflamed. She pressed her lips awkwardly against the rim of the glass to drink again.

Injections, Ivy assumed, taking a moment to let her gaze trail over this alien woman. Expert highlights, ultra-long hair—probably extensions—expensive designer purse, an air-brushed tan over too-thin limbs. False eyelashes. High, full breasts, perfectly rounded. Ivy wondered if Jeremy had paid for those. Paisley clearly took good care of herself, but instead of looking well-groomed, her look came together in an *I'm-trying-too-hard* manner.

How had Jeremy fallen for such a clichéd look? Poppy had described her as pretty, and maybe she was, in an Insta-gram kind of way. *All veneer, nothing beneath the surface.* Ivy laced her fingers together, striving to keep her emotions under control. "Tell me why you're here."

Paisley nodded. "It's part of the program, you know."

A waft of perfume—too strong for a warm day—assaulted Ivy's nose. Staring at her, Ivy waited. *What on earth is she talking about?*

"But I have to tell you what happened first."

"Spare me the details," Ivy snapped, surprising herself at the harsh bite of her words. "I can imagine."

"I-I have to. See, I came to a charity ball at this house." Paisley gulped air in her headlong race to unburden herself. Her words spilled out, tumbling over each other like rusty

JAN MORAN

jacks. "With a guy I used to date. Sort of, I mean, he's a partner where I work. That's how I knew about this place. The
town was so cute, and I saw Carol Reston here. I got her auto-
graph, you know, though she probably doesn't remember
me."

Ivy's thoughts centered on Jeremy. *How could he?* With
this woman—this *girl*—who was not much older than Misty.
Paisley was blabbering like a child who'd been caught in a lie.

"Go on," Ivy said before grinding her teeth in a death
clamp to avoid shrieking something angry and archaic, like
Have you no shame? She felt so old right now.

The clock ticked off the interminable seconds.

"First, I want you to know that I planned to get Jeremy,"
Paisley said, her voice gaining strength. "He wouldn't have
looked at me—well, he *looked,* but he probably wouldn't have
acted on…well, you know, if I hadn't planned it all. I'm not
proud of that. Still, he *was* French, and you know how they
are."

Ivy had a sudden maniacal desire to slap Paisley's face,
yell and shove books off the bookshelf, hurl the small vase of
flowers against the wall, kick in a door, smash the clock, and
drive this feeble siren out of here with the force of her fury.

But she resisted.

Deep within, Ivy *needed* to know what had happened, in
what was surely a perverse longing that would not benefit her
mental health. To keep from screaming, she drew one hand
under the table and clenched her fist until her nails dug into

her skin. She drew a breath and said, "Go on."

Paisley flicked off ragged pink nail polish chips from her disastrous manicure. "Jeremy didn't stand a chance. I-I planted myself in his hotel room after a long night at the bar with his clients. I worked for them, you know, taking notes in meetings, though I used to be an actress, you know."

"No, I *don't* know," Ivy snipped, the sharp words slipping out.

Paisley instantly deflated. "That's what my acting coach used to say. Stop saying *you know*. But it's hard, especially when you're nervous." She raised her thumb to her mouth and slipped the nail between her teeth. After ripping off a hangnail, she seemed to become aware of her actions and dropped her hand.

The clock thundered on, measuring off seconds that stretched into infinity.

"Please. Finish." Ivy counted silently to herself.

"Okay. So I'd heard one of the partners talking about this property," Paisley said. "They thought it was a great development deal, and they talked about how much money they could make from it. I didn't have any way of making that much money. I thought if I took the deal to Jeremy, I could get a referral fee, help build and decorate it, and maybe be a part-owner." She glanced away, and her voice shrank. "Maybe even get married."

Ivy almost shot out of her chair. "You knew he was married. And had a family." She gripped the arms of the chair.

"He told me right away. But I acted like it didn't bother me, that what we had—"

"That's enough." Ivy flung up a flat palm toward Paisley.

"Look, he was trying to break up with me. The guilt was killing him. He wasn't really a player, you know, not like other guys I've been with."

Ivy grasped at this knowledge like a lifeline. *At least he felt guilty.* It was a tiny consolation, though not worth much. "Why are you telling me this?"

"Because I have to," Paisley whined. "I've done eight steps. You were at the top of that list."

"I don't follow." *Where is this girl going with all this?*

Paisley's face grew red, and her eyes filled with tears. "I numbed myself with alcohol. I knew I didn't really love Jeremy. I mean, he was so old. And I've learned I wasn't capable then...for a lot of reasons I probably shouldn't tell you about. See, I was reaching for something that wasn't mine to get."

"No," Ivy said, holding back.

Paisley sniffed. "Jeremy wrote me a letter saying he was breaking off our relationship because…" She paused to fumble in her cavernous bag for a tissue and wipe her stained cheeks. "You were the most important thing in the world to him. See, he planned to quit the assignment, put the property up for sale, and confess everything to you. He wanted to start his life over with you. You know, since Misty and Sunny were gone."

Her daughter's names on this woman's lips was yet another deceit. "You're lying. He didn't do any of that."

"That's because I took some pills right before your birthday, woke up in the hospital, and pleaded for him to come. He did. And that's when he died." She pressed a fist against her mouth. "I felt like I killed him."

Ivy passed a hand over her forehead, shifting into a clinical explanation that was factual and safe. "He had an aneurysm. A weak spot in a blood vessel in his brain."

After taking a drink of water, Paisley continued. "I drank myself into a haze after that. Finally, I had to get help. And I'm doing pretty good on the twelve-step program. But I will always be an alcoholic, you know."

As much as she hated to admit it, this was beginning to make sense to Ivy.

"Step eight," Paisley said. "I made a list of everyone I harmed, and I'm ready to make amends. I couldn't sleep last night thinking about it, so I jumped in the car and drove right here before I could change my mind."

"You don't have to make amends to me." Ivy wanted nothing to do with this troubled young woman.

"No, I do. I've started step nine, which is…" Paisley paused for another swig of water. "To make direct amends to people I've harmed unless it would injure them. That's a direct quote from the A.A. program," she added. Digging into her purse again, she drew out an envelope.

Ivy caught her breath when she saw the written address. It was Jeremy's handwriting. "I don't need the details." She peered down her nose at the letter.

Paisley slid it across the desk. "This will make amends. Just read it."

Instinctively, Ivy shoved the envelope back as if it were red-hot and radioactive. "I will *not* read a letter my husband sent to you. And asking me to do that *will* harm me, I assure you. You've already broken my heart. What more do you want?"

Paisley's mouth dropped open. "But this is really important." She pushed the envelope back toward Ivy.

"Only to you," Ivy said, unleashing her emotions. "You want me to absolve you, to forgive you, to make your life right. But I can't. I *won't*. Actions have consequences. What you did tore my heart out. Was it not enough to lose my husband? And then, to find out about *this* place." Ivy waved her hand around the room. "And *you*. How dare you think that I might feel sorry for you? Why, you just said you didn't love Jeremy. How could you mourn him?"

Without answering, Paisley bowed her head.

Shaking with fury, Ivy jabbed a finger at her. "You. Don't. Know. How."

With a great gulp, Paisley broke down sobbing. "You're right," she wailed between her tears. "I've failed the program. I'll leave."

"Yes, you should." Ivy sprang from her chair to pace the room, hatred flaring in her heart for this, this...*creature*. For Jeremy, again. She couldn't even offer pity to this mess of a woman.

"Look at yourself." Letting out a huff, Ivy flung her hand toward Paisley. "I can't turn you out like this. You're an emotional mess, and you haven't slept. In your condition, you might kill someone on the highway back to L.A. I won't have that on my conscience. Go to your room and rest. And leave when you're fit to drive."

Paisley nodded through her tears and stumbled toward the door. "Just read the letter. Please?"

"Go." Ivy turned away, fuming. When she heard the door click, she whirled around and shook her fists at the ceiling. "Why?" she cried out. "Why?"

Snatching the envelope Paisley had left, Ivy flung it into the trash.

There was nothing in it she ever wanted to see.

Her every limb suddenly shaking with pent-up anger, Ivy sank to the floor. The intricate pattern of the Persian rug rushed up to meet her, blurring before her eyes as she doubled over with agony. Pressing her hands against the carpet, she let out a gut-wrenching moan. This selfish, cowardly woman and her poor-me story brought out the worst in Ivy. She wanted to be forgiving, but when faced with the woman that Jeremy had betrayed her for, all the hurt and anguish and fury burst through her emotional defense. As the fresh details of Jeremy's deeds constricted her heart, a wail of agony escaped her lips.

This was more than Ivy could manage or process. Leaning against the bookcase, she clutched her legs and bowed her head against her knees. She closed her eyes against the world, while the steady ticking of the antique clock metered her hammering pulse. Her scarred heart was splintering once again. After this fiasco, she wondered if she would ever be strong enough to love or trust a man again.

A moment later, the library door swung open.

Poppy slid a hand over Ivy's shoulder. "Auntie, that woman has gone to her room," she said softly. "Let me help you to yours."

"You're an angel," Ivy said, lurching to her feet.

Poppy frowned at the trash bin, where the envelope was poking out. "What is that in there?"

"Leave it," Ivy said, spitting out her words. "That's all in the past." But with Paisley still under her roof, was it really?

Chapter 6

BENNETT TILTED HIS HEAD TOWARD the gaping hole in Ivy's ceiling. "Tape it up for now?"

"After we remove the soggy material," Forrest said. "Reed can measure the opening and cut a length of plastic sheeting to cover it."

"Sure, Dad." Reed snapped off a steel measuring tape from his work belt.

Forrest picked up his tools. "Allow for plenty of overhang."

Bennett smoothed his hand onto Ivy's shoulder. She'd been through a lot in the last day.

"That should abate that musty odor," Forrest said to Ivy,

who sat on a bench watching her brother and nephew.

Ivy nodded. "Sure, okay."

Ivy's voice sounded flat, and Bennett was worried about her. Paisley had left this morning after cocooning herself in one of the old maids' rooms near his apartment over the garage. He couldn't believe Ivy had let her stay, but that was one more reason he admired Ivy. Though he knew she wanted nothing more than to slam the door in Paisley's face, she'd heard her out. Ivy was angry—and rightly so.

This was the first time Bennett had seen Ivy that upset. She was livid, but she managed to keep her anger under control and not let it overwhelm her sense of reason.

Last night he'd coaxed her out of her room for a short walk on the beach, and she'd told him the entire story. Paisley even had the gall to give Ivy a letter that Jeremy had written to her.

Just the thought of that made him furious, too. *How the hell did that cheeky woman think that would help Ivy?* From what he could see, Paisley was trying to shove her guilt onto Ivy. Jeremy had probably made it sound like his indiscretion was Ivy's fault. A classic move of shifting the blame onto someone other than himself.

Reed, who favored his father in build and appearance— an open and friendly face, broad-shouldered, with a baseball cap pulled over his short brown hair—climbed the ladder. "I can cut out the wet material, but won't it dry?"

"Won't be the same," Forrest said, his hands on his hips.

Forrest had come over after work with Reed, who was working for his father after completing a degree in construction management.

Reed exchanged his tape measure for a flashlight from his utility belt. He climbed higher into the hole and flicked it on. "You want the stuff that's up here before I close it up?"

"What's up there?" Ivy said, rising from the bench.

"Not much. Just an old bag."

"Pull it down," Forrest said. "Let's have a look."

Reed dragged a brown leather satchel through the opening. He handed it down to Bennett.

"Awfully dirty," Bennett said, taking it by the handle. "Ivy, do you have something to put this on?"

"I'll get a towel," she said.

Watching Ivy walk away, Bennett wished Shelly were here to lend support. He'd never liked Jeremy, but Ivy *had* been married to him for twenty-five years. She'd lived with him as her husband and the father of her children. Bennett had never seen those sides of the man, who had been driven to tear down this house and erect a monument to his greatness. And for what? Greed and some kind of new life with a plastic woman like Paisley? Bennett dragged his knuckles over his face. If he ever had the good fortune to call Ivy his wife, he'd never treat her like that.

Whoa. Bennett blinked in surprise. Where had *that* thought come from? He scratched the stubbled shadow on his chin. If he were honest with himself, which he tried to be, he knew it was true. But judging from the wild look in her eyes last night, if he let her know too soon, she'd slam the door on their relationship. Just when he and Ivy were growing closer, Paisley had rekindled Ivy's heartache.

"Use this," Ivy said, spreading out a tattered towel. "Found it in a box of linens on the lower level. Probably fifty years old."

"Or more," Bennett said, brushing her hand as he helped her spread it out on the bench. A corner of her mouth curved up at him, and his heart skipped a beat. That's all she had to do to make his day.

"There you are," Bennett said, placing the satchel on the towel. The musty odor filled the room. "Want to look inside?" When Ivy nodded, he worked at the old latch, which was stuck.

"Try this," Forrest said, handing him a pocket knife.

After flipping open the knife, Bennett used it to scrape off the rust that impeded the latch's functioning. When he was done, he tried it again. "Got it." He opened the accordion top and held it open for Ivy to look inside.

Her eyes widened with curiosity. "Help me lift this out."

Bennett grasped a large leather volume and slid it from the case with care.

Opening the cover, Ivy exclaimed. "An old photo album." Sepia-toned, black-and-white images mounted on crumbling pages stared up at them. "This must be Amelia's family."

"Or her husband's," Bennett said.

"Maybe both." Ivy peered closer and ran her fingers along the edges. "Look at their clothing. Turn of the century, I'd say." She turned a few pages. "And 1920s, maybe thirties, judging from the women's hats."

"Can't help you there," Bennett said with a chuckle.

"The styles can help date these photos." Her eyes lit with interest. "Megan will love this. I'll take some photos and send them to her."

Megan was away on another film project, but she and Josh were looking for a home in Summer Beach. They had asked Bennett to forward listings of beach bungalows they might be interested in, which he had.

He leaned over Ivy's shoulder. "That's Amelia and Gustav. They're fairly young in that photo. Probably before they moved here."

"I wonder if this is their wedding photo. There's writing below it, but the ink is so light." She sighed. "And it's in German. I can't read it."

"Maybe we can find someone in Summer Beach who knows German." Offhand, he couldn't think of anyone, but Nan might know of someone.

Ivy turned another page, sending tiny bits of paper fluttering. "This is fascinating. I wish Shelly could see this."

"We all miss her." Forrest moved beside her and put his arm around her. "Even more since she'd been back for a while. Want me to call her?"

Ivy patted his hand. "I know she'd love to hear from you."

Bennett watched the two siblings. Ivy had told him how protective Forrest and Flint had been over their youngest sister. Everyone in the family had doted on Shelly when she was little. Even then, Ivy said, her sister had an independent streak, shrugging off their attention and going her own way.

Ivy closed the photo album. "I'll look at this later. I want to join our guests in the music room before it's too late."

"I'll go with you," Bennett said. The late afternoon wine and tea gathering had proven popular among guests. The locals who were staying at the inn—among them, Imani, Jamir, and Gilda—enjoyed sharing Summer Beach highlights with the out-of-town guests. As mayor, Bennett appreciated the goodwill they spread.

Celia often brought in music students to play the piano or violin or harp, and Ivy had insisted on putting out a tip jar. Bennett smiled to himself. That made the youngsters feel grown-up and motivated to practice before a live audience.

"You folks go on," Forrest said. "Reed and I will take care of closing this up. We can repair this over the weekend, but we can't match this spot to the rest of the ceiling. It's too old. If you want it to look nice, you'll have to replace the entire ceiling."

Ivy frowned. "How much will that cost?"

"Just materials," Forrest said. "And I'll cover that. Don't worry, Ivy. Anything I can help you with here, I'm happy to do."

Ivy hugged him. "I can't tell you how much I appreciate this."

"You don't have to," Forrest said. "You've been through a lot."

Bennett knew Ivy wasn't the type to ask for help. In fact, Poppy had called her dad to repair the ceiling. Maybe it was because Ivy had lived away from the family for so many years, or perhaps that was her nature. She was self-sufficient, and he liked that about her. But he also enjoyed taking care of a woman—not that Ivy needed it.

Having the opportunity to pamper and provide for a woman who didn't need it? That made a man feel even more accomplished.

"A glass of wine is calling you," Bennett said to Ivy, holding his hand out to her. "My brain is fried from too many spreadsheets today." He'd spent much of the day with Boz and Maeve carefully reconstructing the timeline of Ivy's zoning approval in preparation for the mediation. And they were beginning the annual budget preparations as well.

"We've got this," Forrest said.

Bennett escorted Ivy downstairs to the music room, where one of Celia's students was playing Beethoven's *Ode to Joy* on the piano. The teenager looked to be about sixteen years old, and she was clearly nervous. Bennett recognized her. She was the daughter of the couple who ran a beachside restaurant. When the girl finished her piece, Ivy began clapping, and other guests joined in.

"That was lovely," Ivy said to the young woman, who gave her a shy smile.

"It pays to practice," Bennett said with a wink. He slid some cash into the tip jar, and the girl beamed. She started the next piece with confidence.

While Ivy circulated and welcomed the new guests, Bennett poured a glass of wine for her at the honor bar, which was an antique silver platter where Ivy and Shelly placed assorted libations, along with a box for guests to deposit whatever they wished. It was a quaint throwback that he'd seen on his overseas trips to London and parts of Europe.

Poppy had also arranged cheese and crackers, grapes and apples, and cookies on a tray. Today's variety was oatmeal-raisin. Shelly had been baking cookies for the afternoon gatherings before she left, but now Mitch was delivering them. Bennett scooped up the last one.

Bennett brought Ivy a glass of Cabernet Sauvignon from Sonoma Valley, and she accepted it with quiet gratitude. After the last couple of days, she deserved a little relaxation and pampering. "Saved the last cookie for you."

"I'm not hungry," she said. "Mitch should be here soon with more."

Ivy turned to greet Imani, who was wearing a pink and green batik-print sundress, and they chatted for a moment about Jamir.

"How're you holding up, Mr. Mayor?" Imani asked.

Bennett knew she was referring to the mediation preparation. "There's a lot I'd rather be doing."

"I hear you," Imani said. "Have you seen the schedule yet? I'm wondering who's first, us or the city?"

"Don't know yet."

Imani nodded. "Probably you guys. You have deeper pockets."

"You know what she wants." Glancing at Ivy's solemn face, he quickly changed the subject. "How's the flower business?"

"Blossoming," Imani said with a twinkle in her eye.

Bennett groaned at the pun he'd walked right into. To Ivy, he said, "I see Celia's back from San Francisco. Any word from Tyler?"

"They're talking now," Ivy replied, smiling. "Celia saw Tyler at the marina in San Francisco. But with school beginning soon, she wanted to return in time to start the music program."

"That's a good sign." Bennett couldn't imagine why his neighbor had taken off after the fire. Outwardly, Tyler was relaxed and friendly, but Bennett knew that Tyler was tightly controlled and exacting. He'd been in technology, which required attention to detail. Bennett imagined that Tyler felt out of control in the wake of the fire. Maybe that was it, he mused, hoping they didn't have deeper problems and that Tyler would return soon.

Gilda motioned to Ivy and started toward them. She held

Pixie in one arm and a glass of wine in the other.

"Good to see her out of her room," Bennett said quietly to Ivy.

"The contractors have started rebuilding her house, so she's been out checking on it." Ivy sipped her wine. "How's your home?"

"The work is slow, but I don't mind," he added with a grin. He liked being near Ivy and would miss seeing her every day after he moved back into his home.

Ivy smiled, though her eyes held a trace of sadness. Would she miss him, too, he wondered? Although it wasn't as if Summer Beach were a large town. He could still see her every day. They'd just have to make a point of it. He hoped she would.

As Gilda approached, Bennett saw Mitch enter the music room with a box. "If you're okay with Gilda, mind if I catch up with Mitch?"

"Go on," she said. "I'm fine."

As Bennett made his way toward Mitch, a smell of fresh-baked goods trailed him. "I hope you've got more cookies in there."

Poppy smoothly intercepted the box. "I'll put these out." She lifted the lid. "Oooh, chocolate chip and peanut butter."

Mitch grinned. "For guests only. And you, Poppy." He threw an elbow out to block Bennett.

"What am I?" Bennett asked, slinging his arm around Mitch's shoulder.

"Rabid devourer of cookies." Mitch laughed. "But hey, keeps me in business." Mitch glanced around. "Can I talk to you?"

"Sure," Bennett said, snatching a chocolate chip cookie.

"Not here." Mitch jerked his head toward the door that led to the veranda and terrace. "Let's take a walk."

They threaded through the crowd and stepped outside. The humidity and rain had passed. As he and Mitch strolled toward a pair of beach chairs on the terrace facing the ocean, Bennett filled his lungs with fresh air from the on-shore breezes. He'd had a run this morning, and it had felt good after missing his run yesterday due to the storm. He didn't feel any guilt as he ate the warm cookie.

"What's up, Mitch?" he asked as they eased into the chairs.

"I hired a new person at Java Beach to help Katie. That way, I can go to New York for a few days to try to see Shelly."

Bennett sipped his wine. "Think she'll agree to see you?"

"Not yet. But Shelly posted a preview of a floral design job she's doing for a big wedding. I'll figure out a way to get in." He grinned. "I learned all the tricks…you know where."

"As long as you're using that knowledge for good." Mitch had been opening up more about his past and his time in prison, and now he was even making jokes about it. "Still, you might want to think that through."

Mitch pitched forward, leaning his elbows on his knees and clenching his hands. "I have no idea what to say to her, though."

"Maybe you should get a woman's perspective."

"I talked to Ivy a few days ago."

"That's good," Bennett said, nodding. "No one knows Shelly better."

"But they're not talking very much."

"Shelly's in a tough spot right now."

Mitch frowned. "Why do you say that?"

"Just getting over an old boyfriend, from what I understand." Bennett raised an eyebrow at Mitch. "And that guy's in New York."

"Ezzra is his name."

"If I were you, I'd watch out for him."

"Yeah?" Mitch frowned. "What's he do?"

"He's a podcaster."

"I'm not worried." Mitch chuckled. "I'm packin'…a rolling pin."

Bennett reached up and mussed Mitch's spiky hair.

Mitch ducked out of the way. "Seriously, those can be lethal."

"You stay out of trouble in New York," Bennett said. "Leave the deadly kitchen equipment here." He stretched his legs out and watched the sun slip toward the horizon. "I hope you can convince Shelly to come back. Ivy really misses her."

"She's gotta follow her heart, man. Shelly does what she wants, and I wouldn't want her to be any other way."

Bennett grinned at his younger friend. "I think her heart

knows where it wants to be, and I don't think that's New York. Just saying."

"All I want her to know is how much she means to me," Mitch said. "Then, it's her decision."

Chapter 7

"THANKS FOR STAYING AT THE Seabreeze Inn," Ivy said to the couple departing for their home in Phoenix. They'd arrived last week for a long weekend respite from the intense desert heat.

"We'll tell our friends about your lovely home," the woman said. "I'm so glad we found you on iBnB. After seeing the glowing reviews, we just had to try your new inn. And we loved the Sea Breeze juice cocktails. Do you have a recipe for that?"

Ivy smiled and brought out a printed recipe card from behind the reception desk. "Here's the recipe. It's my sister Shelly's. We enjoyed having you, and we'd sure appreciate another review," Ivy added as she helped them with their bags.

With a background in marketing and publicity, Poppy had stressed the importance of social proof in the form of reviews. Even a line or two would boost their online position, her niece told her, to push them higher in the recommendation algorithms. All that computer jargon made Ivy's head hurt, but she couldn't deny that Poppy was right. With a few positive reviews, they'd seen a sharp increase in bookings, and Ivy was thankful that they were now meeting their weekly financial goals. As a result, she was on track to pay the overdue taxes before the foreclosure deadline. Anything could happen, of course, but Ivy could rest a little easier.

After depositing the couple's bags into their rental car, Ivy waved as they drove away. She couldn't believe how fast the days passed. This last week, between reviewing notes with Imani to prepare for the mediation, helping new guests become comfortably situated, and directing guests to the beach, marina, shops, and restaurants, Ivy had been busy from sunrise until she fell into bed at midnight. And now it was the beginning of another week again.

Thinking about Shelly, Ivy pressed a hand against her heart as she climbed the stone steps to the front door. Mitch had gone to New York to talk to her sister. She'd texted Shelly, but she'd received only a brief, emoji smiley-face response. Ivy had no idea if Mitch had connected with Shelly. Mitch had let Bennett know he'd arrived, but that was it.

It had been several days, and Mitch was expected back

today.

This radio silence from Shelly was making Ivy anxious. As much as she missed her sister, she only wanted her to be happy. Maybe Shelly's life didn't include the Seabreeze Inn, but Ivy would always be grateful that Shelly had helped her bring the old house back to life. Still, Ivy missed her sister's laughter and companionship.

At least Ivy had plenty to do to keep from obsessing over Mitch's visit. With the landscape cleanup needed after the heavy rain last week, she'd fallen behind. Thankfully, Forrest had measured her bedroom and ordered supplies to replace her damaged ceiling. And fortunately, the roof was in reasonably good condition, so no other rooms had sustained damage.

Today, after putting out breakfast, leading the morning walk, seeing off departing guests, and confirming arrivals, Ivy had a brief lull in her schedule. Poppy was watering plants, and most of the guests were out enjoying Summer Beach. Only Gilda remained on the veranda with Pixie and her laptop.

Ivy had been dying to go through the satchel Reed had found in the attic, so she lugged it downstairs into the reception room—an area quaintly marked *parlor* on the architectural plans.

The sweet aroma of Imani's tuberose and lily arrangement in the foyer filled the air and made her smile. Ivy had decorated this room with wicker furnishings and antique pieces she'd found on the lower level. She'd added marine-blue and seafoam-green cushions for color, along with her seaside paintings.

Sitting down, Ivy spread the old, leather-bound photo album on an antique table and put on her indigo-blue and cadmium-yellow reading glasses. These always made her think of Monet's later Water-Lilies paintings. She ran her hand over the padded leather cover, which was etched with a *fleur-de-lys* design. As she turned the brittle pages, bits of paper chipped off.

Peering closely, she studied each page, but all she saw were faded, sepia-toned family photos from a long-ago era. Though these were fascinating snapshots in time, the images shed little light on the mystery of Amelia Erickson.

What am I missing? Why would Amelia have hidden this in the attic and then wallpapered over the enclosure? She could understand that the home's former owner might have forgotten about the album. Still, tradespeople wouldn't cover an attic opening without specific instruction.

Amelia definitely wanted to hide the attic entry. Although the woman had suffered from dementia—judging from a letter Ivy had found, Amelia's illness was most likely Alzheimer's—she took deliberate action by hiring contractors.

Carrying a watering can for plants, Poppy sauntered into the room. "That looks interesting." She put down the water and sat next to Ivy.

"It is. Looking at the dress styles, it seems many of these were taken in the 1920s." She tapped a photograph of a large home. "This might have been their house in San Francisco.

See, that looks like the bay in the distance. Before all the high-rises were built."

"And that looks like a fancy party," Poppy said, pointing to another one. "Look at all those beautiful dresses."

"Probably a lot of important people of the day there." Ivy looked closer. "With a magnifying glass, I bet I can make out the art on the walls. And look at what she's wearing. Gorgeous gown, ropes of pearls, a pearl-and-gemstone collar at her throat."

"We've seen her taste in jewelry and art up close." Poppy quirked her mouth to one side. "As Shelly said, some like it hot."

"Maybe, or maybe not." Ivy made a face. She was reluctant to assume that Amelia was trading in stolen artwork and jewelry.

"She sure didn't show off what she had here," Poppy said. "Not like in these photos."

That reminded Ivy of something. "Wouldn't she have kept records and photos of her collection? Art collectors usually catalog their collections."

"Like museums do?"

"Much like that. A work's provenance adds to its value. Collectors also track where they've lent pieces, what they paid for them and when, and where they purchased them. All sorts of details about the artworks, too."

"That's exactly what you need to find."

Ivy leaned back in the chair and took off her glasses. "If I were Amelia—or Gustav—where would I keep such a cata-log?" She knew some collectors even printed and bound their art catalogs.

Poppy pressed her hands on the table. "Probably at their home or office. Maybe an attorney's office."

"Or a bank vault." Ivy got up and paced the room. "The executor of her will probably had a copy."

"But that's her legally owned collection," Poppy said. "Where would she have kept a list of the stolen—or *bor-rowed*—works?"

Ivy returned to the photo album. "Where, indeed?"

They turned a few more pages until they came to even older photos on stiff backings. "These images have been en-hanced by hand," Ivy said. "Look, the children have rosy cheeks and tinted eyes. My grandmother called these tintype photos."

Poppy picked up one. "This must predate the First World War."

"Actually, they're from the 1800s." Ivy turned over the images. "This one was shot at a studio in Berlin. Must have been in the early days of photography."

As Ivy stared at the old photo, an idea struck her. "Do you have time for some research?"

"I'll make time," Poppy said. "Do you think this studio is still around?"

"I doubt it. But you could research the names on the back of the photos or those written beneath the mounted ones."

Ivy turned a page to a young couple with serious expressions in formal dress. The woman wore a veil, though the style was far different than current wedding fashions. "This could be Amelia and Gustav on their wedding day. Before the First World War, and before they came here. Look how young they are."

Ivy spied another photo of an older man standing in front of a stately building. She studied the faded script beneath it. "That's a museum. And this says *Vater*. That's German for father. Probably Amelia's dad."

As Ivy stared at the old image, something about the man struck her, but she couldn't articulate what that was. Assuming that it was Amelia's father, of course.

Poppy leaned closer. "These are amazing. Mind if I take some pictures and post to social media? People love learning about the history of old houses."

"Go ahead," Ivy said as Poppy pulled out her phone to snap some shots. "Maybe someone will recognize something."

Just then, Ivy heard a whooshing noise at the front door, and a handful of envelopes shot through the mail slot.

"Mail time," Poppy said, jumping up.

Ivy sensed this album had a significant meaning. Important enough to hide it and plaster over it. Again, she wondered what she was missing. Somewhere in this house was the key to Amelia's strange behavior. But where?

Thumbing through envelopes, Poppy returned. "The usual. Utility bills, junk mail—and a letter for you."

Ivy took it. "No return address." She slid a nail under the flap to open the envelope. "Expensive writing paper."

"From a guest?"

Ivy opened the folded paper. "Watermarked and monogrammed, too." As she scanned the letter, her pulse quickened with anger. "It's from Paisley Forsythe." She tossed it on the table, dismissing that woman from her mind.

"What?" Poppy's eyes widened. "May I?"

"I don't care." Ivy shoved the letter across the table toward her. "Throw it away when you're finished. That woman brought out the worst in me." Working overtime, her brain had conjured an image of Paisley in Jeremy's arms, and she hadn't been able to purge it.

Poppy flicked a gaze toward Ivy. "All things considered, I thought you handled her pretty well. I don't know if I could have been as cool as you were. But you sure gave it to her in the end. Even Shelly would have been proud of you."

"You heard all that?"

"The walls are thin, Aunt Ivy. And I thought you might need help with her."

"No secrets here, I guess." When the corners of Poppy's mouth turned down, Ivy jumped up and embraced her. "I didn't mean that, really. See what she does to me?"

With eyes full of empathy, Poppy nodded. "I've never seen you that angry. Or that hurt."

"I've never met my husband's mistress." Ivy closed the old photo album and slid it back into the satchel. Pausing, she looked up. "She's pleading with me to read the letter *my* husband wrote to *her.* In some alternate world that exists in her mind, she thinks that will help me. What it would do is rip open my heart again." She pressed her lips together in disgust. "All she wants is for me to forgive her because she feels guilty. Well, I can't. Not yet, anyway."

"Did you read the letter?"

Ivy shook her head. "No, I threw it away."

"Aunt Ivy, I'm really sorry, but..." At a seeming loss for words, Poppy paused, then tidied up the tiny pieces of old paper that the photo album had shed. "I can't imagine what you're going through. I feel so bad for you."

"I appreciate that." What could anyone say that would make her feel better? Ivy wrapped her arms around her torso as if that would help keep her anguish from exploding. "I'd thought that confronting Jeremy's mistress would bring closure, but all it did was raise more questions about Jeremy's lack of judgment. Had he been that superficial to take up with a woman like Paisley?" She shook her head. "I keep wondering if it was something I did—or didn't do—that drove him to do that."

"Paisley confessed she set a trap for him," Poppy said. "I overheard that bit."

As feelings of loss and defeat threatened to overtake her again, Ivy flopped into a chair while Poppy read Paisley's letter. She gazed out the window, thinking about how the events had unfolded.

Resting her chin in her hand, Ivy said, "As terrible as it sounds, if I had to hear about their affair, I wish it had been from Jeremy." Her husband hadn't been perfect, but he'd been her confidant, partner, and lover for all of her adult life. Even now, she often felt unmoored without him. She was sure they could have worked this out. Eventually, with his support, maybe she could have found it in her heart to forgive him.

Ivy closed her eyes and sighed. That was the kind of woman she wished she were. But right now, she simply wasn't. The wound was too fresh and too deep.

Even though Ivy had landed in Summer Beach, she was still essentially alone. She hoped this feeling of being adrift wasn't spurring her attraction to Bennett, even though he made her feel gloriously alive again. When she couldn't sleep, or her emotions engulfed her, she clung to moments they'd shared. *A kiss the night of the fire, sharing wine and watching the waves, a slow dance on a moonlit beach.* And she'd had a summer crush on him all those years ago.

But could she trust her heart again?

Poppy put down the stationery and perched on a chair next to Ivy, taking her hand. "Forget that letter for now." She furrowed her brow. "What I've learned from being here and working with you is that *adulting* can be crazy tough. I just want you to know how much you inspire me. I love you, Aunt Ivy."

"I love you, too, sweetheart." Ivy hugged her niece, grateful that she was here.

Poppy gave her an encouraging look. "I know that you'll find someone more deserving of you next time. My mom always tells me there's plenty of fish in the sea. Just look at Bennett."

Ivy smiled at her niece's optimistic outlook. Now, Ivy knew the older she became, the harder it would be to find a life partner—if she wanted one at all anymore. "And you inspire me to keep going every day. Now, if we don't cut this out, we'll both start crying."

As the two women hugged each other, the front door swung open.

"Anyone home?" Mitch called out.

"In here," Ivy said, surprised to see him so early. "Did you take a red-eye flight?"

Mitch ran a hand over his messy hair. "Yeah, I left early. Just got in. Couldn't sleep." He stifled an enormous yawn.

"And? Did you see Shelly?" Poppy asked.

Ivy was anxious to know what had happened between them, but she saw how tired he was. "Need some coffee? Might not be as good as Java Beach, but it's fresh and ready now."

"You have no idea how good that sounds," Mitch said.

As they were walking to the kitchen, a guest returned, saying he had lost his key. "I'll take care of him, Aunt Ivy," Poppy said.

In the kitchen, Ivy poured coffee for Mitch. "I have bagels and lox if you're hungry."

"Famished. Little packages of manufactured pretzels don't sustain you for long."

Ivy smiled, thinking about how she missed cooking for her daughters. Mitch was a little older than her girls, though not much. Yet because of his life experiences, he seemed much older. She brought out a cutting board and sliced open a poppy seed bagel, then brought out lox and cream cheese and vegetables from good old Gertie, the vintage refrigerator.

She hadn't expected that Shelly would drop everything and return with Mitch, but she was still hoping for good news about her sister.

While the bagel was warming, Ivy arranged slices of salmon and a chunk of cream cheese on a plate, along with capers and sliced tomatoes and onions.

"Wow. Looks as good as what I'd find at a New York deli." Mitch dug in, clearly relishing the food. Between bites, he told her what had happened. "I was going to surprise Shelly, but I realized I couldn't barge in while she was working. When I texted that I was in town, she agreed to meet me in Chelsea, where she was choosing flowers for her work. Have you ever been there?"

"Several times. I love the Chelsea market."

"We talked for a long time, and I didn't hold back. Told her everything—even the parts I'm not proud of. That's my history, and I can't change it. She listened, and then I asked her about Ezzra. She told me they'd been dating for years, but that he couldn't make up his mind." He paused. "Maybe it's my ego, but listening to her talk about him, it didn't seem to me like there was a lot of love there."

As she listened to him, Ivy wrapped up the lox and returned it to the old refrigerator, which was still running strong. "Interesting. Why do you say that?"

Mitch ran his fingers along his furrowed brow. "I'm no expert, but shouldn't a partner want what's best for someone they love? And celebrate the other person's victories?" Without waiting for her to answer, Mitch went on earnestly, gesturing with his hands. "Not just the big stuff, but the little things that make us feel exhilarated and high on life. Like the feeling you get after riding the perfect wave...or making breakfast for someone you care about. Or creating a beautiful garden. And knowing that if you wipe out, burn breakfast, or the garden dies, your partner's going to help you start over because they know how much it means to you."

Mitch paused, a faraway look in his eyes. "That's what I want for Shelly. I hope I'm that guy, but if I'm not, I want her to find him because she deserves kindness and love. I'm not a complex guy, and I'm no Shakespeare, but that's how I see it." He fell silent.

"Actually, that's beautiful," Ivy said, caught up in his words. His feelings were pure and straightforward. She wished she'd heard those words from Jeremy, but that was in the past. As for Bennett, Ivy realized that Mitch reminded her an awful lot of him. Or maybe it was Bennett's influence on Mitch.

"What do you think?" Mitch asked.

a sheaf of papers in her hand.

"Brought you more homework," Imani said, handing them to her. "More prep work for the mediation tomorrow."

"Not again." Ivy groaned. The mediator had moved up the schedule due to her vacation. Ivy's case with Darla was first, and the more complex case with the city had been pushed to the following month. "But thank you for making sure I'm prepared."

Imani glanced around. "I thought I might have missed you. Where is everyone for the beach walk?"

"Sleepy guests this morning, I suppose," Ivy said. "Do you have time for a quick spin down the beach and back?"

"Not today. I'm off to the flower market. One of my clients is throwing a huge party, and I have a special shopping list from her."

As Ivy thumbed through the papers, her heart sank. "Looks like I have a lot to do, too."

"Take a walk. Clear your mind before you start working on those questions." Imani hurried toward her car.

Ivy deposited the paperwork in the kitchen and stepped outside again. Imani was right. Though Ivy had much on her to-do list today, it was such a glorious morning. She needed the rush of the ocean in her ears and the cool morning breeze on her skin.

Thoughts of the mediation, along with Shelly, Sunny—and even Paisley—had raced through her mind all night. Anxious to clear her mind, she charged off at a brisk pace across

Ivy wiped bagel crumbs from the cutting board and put it away. "I think you're right. Honesty and supportiveness go a long, long way. You told her all this?"

"Yeah, when we went to Woodstock. Rented a car and drove there. Very cool place. Hiked and rode bikes by the reservoir. And did a lot of talking."

Ivy smiled, remembering how much Shelly loved going to the quaint village in the Catskill Mountains.

Mitch polished off the rest of the breakfast. "This was great. Maybe I'll put this on the menu at Java Beach. With practice, I bet I could make killer bagels."

Ivy wiped her hands on a dishtowel. Anxious to hear the answer, Ivy asked, "Any chance Shelly might return?"

"She told me she needed time to think," Mitch said, rising.

"That's what I figured," Ivy said, although it wasn't what she'd hoped to hear.

After Mitch left, Ivy thought about what he'd said until Poppy poked her head in the kitchen.

"Any news on Shelly?" Poppy asked.

"Not really," Ivy said, putting away the dishes. "She and Mitch talked, but it seems Shelly is intent on staying in New York. She's lived there for a long time, and New York is special. We had a lot of good times there over the years when I visited. Going to the theatres, great restaurants, fabulous events. In a way, I can't blame her. She loves being in the middle of the action."

"She loves a good mystery, too," Poppy said. "I'm going to text her the pictures of the photo album we found and tell her that we're exploring the attic. She's going to be so jealous she'll wish she were here."

Ivy propped her elbows on the counter and rested her chin in her hands. Poppy was awfully perceptive. "Maybe you're right."

Chapter 8

IVY TURNED HER FACE TOWARD the dawn of another day. She was concentrating on her warm-up stretches on the columned terrace by the Greek-inspired pool, the designated meeting place for the morning beach walk. As the sun rose over the cliffs that cradled the community of Summer Beach to the east, broad strokes of pink and orange formed a watercolor background for silhouetted palm trees in the foreground. She fixed the image in her mind to draw on later for painting.

Standing on one foot, Ivy bent the other leg behind her and grabbed her toes to stretch her quads. As she was stretching her tight muscles, she saw Imani striding across the patio, her bright floral skirt swishing around her calves. She clutched

the sand, inhaling the fresh salt air to cleanse her foggy brain. She wished there were other ways to alleviate the situation with Darla, but so far, nothing seemed promising.

And if she lost the case?

Refusing to entertain the idea, Ivy picked up her pace, her legs burning with exertion. Instead, she focused on the beauty of nature surrounding her.

One of the pleasures of Summer Beach was greeting the sun every morning and watching the sunset from the veranda or terrace every evening. The late afternoon gathering in the music room inevitably spilled outside, and guests loved lingering to watch the sunset.

As she walked, Ivy swung her arms over her head, stretching and filling her lungs. In the distance, she could see the form of a lone runner on the sand, scaring up shorebirds as he passed.

Ivy knew that gait. Watching Bennett run toward her, she felt a sweet sensation bubbling up inside of her. As many tasks as she had to juggle, she looked forward to seeing him on the beach in the mornings.

She'd come to recognize other regulars at the beach, too. The woman with the frisky Labrador mix, the older couple who walked hand-in-hand. Mitch surfed on the other side of the point where the waves were larger. And at the marina, boat owners would be up early checking on their vessels and getting ready to go out on the water to fish or sail.

Ivy was getting into the rhythm of Summer Beach. It

suited her, she realized. Maybe this wasn't Shelly's ideal life; Ivy would simply have to accept that. She'd try calling her later today.

As Bennett ran toward her, Ivy admired his muscular build. He looked good for his age—any age, in fact.

Bennett's pace slowed until he met up with her. "Where's your crew this morning?" He turned and walked with her, as he often did if he didn't have an early meeting at the office.

"Gilda worked late on a deadline, and several guests are in town for the horse races in Del Mar. I think there was a party last night." Ivy was glad that it was just the two of them this morning. She wasn't in the mood for small talk or giving out local directions.

Bennett stroked his stubbly chin. "Might have been the crowd that gathered at the Starfish Café. Heard they stayed pretty late. But that's why people come here. To relax and have a good time."

She lifted a corner of her mouth. "What a good idea that would be."

"Think you could break away Sunday afternoon?"

"Maybe after the weekenders check out. Why?"

Bennett grinned. "I have something in mind. A surprise I think you'll like."

"I'll need it after the mediation."

He caught her hand and squeezed it. "You're going to do just fine. I remember how well you spoke before the city council for the zoning variance."

Ivy appreciated his confidence, but she was still worried. "Imani is fairly certain this case will go to trial," Ivy said. "But we still have to go through mediation."

"This judge usually orders it. Can't see you agreeing to close the inn, though." He kissed her on the cheek. "I've got to run. Meeting with Maeve and Boz again this morning."

She wrapped her arms around his neck in a quick hug, not minding at all that his T-shirt was damp with salt spray and perspiration. "I'm already looking forward to Sunday."

"Me, too," he said, his eyes gleaming. "We'll have fun, I promise."

Bennett started off toward his apartment at the inn, where Ivy knew he would shower and shave and then be off to his office. She couldn't resist turning around and watching him for a few moments.

Ivy continued walking, picking up her pace again to offset the croissants and wine and cheese she loved. While her muffin-top middle was firmer than when she'd arrived in Summer Beach, she'd never be as svelte as Shelly, but that was okay. They were different body types, and she was happy as she was.

Feeling the burn in her thighs, Ivy continued, waving at the woman with the Labrador mix dog that was running at the end of its leash. Ahead of her was another woman she was gaining on.

Ivy recognized the royal-blue head of hair and sparkly visor at once. *Darla.* Usually a brisk walker, Darla was taking a slower pace today. Maybe the mediation meeting was weighing on her mind, too.

As Ivy watched, Darla stopped and put her hands on her thighs, leaning over. Concerned, Ivy sprinted toward her. The older woman looked unsteady on her feet.

"Are you okay?" Ivy rested a hand on Darla's shoulder, ready to catch her if she fell.

"I'm fine, just fine." Darla shrugged her away and tried to walk, but after a few steps, she faltered and stumbled.

Ivy caught Darla before she hit the sand and steadied her. "I've got you. Feeling a little faint?"

"Yeah..."

Ivy spied a group of rocks, the same flat rocks where she and Bennett had shared a bottle of wine one night. "Let's have a seat over there."

As Darla eased onto the rocks, Ivy scrutinized her. The morning was still cool, yet beads of sweat lined Darla's hairline. Her hands were shaking as she tried to settle herself on the smooth rock. Ivy slid her hand over Darla's wrist and noticed her pulse was elevated.

"I probably shouldn't be talking to you," Darla said, wheezing a little.

"We're still neighbors. We can talk if we want."

"Matthew—" Darla paused and pressed a hand to her chest. "He wouldn't like it."

"I think your attorney would understand that you need help right now."

Darla turned a grumpy frown her way. "I'll be okay."

"I'm sure you will be, but I'll wait to make sure."

"Do what you what," Darla growled, trying to catch her breath.

Though her tone was gruff, Ivy detected Darla's vulnerability. "Better yet, I'm going to call Chief Paula and have her send over one of her emergency medical teams to check you out. Any chest pains?"

"Not really. I don't need—" Darla winced and stopped. "Okay, okay."

Ivy pulled out her phone and tapped the emergency number. Darla was an older woman, and for all her bluster, her physical signs were concerning.

When the dispatcher answered, Ivy gave her the details. "We're on the beach side near Java Beach." Ivy told her she'd wait with Darla until aid arrived, and then she hung up.

"Has this ever happened before?" Ivy asked.

"More lately," Darla said.

"Have you been to a doctor?" Ivy observed Darla. Could be a panic attack, or possibly the precursor to a heart attack. If they were at home, she'd give her an aspirin to be safe, but they were too far away, and surrounding businesses were not yet open. In the distance, a siren sounded.

Ivy smoothed her hand over Darla's. "Hear that? The emergency service will soon be here."

Darla shifted on the rock, and Ivy slid her arm around the woman, surprised at how thin her shoulders were. She always wore large clothing and jackets, which meant that Darla might have lost a significant amount of weight.

After a brief hesitation, Darla relaxed against Ivy's side. "Thanks for stopping," Darla said softly. "Wouldn't blame you if you hadn't."

"I have no issue with you, Darla." Maybe that was a stretch of the truth, but the only issue she'd ever had was Darla's attitude. And the lawsuit.

"The nerve of that woman," Darla muttered.

"What woman?"

"Paisley."

Ivy stiffened.

"I didn't like your husband, and I certainly didn't care for that brazen hussy," Darla spit out. "Imagine her wanting to stay at *your* home."

Ivy rubbed her arm, trying to calm her.

"My husband did the same thing to me, you know. Begged for my forgiveness. I told him I would, but between you and me, I never could." She pressed a fist against her stomach. "Not inside. Eats you up, makes you do crazy stuff. I got so used to living that way, that even after he died, I kept right on being angry at everyone."

Ivy could sure understand that. "Except for Mitch."

A smile crept across Darla's face. "He's like my son. Did you know I had a son? He'd be about Mitch's age. I had him late in life. Never thought I could have kids. I waited so long for him, and then the Lord saw fit to take him away from me. That's when Henry took up with another woman, saying I was acting too sad. *Too sad?* I'll have a hole in my heart forever over the loss of my baby. At least Mitch fills it with flowers and kindness."

Ivy sucked in a breath. Darla's story was heartbreaking. No wonder she harbored such anger.

The siren was drawing closer, and Ivy silently urged it on.

Darla looked up at her. "Did you know my sister tried to get me to go to Shelly's yoga class? Told me it would help me release my anger."

"Debra mentioned it, and I told her we'd love to have you."

Darla was quiet for a moment, and Ivy watched her breathing. The siren had stopped nearby.

"I didn't like you at first because you were married to Jeremy." Darla drew a ragged breath. "But people 'round here like you, and you seem to be doing a lot of good for Summer Beach. I hear those kids practicing their music."

"I hope that doesn't bother you."

"I sit outside so I can hear it."

"The kids are part of Celia's music program in the schools. They often perform in the afternoon while we gather to share tea and wine and cheese." She slid a grin toward Darla. "And Mitch brings the cookies."

"Does he?" Darla's face lit with interest.

Ivy hugged the woman close to her. "We can start over, Darla. If there's anything we're doing that bothers you, I'm sure we can sort it out over a cup of tea."

"Or one of Shelly's Sea Breeze cocktails." Darla's face darkened again. "You know, Matthew egged me on to file those suits. Wish I hadn't now. Half the town has turned against me over that."

"Then why don't you tell Matthew you don't want to go on?"

"Do you think it's that easy?"

"I can ask Imani."

"I'd really like that. I'm so tired of fighting." Tears trickled from Darla's eyes. "I don't want to go to that mediation meeting, and I don't wish you any more harm. I heard you might lose the property. Is that true?"

"I can't afford to live there unless I can rent out rooms," Ivy said gently. "But whatever happens, I'll be okay."

Darla gripped her hand. "I *want* you to stay."

A team of two emergency technicians arrived and knelt beside them. While a woman unpacked equipment, a young man asked, "What seems to be the trouble here?"

Ivy explained, and then the medical providers took over. "Let's check you out."

Darla looked back at Ivy. "Promise me you'll talk to Imani and stay?"

"I promise," Ivy said, hugging the older woman. "And I can't wait for you to join us at the inn. You'll have fun." Shelly would be appalled, but having Darla as a friendly neighbor was infinitely better than defending a lawsuit.

As the emergency team took Darla's vital signs, she gave

Ivy a smile of relief.

Just then, Ivy saw Bennett racing across the sand. "I heard the emergency vehicle while I was getting dressed, and when I saw it stopped here at the beach, I thought something might have happened to you."

"No, it's Darla," Ivy said. "I'm glad you came."

Bennett stooped and said a few words to Darla, who beamed at his presence.

The poor woman is lonely. Lonely and feeling left out from the crowd—isolated from everyone around her enjoying life. Recalling the time when she had volunteered at the elementary school for Misty and Sunny, Ivy thought about the children who had developed angry attitudes when they felt excluded. She resolved to make an effort to include Darla.

As the emergency medical providers put Darla on a stretcher to take her to the hospital for emergency care and tests, Bennett joined Ivy. They stepped aside to talk.

"Glad you saw her on the beach," Bennett said quietly. "I'd passed her a little earlier on my run, but she seemed okay then."

"She was feeling faint, so I stopped to help."

"I wish I'd been here to help you. Darla's pretty prickly."

"Actually, we had a good talk."

As the medical technicians lifted the stretcher, Ivy hurried back to Darla's side. She reached out and squeezed the older woman's hand. "Would you like me to call your sister? We have her number."

Darla offered a weak smile. "You'd do that for me?"

"Of course. We're neighbors," Ivy said. The genuine surprise in Darla's voice made Ivy feel sad about not having a closer relationship with her. "We'll tell Mitch you're at the hospital, and I'll follow you there."

Ivy and Bennett waved as the emergency technicians hurried away with Darla.

Turning to Bennett, Ivy said, "Darla told me she doesn't want to go through with the mediation, and she wants to drop the lawsuits. This process has been so stressful for her that I think it finally overwhelmed her. And from now on, we promised to work out our differences over tea."

"Certainly a lot less traumatic for everyone." A smile spread across Bennett's face as he twined his fingers with hers. "You're an amazing woman. I can't wait to tell Maeve and Boz the good news."

Watching the emergency vehicle take off, Ivy shook her head. "I just didn't understand her before."

"Want a ride back to the inn? Or straight to the hospital?"

"The hospital," Ivy said. "I promised her I'd follow." She tapped out a quick message to Poppy to look up Debra's number and call her. Then she followed Bennett to his SUV.

As Bennett drove, he looked at Ivy with a mixture of relief and admiration. "Resolving your differences with Darla is a major obstacle out of the way. Congratulations. And thank you. You've just saved all the parties involved a lot of stress, effort, and money. Matthew is the only one who'll be disappointed."

"He'll have to get used to that. We'll watch out for his influence on her."

Bennett turned a corner onto Main Street. "Aw, Matthew's not so bad. Just cranky. Probably feeling left behind himself."

"You're too soft on him." Ivy arched a brow. "Surely you're not that desperate for votes."

"In order to reach compromises at the city, I try to see both sides of people and their dilemmas." Bennett lifted his hand from the top of the steering wheel in a thumbs up to Mitch, who was standing on the curb and waving them down. "Hang on," he said, pulling to the curb and rolling down his window.

"Darla's on her way to the hospital for a check-up," Bennett said.

"How bad is it?" Mitch asked, frowning.

"They didn't say, but she's awake and talking." Bennett put a hand on his friend's shoulder.

"It's those lawsuits that have got her all wound up," Mitch said.

Bennett tapped Ivy's hand. "I think those are in the past."

Mitch nodded and stepped back. "I'll check in with her."

As they took off again, Ivy said, "Anyone ever tell you you're a pretty good mayor? Aside from hitting on the newcomers, that is."

Chuckling, he added, "Seeing what you've been through makes me want to be even better. I'll swing by the hospital after Darla's been checked out. However, I have to get to the office for a fairly important meeting."

"Go. I think she'll be okay."

After Bennett dropped Ivy off at the hospital, she waited for Darla to be seen. Poppy had reached Debra, so Ivy called to give her an update on her sister's condition, which was eventually deemed to be a panic attack.

Though the hospital kept Darla for observation for a few hours, when Mitch arrived to take her home, a smile lit her face. Ivy rode back with them to help make Darla comfortable at her home. After Mitch promised to bring Darla some chicken soup, Ivy left to return home next door. It had been a tumultuous day, but Ivy was happy that Darla would be okay.

As she was climbing the stone steps, Ivy saw a familiar suitcase just inside the front door, which was standing ajar.

When she spied the airport tag with the JFK code printed on it, Ivy cried out and raced up the steps.

Chapter 9

"YOU'RE BACK!" AS IVY BOUNDED into the house, Shelly swooped her arms around her. Regardless of whether this was temporary or not, Ivy was thrilled and relieved to see her. Shelly looked a lot more relaxed than the last time she'd seen her. Poppy's face was wreathed with a smile.

"I finally figured it out, life *is* better in Summer Beach." Shelly laughed and flashed a keychain with that logo. She took a step back, holding Ivy's hands. "When Poppy said you'd gone to the hospital with dragon lady next door, I knew I'd been gone too long. Soon as I turned my back, you started cavorting with the enemy, huh?"

"It wasn't like that," Ivy said, checking out Shelly. Her

thick chestnut hair was in its usual messy bun, though she seemed leaner than Ivy had recalled. Clad in head-to-toe black—tunic, leggings, boots—Shelly had regained her city vibe. And she certainly hadn't been out in the sun since she'd left. Ivy was so happy, even if this were only a short visit.

"You always were a softie," Shelly said, hugging Ivy again.

"Only with people I love," Ivy said pointedly. "But this was different. Darla nearly collapsed on the beach this morning. You would've done the same thing. And I learned a lot about her past, which explains why she's the way she is—not that I'm excusing her attitude. But I understand it now."

"Wow, can't wait to hear that story," Shelly said, lifting an eyebrow. "Did you talk about the lawsuit?"

"We did." Ivy smiled. She'd half expected Darla to renege on the promise, but as soon as Mitch and Ivy had taken her home, she had called her attorney. "Darla decided to drop the case. Seems it was causing a lot of stress for her, too. The doctor said she had—well, I can't recall the medical term, but basically, it was an anxiety attack. Or maybe it was a panic attack. Anyway, she needs further treatment for that." Ivy had heard Matthew berating her through the phone for her decision, but Darla stood fast in her decision.

Poppy huffed. "As long as she keeps to herself, we're fine."

"If Darla counts Matthew as a friend, she needs better friends." Ivy swung a look between Shelly and Poppy. "I've invited her to join us for yoga in the morning, as well as wine and cheese in the afternoon. I think this will benefit all of us."

Shelly smacked her forehead. "You *what?*"

"We're partly to blame for this," Ivy said. "Just like with kids, our reaction to her fueled her actions." But she was anxious to hear more about Shelly. "Enough of that. I'd love to hear what's going on with you."

"I know I've been kind of *incommunicado,* but I had a lot to think about." Shelly ducked out and brought in the bag she'd left outside. "Before I start, are you two up for a Sea Breeze?"

"After this day, I'll take mine fully loaded," Ivy said. "I hadn't expected to spend the better part of the day at the hospital, but I couldn't leave Darla alone." She smiled at Poppy. "Thanks for covering for me."

"No worries," Poppy said. "You had a few messages, but those can wait. I still have some guest inquiries to respond to. Why don't you two go catch up? Shelly, I've got your old room. I'll put your bag in there."

"Mind sharing again?" Ivy asked. "We're full right now."

Shelly looped arms with Ivy and started for the kitchen. "I'd sleep in a hammock at this point."

In the kitchen, Shelly mixed her special concoction with ruby red grapefruit and cranberry juices, a slice of lime, and a shot of vodka. She and Ivy carried their tall glasses onto the edge of the terrace, where they sat side by side on a step, squishing their toes into the sand and watching the ocean waves roll onto the shore and rush back out again.

"I'm kind of like those waves," Shelly said. "Advance and retreat, over and over."

Ivy nudged her. "There's nothing wrong with wanting to revisit a decision."

"That's not why I left—"

"I know that you—"

"Big sis, I love you, but let me finish." Shelly shot her a firm look. "You're always trying to make everything okay, and while you're good at that, sometimes you simply can't. It's not your place, anyway. I have something to say, but give me a minute to think."

Ivy parted her lips to disagree, but Shelly shot her *that look*. She took a sip of her icy cocktail to cool off. Though she hated to admit it, what Shelly said was true. She'd spent all of her adult life trying to smooth out the bumps of life for everyone but herself.

If Jeremy had been unhappy with anything—the press of a laundered shirt collar, the firmness of his pillow, the phone service, or anything outside of his workplace—it fell to her to resolve the problem. He simply expected it. She'd fought against this expectation in the beginning, but he'd complain and sulk until she finally gave in to keep the peace. Since she didn't work when the girls were young—few of their social circle except Ivy considered artwork or child-rearing real work—her painting had tapered off until the girls left for college.

Unfortunately, the girls had modeled their father's behavior, too. Ivy took another sip, savoring the chance to relax and enjoying the silence between her and Shelly.

As teenagers and college students, if Sunny or Misty had a problem, they demanded *mom to the rescue*. As an innkeeper, that made her a gracious host, but from now on, Ivy resolved to limit that behavior to her guests in a professional capacity. Shelly had a point.

Ivy thought of her responsibilities to her late husband and adult daughters. Thankfully, Misty had quickly grown out of her demanding habit after she moved out and discovered that mom couldn't solve her adult problems. *And Sunny? Still learning.* People *needed* to know how to solve their own problems or save themselves.

Shelly scooted her legs up and drew a deep breath. "Okay, I'm ready."

"I'm listening."

"I got scared," Shelly began. "When the police called Mitch in for questioning, instead of facing Mitch's problem with him and trying to understand his background, I ran away. I didn't know how to deal with his potential legal entanglement. When I learned he'd been in prison for theft, I jumped to a conclusion—which was exactly why he hadn't told me. I know you think he's a good guy, but *I* have to believe in him. And for me, that takes time. I've been burned by a lot of guys, especially Ezzra. And if I ever get married, I want a shared union. I won't be anyone's housekeeper."

"You mean, like I was?"

Shelly nodded and glanced at the big house behind them. "Unless they're paying me by the night."

Ivy choked on the drink she was taking. "You might want to rephrase that."

Shelly reached over and mussed Ivy's hair. "I meant, as an *innkeeper.*"

"Hey, just saying," Ivy said, chuckling and smoothing her hair back.

Shelly quirked up her lips. "I also had to make sure that living in Summer Beach was really my decision and not something I was doing for you—and to avoid Ezzra."

Ivy nodded. "I've wondered that myself. If given a choice, would I have wanted to return here? Maybe I should be near my children."

"Sunny has no idea where she wants to be. And as an actress, Misty will probably land somewhere besides Boston."

"She's mentioned that."

Shelly ran her fingers thoughtfully across her forehead. "Given the crazy twists that life serves up, should we really make decisions based on reactions?" She waved a hand at the old house. "Sometimes you have to, I guess. But I want to design my life. Live my plan, if I want one at all. Act, not react."

Here it comes. Ivy braced herself for the inevitable. But it was okay. Shelly had a life to live. "So, you're only here for a visit?"

"Let's call it another test run." Shelly smoothed a hand onto Ivy's shoulder. "When Mitch and I went to Woodstock,

I told him I wanted to be friends first. I want to get to know him—or any other guy I date."

"That's practical," Ivy said, though she wouldn't have applied that description to Shelly much in the past. Had her sister changed that much in just a few weeks?

Shelly stretched out her legs. "I want children, but why do I have to get married for that? I have single friends who've had artificial insemination or adopted children. A lot of sweet kids could use a forever home, but they don't always get one. What I'm saying is that the life I choose might not look like yours—with wedding bells and two kids and a dog—but I can still create a life I want and love."

As Ivy let Shelly's words sink in, she twined her fingers with her sister's. Ivy had to accept and respect Shelly's decision, just as she would her children's. She'd always known that Shelly didn't fit the traditional mold. "Whatever you decide to do, I'll support you. And I admire you for being honest with yourself and staying true to your course."

Shelly's expression relaxed. "We've all got a North Star. We just have to find it."

Ivy grinned. "But don't rule out the dog."

"Pixie might have influenced my decision," Shelly said with a sly smile. "And how is that troubled little pooch?"

"Her kleptomania is nearly under control. It's been days since anything has gone missing. For long, that is. Gilda has been making Pixie return stolen goods, so the pooch can see how happy people are to have their belongings returned.

That's a novel approach, but now she's snatching and returning. Sort of like catch-and-release. It's…interesting."

Shelly started laughing. "See the fun I've missed? This is much better than bar hopping in New York. Although there was a time for that." The smile slipped from her face. "Actually, that was never as much fun as it looked on social media."

Ivy bumped against Shelly's shoulder. "But you always looked hot."

Shelly grinned. "I did, didn't I? You know, getting dressed was the funnest part—if that's a word."

"It's not, but go on." Ivy smiled at her sister, who'd been inventing words since childhood.

Sipping her drink, Shelly continued. "I talked to Mom. Even though they'll be sailing around the world soon, she pointed out that it would be good to be around family if I decide to go it alone on parenthood. With all the cousins, I'd have built-in babysitters."

"Wish I'd had that," Ivy said, recalling when her girls were young. They'd stayed in Boston because of Jeremy's position and the proximity to his work in Europe. "Sounds like you've done a lot of thinking."

"Yeah. Except for when I was working, I had a lot of time. Took some long walks through Central Park, watching the birds and kids." The late summer sun was low on the horizon, and it was nearly time for the evening gathering. Shelly shaded her eyes. "How's business been?"

"Nearly full occupancy. I'm glad we renovated the maid's

quarters. With the money we've made from those—and the events we've had—we're in the black on cashflow now."

Shelly frowned. "Enough to pay the tax bill on time?"

Ivy smiled and reached for Shelly's hand. "Relax. We're going to make it. Barely, but we'll do it."

"Yes!" Shelly did a fist pump. "Won't it feel good to have that out of the way?"

"You bet. All that's left is maintenance, insurance, and taxes. That's manageable. And if a major repair comes up, then with the rental history we're building, we can probably get a loan."

"Who knew you'd be so good at business?" Shelly nudged her. "Must be satisfying to see your idea come to fruition."

Ivy slung an arm across Shelly's shoulder. "We did it together. You and Poppy put out just as much effort as I did. But yeah, it will feel good not to get the nasty-grams from the tax department." Then, and only then, would Ivy feel like she could let up and take a day off without guilt.

"Besides all the work and craziness, it's been a lot of fun," Shelly said, cupping her chin in her palm as she reminisced. "Those old paintings and the jewelry…"

"Uh, that's not all."

"Poppy mentioned you guys found an entry to the attic."

Shelly's eyes brightened as Ivy told her about the rain and the leak in her room. "And in the attic, we found a satchel with an old photo album loaded with pictures of the Ericksons and their family."

"I'd love to see that. Did you show it to Megan?"

"She's been away, but she's coming back soon."

"Any other treasures up there?"

"Not that we could see."

Shelly whipped around to scrutinize the house. "Look at that roofline," she said, tracing it with her hands in the air. "It's high enough for another level. Have you explored?"

Ivy poked her sister in the ribs. "Without you around, when have I had the time?"

"Come on, let's go," Shelly said, sitting up straight.

"Now? We've got the wine and tea hour, and everyone will want to see you. Besides, Reed has been up there, and he didn't see a thing."

"He walked the entire length of the attic?"

"Well, no… But it's probably filthy up there. And everything got wet with the rain." Still, the excitement in Shelly's eyes sent a ripple of renewed curiosity through her.

Shelly stood and put her hands on her hips. "What's the matter with you? Where's your sense of adventure? This is why you need me."

Even though the idea was tickling her interest, Ivy resisted. "Listen, I'm going to write that big tax check next week, and I don't want anything taking us off task. Remember what happened last time we started tearing down brick walls? We had the FBI crawling all over us in a nanosecond."

"It wasn't that fast, and you don't have to call them. Besides, I think you swung the first hammer."

"Well, I'd have to change…"

"Woo-hoo! We're going up!" Shelly grabbed Ivy's hands and pulled her to her feet.

"Wait, the glasses." Ivy picked up their glasses and shoes, and the two hurried into the house.

Poppy met them at the door. "I was wondering what happened to you two. I've put out the cheese and crackers in the music room."

"I'd planned to surprise everyone at yoga in the morning." Shelly's eyes glittered with excitement. "We're going to explore the attic. Come with us. Right now."

"I can't believe I'm doing this," Ivy said. "I've got to see Imani about Darla's decision and welcome the new guests. You two go find flashlights and a ladder. Come get me when you have everything."

While Shelly and Poppy scurried off, Ivy made her way into the music room. Sweet strains of violin music soared through the house, just as it might have in Amelia's day. When Ivy walked into the music room, she greeted Celia first.

"What do you think of our Julliard-bound violinist?" Celia asked, pride evident in her voice. Her sleek black hair was wound into a topknot skewered with jewel-toned cloisonné combs.

"She's quite talented," Ivy said. Celia and her husband had endowed several music scholarships at various universities and music conservatories.

Celia leaned in toward Ivy. "I wanted to tell you that Tyler has been calling me every evening. He's been working on his anxiety, and we're really talking now."

"That's good, yes?"

"I think so." Celia beamed. "The house repairs are going well, too, so I don't know how much longer I'll need my room. Although I've loved staying here at the inn, even if Tyler didn't."

"We'll still see you here for your music program, I hope." Ivy heard a thud upstairs and wondered what Shelly and Poppy were doing. *Just a few more minutes,* she told herself.

"Absolutely," Celia said.

After chatting a little more about the young musicians, Ivy quickly moved on to see Imani, who was standing by the antique fireplace. Ivy loved her style; Imani looked like the picture of summer. Today she wore a bright yellow and orange batik-print sundress with strands of chunky coral around her neck.

Imani hugged her with enthusiasm. "Hey lady, I don't know how you convinced Darla to drop her case against you, but I sure got a blistering call from Matthew."

"You know that Darla nearly collapsed on the beach from stress this morning?"

"I've heard all about that," Imani replied. "Word travels fast here. I have a customer whose husband is one of the emergency medical service providers that attended to Darla."

Ivy pursed her lips. "Darla's heart wasn't really in those lawsuits. From what she said, I think she was complaining to

Matthew one day, and he badgered her for the cases."

"Why, of course, he did. That's Matthew. He's an opportunist. But we all know that about him and steer clear."

"Then why is Darla friends with him?"

"Old ties, I guess." Imani shrugged. "Matthew is always pleading poverty—though he has plenty of money—and offers to sue someone for her. Then he keeps the pressure on her. This is not the first time. Darla might have a quick temper, but she usually calms down."

"Well, she can't take the stress anymore," Ivy said. "Mentally or physically. The hospital kept her for observation and tests before releasing her, but it could've been much worse."

"Maybe that's a blessing. Darla can use her health issues to make Matthew back off." Imani smiled as she sipped her white wine. "So, does this mean you two are friends now?"

Ivy lifted a shoulder, then let it fall. "I'm hoping for cordial, but I'd like to have a friendly neighbor. She's not so bad, after all. When you understand a prickly person's history, you develop compassion for them." Now she saw why Mitch was friendly with her.

Imani laughed. "Sounds like you're becoming one of us here in Summer Beach. We're like a big family with its spats and arguments, but we take care of each other."

Ivy was just about to excuse herself to see how Shelly and Poppy were doing when her phone buzzed in her pocket. She glanced at it. *Sunny.* Calculating the time difference, her heartbeat quickened.

"Excuse me, Imani, it's my daughter calling in from Europe. I have to take this, but let's celebrate our victory over Matthew—maybe even include Darla," she added with a smile.

After stepping into the hallway, Ivy tapped her phone. "Sunny, is everything okay? Awfully late there for you." It was after midnight for her.

"Oh, Mom, I'm so glad you picked up." Sunny was crying into the phone. "I really n-need your help."

Every nerve in Ivy's body snapped onto high alert. "Tell me what happened."

"Oh, everything is so awful..." Sunny sobbed hysterically.

"Are you okay?" Ivy had to restrain herself from screaming into the phone. She rushed into the library and shut the door. That something should happen to her children was her worst nightmare. The line crackled, and she couldn't make out anything Sunny said. Ivy pressed a hand against her heart, willing Sunny's safety across the Atlantic Ocean.

"Sunny!" she yelled. "Are you hurt?"

"Noooo," Sunny wailed. "But, I'm stuck on Ibiza. I came here to be with Reggie, only I found out he's here with someone else. And they're *engaged*." A heartbreaking sob soared over the phone line.

Ivy lowered herself into a chair with relief. Shelly and Poppy could wait. "But, you're physically okay?"

"Aren't you *listening*? And then, and then..." Sunny gulped for breath. "Mom, I can't even compete. He's in love with another *guy!*" Another wail erupted from Sunny, and Ivy held the phone away from her ear.

"Take a breath, he's not worth getting this upset over."

"Mom, he's a *prince.* Prince Reginald. Not that his family is actually in power anywhere, but I could've been a *princess.*"

Ivy sank her face into her hands. *What in heaven's name has gotten into Sunny?* This was beyond grieving for her father. *She's lost.*

"Sunny, forget Reggie, forget Ibiza. Get on a plane and go back to work."

"I-I can't do that," Sunny said in a small voice.

"Why not?" Ivy's heightened perception kicked into high gear. "You're still working as a nanny, yes?"

"When I left, they told me not to come back."

"*What?*" Ivy sucked in a breath to check herself. "Why?"

"They said I didn't give them enough notice that I was going on holiday."

"And did you?"

"Of course, I did," Sunny cried. "I told them on Wednesday that I was leaving on Friday. Three whole days. I mean, it's August, and *everyone* goes on holiday in August. They should've known I would. But they said they didn't have enough time to find someone else for the kids."

Her daughter was floundering. Ivy had to think quickly to help Sunny gain control of her situation. "Do you have a place to stay?"

"I was planning on staying with Reggie. I was going to

surprise him."

"Well, you did that. Where are you staying tonight?"

"Nowhere, really. I met some Russians and slept on their boat last night. I can go there tonight, or find another place."

"Do you have any money?"

"Duh, that's why I called!"

"Don't *duh* me, young lady. You're the one who got yourself in this situation." Ivy raised her gaze to the ceiling and mumbled, "Oh, please give me patience."

"My credit card isn't working."

"Do you mean you've reached the limit?"

"Yeah, I guess so."

"Not what I asked. Yes or no, did you spend enough to reach the limit?"

"I had to buy plane fare here," Sunny replied in a small voice.

"Round trip?"

"I thought Reggie would offer to take me back."

Ivy closed her eyes and sent up a little prayer for the strength to deal calmly with her out-of-control daughter. "Here's what we're going to do," she said, standing as she spoke. "You have no money and no job, so it's time to come home and sort out your life. I'll give you my American Express card to get a hotel room, then get a plane ticket and come back to the states. Misty said you can stay with her in Boston, or you can come here."

Sunny sniffed. "All my friends are in Boston. I'll stay with

Misty."

"Understand that you need to make life decisions now." Ivy fought to strike a balance between firmness and love. "There's still time to start school next month, or you can find a job. This time I mean it, Sunny. The party's over."

A long moment of silence hung between them before Sunny burst out, "Dad would have *never* talked to me like this."

"Yes, he would have."

"No, he was perfect, not like you. Just my luck, the *wrong* parent died."

She doesn't mean that. Ivy curled her fingers into a tight ball and counted to five, trying to keep the hurt and anger out of her voice. "Don't pull your father into this. He wasn't perfect, but neither am I. Or you. No one is. Now, I'll text my credit card details to you. If you spend more than two more nights in Ibiza, I'll cancel your use of it, and I mean it. I'll also text Corrina's number. She's my travel agent and a good friend. I'll call her, and she'll be in touch with you."

A shaft of light from the hallway slanted across the room, and Ivy turned.

Shelly had opened the library door and was motioning to her. *Are you coming?* she mouthed.

Ivy pointed to the phone and mouthed back, *It's Sunny.*

"Fine." Sunny's tone shifted again, this time to one of spoiled belligerence. "If that's my only option—"

"It is. I love you, Sunny. Get yourself together and come

home."

Click. Sunny hung up.

Shelly placed a large yellow industrial flashlight on the table and perched on a brocade wingback chair. "Is Sunny okay?"

"She chased a prince to Ibiza—but that's a long story. I'm giving her my credit card so she can get a flight back tomorrow or the next day." Ivy tapped her phone and sent her credit card details to Sunny, along with a quick note to Corrina.

"Ouch, that's going to cost you." Shelly shook her head. "August is high season there."

"Corrina always finds great deals, even on short notice," Ivy said, hoping it wouldn't be too much. "I'll hold off writing the check to the tax authority until the following week. Or two. Getting Sunny back safely is more important." Which was true, of course, but Ivy had been looking forward to writing that check for the tax bill and regaining control over her finances.

Ivy never thought she'd be thrilled to write a check for back taxes, but she was. The worry of losing the house had kept her awake many nights. This would also resolve the last of Jeremy's financial disasters. Instead of paying the taxes, her husband had probably spent the money on Paisley. Feeling her energy wane at the thought of his girlfriend, Ivy scrubbed her hands over her cheeks. She had to extricate that woman from her mind.

Shelly raised an eyebrow. "Is Sunny coming here?"

"She's staying in Boston with Misty. She says that's where her friends are."

"I remember being that age. No one could tell me anything. Come on, sis." Standing up, Shelly held out her hand. "Forget Sunny's drama. She's a big girl, and she'll be fine. Just like we were. Now, let's go explore that attic."

Chapter 10

BENNETT SWUNG OUT OF HIS SUV in the car court behind the inn, anxious to see Ivy and congratulate her on Darla's dismissal of the lawsuits against the city and Ivy. As soon as he'd heard Nan say that Darla had backed off the cases, he'd called the city attorney. In turn, Maeve rang up Matthew, who had begrudgingly confirmed the rumor.

Bennett shook his head and smiled to himself. Such was the gossip news circuit in Summer Beach. Nothing stayed secret for long in the town, including the fact that Shelly had just returned. One of Mitch's customers at Java Beach had seen her get out of a ride-share car with a suitcase. Bennett smiled to himself. For Ivy's sake, he hoped she would stay.

As he stepped from his vehicle and shut the door, he saw Poppy emerge from the storage shed carrying an aluminum ladder toward the kitchen door. He strode after her.

"Need some help with that?"

"It's pretty light but sure. It needs to go upstairs into Aunt Ivy's room." Poppy stopped and leaned the ladder against the side of the house.

Bennett frowned. "Problems with the ceiling again?" Though the rain had stopped, the ceiling and roof still had to dry.

Poppy's eyes blazed with excitement. "We're going to explore the attic."

"Now?" Bennett hoisted the ladder over one shoulder and held the door for her.

"Shelly just arrived, and she's excited to see what's up there."

"Same old Shelly." Bennett chuckled and hefted the ladder under his arm. He followed Poppy up the back stairs to Ivy's room.

As he was setting up the ladder, Ivy and Shelly walked in. With one look at Ivy's face, he knew something was troubling her.

"Hey, Mr. Mayor," Shelly said, opening her arms wide to him.

"Great to see you back in town," Bennett said, giving Shelly a warm—though thoroughly respectful—hug. After talking to Mitch, Bennett knew something had happened between the two of them in Woodstock. Mitch was still crazy about Shelly, but she'd put the brakes on their relationship, just like Ivy had. These two women sure made a man work for their hearts, but he respected them all the more for that.

"Why, you need the votes?" Shelly asked in a teasing tone.

"Yours would be hard-earned, I'm sure." Bennett chuckled.

While Shelly and Poppy speculated about what they might find in the attic, Bennett turned to Ivy. Her forehead was creased with exasperation, and her attention was riveted on her phone. He tapped his fingers along her arm. "I'd planned to congratulate you on the lawsuit—or the lack thereof now—but, are you okay?"

Ivy leaned her head against his shoulder. "It's Sunny. She called to say she's stuck in Ibiza, and she's absolutely frantic. I know she's spoiled, but I'm concerned about her."

"Anything I can do to help?"

Turning up a corner of her lip, she gazed at him thoughtfully before shaking her head. "I'll let you know if there is. She's agreed to fly back to Boston as soon as she can book a flight. I'd like to see her start school in September. She's so close to finishing."

Bennett could see the love in Ivy's eyes as she spoke about Sunny, yet she was also clearly frustrated with her daughter. Not having children, he could only imagine what she was going through, even though he was close to his nephew. His sister Kendra always said that Logan behaved better with Bennett than with his parents. Bennett supposed that's just how kids were. Family dynamics were tough to dissect.

"Would Sunny come here?" Bennett wondered how Sunny would react to him. He and Misty had hit it off when they'd met over the Independence Day holiday, and he'd seen the love between Ivy and Misty. But from everything he'd heard, Sunny could be challenging.

"I wish she would, but no. Her friends are in Boston." Flinging up her hands, Ivy let out a mock scream of frustration. "That girl drives me crazy. If she could get out of her own way, she'd have so much to offer."

"Hey, you two," Shelly called out, flicking a flashlight around the bedroom like a strobe light. "I'm going up into the attic."

Bennett frowned. "The ladder is strong enough, but the floorboards could be damp up there. He paused, sizing up the situation. "Are you sure you want to go up there tonight?"

Shelly stepped onto the ladder. "Think there might be ghosts up there?"

"They usually come out at night," Poppy said. "I wonder why that is? If I were a ghost, stuck hanging out in this dimension, I'd want to catch some rays at the beach."

Ivy let out a strangled laugh. "You have a point, but I *don't* believe in ghosts."

"Well, I do," Shelly said with a quirky grin. "And I hope I run into the ghost of Amelia Erickson so she can explain why she hid so much in this house. I'd like to ask her if there's a box of cash or gold coins somewhere."

"Ghosts?" Ivy shuddered in response. "Then you're definitely going first."

Bennett watched the exchange between the two sisters. It was good to have Shelly back in town. Her infectious laughter sparked the atmosphere with fun, and the guests loved her. Bennett hadn't seen Ivy so happy since Shelly left—even if she was worried about Sunny right now.

"Want me to go up first?" Bennett said to Shelly. When she made a face at him, he spread his hands and added, "I'm a guy. I have to offer."

"Absolutely not," Shelly said, leaning against the ladder. "Why should you have all the fun?

Ivy's phone dinged, and she scanned a message. "Corrina has already located a reasonable flight and sent it to Sunny." She let out a sigh of relief. "She'll be on a plane soon."

Shelly climbed up another step. "See? Everything is working out."

"I wish she'd come here," Poppy said, a smile brightening her eyes.

Shelly made a face. "No, you don't."

"Shelly!" Ivy put her hands on her hips. "That's my daughter."

"What? I'm being honest," Shelly said. "I love her, but that girl would seriously disrupt our *chi* here."

"You have a point, but you don't have to worry," Ivy shot

back, grinning. "She'll stay in Boston and mess up Misty's *chi* instead."

Bennett laughed at their bickering. "Sounds like the arguments I have with Kendra." He loved his sister for calling him out.

"What do you two argue about?" Ivy asked, seemingly eager to change the subject.

"Science wasn't my best subject, but she aced it." Bennett ran a hand through his hair, recalling the heated discussions around the dinner table. "Occasionally, I've made un-scientifically-informed comments, and she's only too happy to let me know I'm wrong. In extreme scientific detail." He adored Kendra, and she liked teasing him. "Now that she's a scientist, I'm pretty proud of her."

"Lot of science in horticulture, too," Shelly said, taking another step up the ladder. She poked her head through the opening. "Wow, this attic is like another room." She reached in and knocked against the wood. "Floor seems solid enough. Awfully musty, though."

"How far across the house does it go?" Ivy called out. She and Poppy moved closer.

"Not too far," Shelly said. "Looks like a partial attic."

Bennett was curious, too. He took a step closer. When he had the listing, he hadn't thought to look in the attic. The home inspector had gone up there, but he hadn't mentioned anything special. Other than the fact that there were no signs of recent leakage.

Until now.

Suddenly, Shelly let out a cry and clambered back down the ladder.

Bennett braced the ladder. "What's wrong?"

Emerging from the opening, Shelly shuddered as she descended. "I felt a gust of cold air. You know what *that* means."

Poppy nodded sagely. "Ghosts. I had a feeling."

"Oh, come on, you two," Ivy said, exasperated. "There are no ghosts here. For heaven's sake, I have to *sleep* in this room."

"Better you than me." Shelly stepped off the ladder.

"Gee, thanks for your concern," Ivy said, batting Shelly on the shoulder.

Shelly held out the flashlight. "Who's next?"

Poppy backed away. "This is all you two. I have to check on guests."

"Why don't we wait until morning?" Bennett said, though his curiosity was piqued, too. "After a late night of haunting, ghosts probably sleep in on Saturdays. We'll have it all to ourselves."

Ivy scrunched up her nose, making a face at him as she swatted his arm. "Don't you start, too. I can't have the thought of apparitions floating in my head. I've had enough nightmares with Pixie and thunderstorms."

"Let's close it up, then," Poppy said.

Shelly started up the ladder again to press the tape back into place.

"Need a hand?" When she threw him a look of consternation, he shook his head. "I'm a guy."

"And I'm glad you are," Ivy said, kissing his cheek.

While Shelly and Poppy secured the covering over the hole in the attic, Bennett hugged Ivy to him, and she pressed her hand against his chest in a movement that felt so natural. The warmth of her hand was like a salve to his scarred heart, soothing him in a way no other woman had since his wife had died. He breathed in the scent of her perfume, which smelled like fresh jasmine.

Smiling at Ivy, he placed his hand over hers. Their relationship wasn't forced. Instead, he was letting her take the lead and following as she grew increasingly comfortable with him. Even though his testosterone was barking orders to charge in and sweep her off her feet like some old-fashioned movie hero, he'd known Ivy long enough to know that grand gestures didn't work with her.

Rowan Zachary was proof of that.

Bennett still couldn't get over the actor trying to give Ivy a new Mercedes convertible for saving his life. Sure, she'd dragged the guy from the pool during the wedding a few weeks ago—*that* had been a night to remember, he thought. But Rowan wanted more from Ivy—and that was clear to Bennett.

When Ivy had chosen the old, cherry-red Chevrolet he'd restored for her over the expensive sports car, Bennett had known she was the woman for him. The kind who valued effort over cold cash. He smoothed wisps of hair from Ivy's lovely face.

Speaking of cold cash… Ivy wasn't anything like Paisley Forsythe, who had flounced back to Summer Beach—but for what? To absolve her conscience? He wasn't buying it, and he wasn't convinced they'd seen the last of her. He hoped he was wrong, but he prided himself on being a good judge of people.

And still, Ivy took his breath away every day.

Bennett let his hand slide down Ivy's back, imagining the curves beneath her clothing. She wasn't a skin-and-bones stick figure like Paisley, who had enormous augmentations stitched to her chest. Some men might like that, but he preferred Ivy's natural beauty. Her softness made him feel like more of a man, and he could just imagine snuggling with her in front of a fireplace on a rainy night. It would be autumn before long, and then—

"Hey, are you still here with us?" Ivy asked, catching his hand and squeezing it.

"Sure, what?"

"Tomorrow," she said, her eyes twinkling at him now, almost as if she could read his mind. "We'll all gather here after breakfast to explore in the morning."

"You're on," he said, bringing her hand to his lips and kissing her fingertips. Before he let himself be whisked away by Ivy, he remembered his manners. "Now, how about we celebrate Shelly's homecoming?" He nodded toward Shelly. "That is, you are staying, right?"

Ivy and Poppy turned to Shelly with an inquisitive glance.

"I guess Summer Beach is stuck with me." Shelly turned a thoughtful look toward Ivy. "I love New York, but I'm ready for a change. Sometimes life serves up just the weird circumstances we need."

Bennett wondered what Shelly meant, and what that might mean for Mitch.

Above them, the taped plastic fell in a dramatic swoosh.

"And that must be a signal for you," Shelly said, laughing.

Bennett shook his head. "Where's the tape?"

"Here," Poppy said, handing him a roll.

He climbed the ladder and secured the heavy plastic cover that Forrest and Reed had put into place to keep out the musty odor and drafts. After doing that, he folded up the ladder and leaned it against the wall. Brushing off his hands, he asked, "How about a beach barbecue tonight?"

Shelly's eyes lit with keen interest. "With Sea Breezes by the fire pit?"

"One more, and that's my limit," Ivy said, leading Bennett towards the door. "Look at the trouble we get into," she added, angling her chin toward the ceiling.

"Hey, that was here when I arrived," Shelly said.

As they started for the door, Bennett glanced back at the room. The sheer draperies at the windows shifted. He nodded toward them. "That's Shelly's ghost. Nothing more than a drafty old house."

Ivy stared after the rippling fabric with parted lips.

Bennett walked to the window, pushed the sheers aside, and looked out over the sea. "An onshore wind has come up on the ocean. Look at the whitecaps."

"Well, yeah. But that window is closed." Shelly folded her arms.

"Stop it." Ivy chopped the air with her hand. "A draft. That's all it is." Turning toward the door, she said, "Let's get out of here."

"Glad I'm not sleeping in here," Shelly mumbled as she followed.

Ivy whirled around and leveled a finger at her sister. "Watch it. I'll send the ghost to your room."

Bennett couldn't quite discern if Ivy was serious or not, so he broke the tension with a chuckle. "I've sure missed this. Welcome back, Shelly." He held out his hand to Ivy. "Come on, I'm cooking tonight."

In Shelly's absence, Bennett had fallen into a routine with Ivy and Poppy in sharing the cooking during the week. However, he cooked more often on the weekend. He'd forgotten how much he'd enjoyed being in the kitchen with someone. He and Jackie had loved dabbling in the kitchen together, and being with Ivy brought back those memories.

As he and Ivy made their way through the hallway, he wondered where this relationship would go. With each passing day, Bennett was more determined than ever to have Ivy in his life—for as long as life would allow. While he counted patience as one of his good traits, breaking through Ivy's reserve was proving more difficult than he'd thought.

Chastising himself, he pulled his thoughts back from that path. *Not even six months yet.* And Ivy was still getting over Jeremy's death. When she was ready, he wanted to be the one she would choose. But holding back on telling her how he felt about her—without scaring her away as Rowan Zachary had—would require restraint.

Patience. Extreme patience.

As if she could read his mind, Ivy squeezed his hand. "Glad you enjoy this crazy family."

Out on the terrace, Bennett prepared the grill. Coaxing the coals to life, he soaked up the fresh breeze off the ocean. As he did, he thought about Ivy. With Shelly gone, she had been working long hours, and he seldom saw her bedroom light go off until long after midnight. Now that Shelly had returned, he wanted to take Ivy away for a day off.

An idea formed in his mind. A different beach, not too far away. They could take the vintage Chevy, put the top down... He fanned the flame in the grill to life and went back into the kitchen.

Ivy had brought out the ruby red grapefruit and cranberry juices and limes. She was mixing cool drinks at the kitchen counter for everyone. "How would you like yours?"

"Over ice with a small shot," he said. "We're celebrating no-more-lawsuits."

"Forever, I hope. I'll join you in that celebration." Ivy

passed an icy cocktail to Shelly, who'd plopped onto a stool.

"Almost as good as mine." Shelly held the drink aloft. "To being home, because life is truly better in Summer Beach."

The three clicked glasses, and Bennett added, "It's not too shabby. Good to have you back."

"Let the adventures begin again," Shelly said, hugging Ivy.

"I'll start dinner." Bennett took an armload of fresh fruits and vegetables he'd bought at the weekly farmer's market in the village from Gertie, one of the vintage turquoise refrigerators. After adjusting the separate hot and cold taps, he began to wash the produce in the deep kitchen sink. Strawberries, blueberries, and raspberries. Romaine lettuce, spinach, and arugula, along with red cherry tomatoes and sweet mini peppers in a range of hues from red to orange to yellow. He set aside several perfectly ripe avocados.

Bennett glanced at Ivy. His home would be ready to move back into soon, and he didn't want to waste the precious time he had with Ivy. Not that she would be far away, but it wouldn't be like this—every evening, preparing dinner together. Not until their relationship advanced. This was an anomaly, he knew.

As he ran the produce under water, Ivy joined him at the sink, which was a deep, old-fashioned model with plenty of room for two sets of hands.

"Need some help?" Ivy slid her hand along his and took a

stalk of romaine from his hands, brushing his fingers as she did.

"Sure," he said as a tingle from her touch sizzled through him. This was exactly what he wanted—a woman to share all the ordinary things in life. Any woman could be fun for a weekend—as he'd learned the hard way—but it took a special woman to feel like yourself. He'd been looking for a partner to bond with on a deep emotional level that he scarcely knew how to explain. He knew it when he felt it. *More than in his heart—she was in his soul.* He wasn't the kind of guy who went after the flashiest arm candy, but to him, Ivy was the most beautiful woman he'd seen since Jackie's death.

Ivy must have felt what he was thinking because she leaned into him and rested against him for a moment. "This probably sounds silly," she said. "But this is nice, just like this. Nothing fancy, just…"

When her voice trailed off, he grinned. "Just good, fresh vegetables, right?"

She smiled up at him, her face lit from within with joy. "The very, very best."

Her eyes shimmered, taking his breath away. He wanted to take her in his arms right then, but Shelly piped up behind them.

"So, what's for dinner?" Shelly spun around on the stool. "I'm famished."

Bennett turned his attention back to the supper preparations. "A seasonal summer salad with berries for a starter.

Then I'm grilling skewers of zucchini, Portobello mushrooms, and shrimp. And I have wild salmon marinating in olive oil, herbs, and lime."

"Yum. Want me to chop and assemble the skewers?" Shelly asked.

"Relax," Ivy said. "You've just flown in." She brought out a clean dishtowel to dry the vegetables.

"I'll help," Poppy said. "How many for dinner?"

Ivy glanced around. "Just the four of us, I suppose."

Shelly swirled her drink, clinking ice cubes. "We could always call Mitch, I suppose. I mean, we're all friends here, right?"

Bennett picked up on her request. "Plenty of food. I can give him a shout." Shelly shot him a quick nod as he dried his hands and pulled out his phone to text Mitch. After a few taps, Bennett said, "Done. Hope he gets it."

As a shy smile brightened Shelly's face, Ivy touched Bennett's hand.

Shelly still has feelings for Mitch, Bennett thought. He hoped Mitch would pick up the message and come over—unless his friend was protecting his heart, which was entirely possible. Bennett wondered if Mitch would join them.

Chapter 11

"NOTHING LIKE A MAN AND his grill," Shelly said. She stepped onto the terrace, nodding toward Bennett, who was tending the fire. He was turning skewers stuffed with vegetables and shrimp.

"Just smell that," Ivy said, inhaling the aroma of garlic and herbs as her gaze settled on Bennett. "Delicious, indeed."

Ivy balanced the salad and serving utensils, while Poppy and Shelly carried dishes and napkins and silverware to the table. The evening was balmy and fresh—perfect for dining *al fresco*. While supper was cooking, Ivy had slipped upstairs to freshen up and change into a turquoise sundress with matching sandals that her mother had given her. Though it was a little shorter than she was used to, she loved the color.

"Going to need a plate over here," Bennett called out.

"Got it," Poppy replied. "You can warm the bread, too." She hurried toward him with a baguette loaf under one arm and a plate from the butler's pantry.

The china was fairly ornate for a beach supper. Still, Ivy loved the blue-and-white pattern Amelia had chosen and decided they might as well enjoy it every day. The intricate design appealed to Ivy's artistic sense.

As Ivy and Shelly set a table on the terrace near the beach, Shelly looked up and grinned. "You and Bennett seem to have gotten pretty close while I was gone. But why are you hiding it?"

"We're not close like *that*, if that's what you're insinuating." Ivy gazed after him.

"Aren't you both consenting adults?" Shelly began placing silverware around the table.

Ivy lifted her chin. "I haven't consented to anything."

Shelly flicked a fork in the air. "You seem a lot more serious than when I was here before. At ease with each other, is what I mean."

Ivy lifted a shoulder and let it drop. "We enjoy each other's company. Where's the harm in that?"

"No harm at all. Wonder what Sunny will think of him?"

"We're definitely not at that point." A knot of concern tightened in Ivy's chest. "But Bennett and Misty got along well."

"Uh-huh. That's Misty."

"His house is being repaired, so he won't be here much longer anyway." Ivy would miss his presence. Watching him putter around with the old Chevy always brought a smile to her face.

Shelly arched an eyebrow. "Maybe that will be a good thing."

"What do you mean by that?" Ivy asked, feeling a little defensive.

"When Mitch and I were in Woodstock, we spent a lot of time talking," Shelly said, sorting the cutlery. "What I realized is that circumstances throw people together. Dating because of convenience. Like when you go out with someone who lives in your building."

As Ivy positioned the salad in the center of the table, she glanced at Bennett under her lashes. "Do you think that's what happened with Mitch?"

"Oh, come on." Shelly waved a butter knife and lowered her voice. "What are the chances that you and I would both find Mr. Right here in Summer Beach? Slim to none. Let's face it. These guys, hunky as they are, they're just friends."

Ivy met Shelly's gaze. "Are you trying to convince me...or yourself?"

"I'm being practical."

Ivy stifled a cough. That wasn't a word she would use to describe Shelly. Her sister must have done a lot of soul-searching. "What about young people who fall in love with next-door neighbors and spend lifetimes together?"

"Rare."

"But it happens."

"That would mean there wasn't one true love for you in the world, just whoever was randomly in your orbit." Shelly made a face. "I don't believe that."

Was there another explanation? Ivy pondered this as she arranged the serving utensils. "Maybe the universe has a way of putting people together."

"Like the Great Oz or a cosmic matchmaker?" Shelly blew wisps of hair from her face. "Why do I have to be matched up at all? Marriage is a social arrangement designed to perpetuate the human race and keep society in line. Women, anyway. I like my freedom."

"Whoa, that's way beyond this discussion," Ivy said. "Look, no one says you *have* to be matched up. Do what makes you happy." She thought about her life with Jeremy, and how she'd thought they were well suited to each other. When the children were young, he'd seemed to delight in all their accomplishments.

Shelly paused and peered at her. "When you were married, did you think you were happy?"

Ivy bristled at Shelly's words. "What kind of question is that?"

"I'm not denigrating you." Shelly stepped closer. "I truly want to know what it was like, how you felt."

"I loved the companionship, the spark that still flared between us. Knowing that he was there for me." Ivy choked a little on that last bit. She noted the earnestness in Shelly's eyes. "Happily married doesn't mean happy every moment. Every couple, like every person, faces challenges in life."

"You sure did," Shelly said softly.

"Do I wish certain things had been different? Of course. But every life has rough spots. To think otherwise is incredibly naïve. But then, maybe I was." Ivy puffed out a bit of air in exasperation. She hadn't told Shelly about Paisley yet. As she folded navy blue napkins, Ivy wondered just when she and Jeremy drifted apart. Maybe it was after the girls left for college. She recalled the emptiness in the house, the unexpected quiet between them. Had the opportunistic Paisley somehow sensed that?

"While you were gone..." Ivy hesitated and looked up at Shelly. "I met her, you know."

Shelly's mouth dropped open. "The other woman?"

"I'll give you the details later. Let's not spoil the evening." Ivy glanced over her shoulder at Bennett. With rounded eyes, Shelly distributed the napkins while Ivy folded.

As Ivy sorted the silverware, she remembered Paisley telling her that Jeremy intended to end their affair. She paused, holding a spoon aloft. *He still had hope in his heart for a future with me.* That meant a lot to her now. Strangely, she had Paisley to thank for that, too.

Ivy flicked another look toward Bennett, admiring his focus on the grill as he turned the skewered vegetables just so.

The breeze sent a wayward strand of hair across her face. Pushing it back, she smiled at her sister, truly happy to have her back. "Marriage or not, finding the right person to share your life with can be awfully nice. Fulfilling. If you have a chance, don't let that go."

"That look. Right there." Shelly pointed her finger at Ivy and grinned. "I swear, you look like you fell in love while I was gone."

Instantly, Ivy felt blood rush to her cheeks. "I don't know that I'd call it *that.*" She lifted her chin, hesitant to label what she and Bennett had. It was far easier to encourage others to find their soul mates. Did she even believe in that anymore? She wanted to think she did, but judging from the ache in her chest, her heart was still scarred from Jeremy. A gust from the ocean lifted a napkin, and Ivy caught it before it took sail. "I think dinner's ready," she said, anchoring the cloth with cutlery.

As Ivy made her way toward Bennett, she tried to squash the panic that rose in her chest. Shelly's choice of words was an icy blast of reality.

Why couldn't she and Bennett simply enjoy each other's company? She stared at Bennett's broad back, taking in the muscular curve of his shoulders and hips forged from running. He had a superb form that she admired… *On an artistic level, right?* She blinked.

It wasn't as if they were bed-hopping at the inn.

She pressed a hand to her mouth. Did people *think* that?

And why should she care?

But she did.

At that thought, Ivy felt a twinge of desire that she was afraid to acknowledge. Love and desire—when these two entwined, the effect was powerful.

"Supper's ready," Bennett said with a flourish of long grill tongs. As his gaze rested on her, a broad smile filled his face and crinkled his eyes.

"Smells fabulous," Ivy said, making her way toward him. Bennett's easy smile was reassuring, calming the warring factions of her mind and heart.

The four of them gathered around the table on the terrace, dining on Bennett's fresh grilled feast. Ivy kept her phone close in case Sunny needed to reach her. Ivy and Poppy took turns bringing Shelly up to date on Seabreeze Inn operations, while Bennett filled in with the latest Summer Beach gossip. Through it all, Ivy saw Shelly studiously ignore the empty place setting for Mitch.

During a lull in the conversation, Ivy caught Bennett's gaze and nodded toward the vacant chair in their midst.

Clearing his throat, Bennett said, "Mitch must have gotten hung up with something at Java Beach. He'll probably be here soon."

Shelly shrugged as if it didn't bother her. "Whatever, we're just friends. Hey, let's talk about that attic. Poppy said you found a photo album. Did you look through it?"

"It's pretty amazing," Ivy said, sliding roasted vegetables

and shrimp off a skewer. "Observing strangers' lives, trying to sort out their family, and figuring out what they were about is daunting. I don't know what to look for."

A massive wave thundered onto the shore, diverting Ivy's attention for a moment. Swinging back to Shelly, she added, "Amelia and her husband seemed to have a beautiful life."

"You always romanticize things," Shelly said, tearing off a piece of bread. "You paint life the way you want it to be."

"Meaning not the way it really is?" Ivy bristled at that idea. "Maybe I paint it the way I think life *can* be."

"Might take more than one to make that happen," Shelly said.

Mitch's vacant chair seemed even more conspicuous.

Ivy sipped her drink. "Some have argued that doesn't matter."

Slightly confused, Bennett looked between the two of them. "Did I miss something?"

"They do this all the time," Poppy said. "Sisters have a separate line of communication. Coral and I are like that."

Ivy waved a hand. "Doesn't matter." Shelly seemed on edge and eager to jump into an argument. Feeling the emptiness of the chair next to her, Ivy raised her glass. "We're celebrating tonight."

"To Shelly," Bennett said. "And to the end of the lawsuits."

"And to finding treasure in the attic," Shelly said. "Think of the millions of dollars of painting and jewels that Amelia hid in this house. Maybe we can keep a trinket or two this time?"

"It's not a very large attic, and it seems fairly empty up there," Ivy said, though she, too, couldn't help wondering what else Amelia might have hidden on the premises. *And why?* "Forrest and Reed are coming tomorrow to repair the damage from the rain."

"Then we'd better start early," Shelly said, sliding a hand over her hair as a gust of wind sailed in from the ocean.

"The breeze is getting cooler," Poppy said. "I'll light the fire pit."

"Sounds good," Shelly said, as if eager to leave the empty place setting behind.

"You two get it started," Ivy said. "I'll take the dishes inside."

"I'll help," Bennett said, stacking the plates.

As soon as they were out of earshot, Ivy turned to Bennett. "Think Mitch is coming? I can wrap up a plate for him."

Bennett put the dishes down and checked his phone. Frowning, he shook his head. "I thought he would've liked to welcome Shelly back."

"They went to Woodstock during his visit to New York," Ivy said, rinsing the dishes in the sink. "Think something happened there?"

"Maybe. Shelly seems to be going to great effort to ignore the fact that Mitch hasn't shown up."

"She keeps insisting that they're just friends, too."

"Mitch cares a lot for your sister," Bennett said, leaning against the counter and crossing one foot in front of the other. "If she's not reciprocating, he might not want to get his heart broken."

Ivy stacked the plates before turning back to him. "She needs time," she said, shaking droplets from her hands into the sink.

As Bennett picked up a dishtowel, he smiled. "Now, where have I heard that before?" Enveloping her hands with the soft cloth, he stepped toward her.

The warmth of his hands on hers drew her in. He slid the towel over the back of her hands, then turned her palms up, gently blotting droplets from her skin, which sent shivers through her. In drying her hands, his motions were so simple, so ordinary, yet the intimacy was overwhelming. Her breath quickening, she took a half step closer, until their thighs touched.

Without a word, he folded her into his arms. She rested her head against his chest, which still held the sweet, smoky scent of the grill. As she listened to his heartbeat, she closed her eyes, wondering what it would be like to fall asleep like this.

"Sometimes, we think we have all the time in the world," Bennett said, tracing a circle on her back.

His gravelly voice rumbled in his chest, sounding unusually thick. At once, Ivy understood. They both knew the searing intensity of loss that could slice through a heart in a second. She drew back from him and nodded.

As her eyes watered, she laughed softly, and he drew his thumb under her eye with a gentle caress. It was then she noticed the emotion welling in his eyes, too.

Startled at the intensity in his gaze, she pulled away and gestured toward Shelly and Poppy outside. A roaring blaze illuminated the fire pit. "We'd better help them manage that fire."

Because the one in her heart was threatening to flame out of control, and she wasn't ready. "All we need is another rampant fire," she said, recalling the devastating Ridgetop Fire. "Between Darla, Shelly, and Sunny, it's already been quite a day."

"I'll take a fire extinguisher," Bennett said, reaching under the sink for a shiny red canister. "Just in case."

Ivy and Bennett joined Shelly and Poppy around the fire and managed to bring the blaze under control. Poppy had positioned beach chairs around the slate-lined fire pit, and they all eased into them. Bennett sat close to her, their arms touching.

Ivy smiled at Bennett in the dancing light, which framed his silhouette. "Perfect way to end the day."

"I'll say." Bennett reached for her hand.

As the flickering warmth enveloped her, Ivy nodded toward her niece, who sat across from her. "Glad you talked me into the fire pit, Poppy. With the waves crashing behind us and the stars above, it's rather magical."

"Guests will love this," Shelly said, shaking her tousled hair in the breeze. "Especially in the winter. When the weather cools, we can have the late afternoon wine party by the fire." She swung out her arms as she spoke. "We'll open the doors and let the music soar out. And these grounds are perfect for events. Speaking of events, how's the planning for the art show?"

"We canceled it," Ivy said.

"Why?" Shelly asked, frowning. "That was your baby."

Ivy glanced at Poppy. "We couldn't manage everything. So, we cut back on activities, and the art show was among those things we cut."

Shelly pursed her lips. "Well, I'm here now, so let's put it back on the calendar."

"I don't know if we can still get the artists here," Poppy said. "People were pretty upset when we canceled."

"Then they'll be dying to come," Shelly said. "I'll promote it on my vlog and social media, especially to the horse racing crowd in Del Mar. We can draw a lot of them in. Do we still have their details?"

"We do," Ivy said.

"I'll take over the yoga class and the exterior gardens again so you can focus on your show." Shelly glanced around the grounds. "You didn't do a bad job around here, but these plants are screaming for me." She put a hand to her ear. "I swear I can hear them. *Help me, Shelly, please...*" With a deadpanned expression, Shelly added, "That was the gardenia bushes. Look at all their crinkled brown blossoms. Do either of you know how to deadhead the flowers?"

Ivy made a face. "Don't start now."

"I'll help you, Shelly," Poppy said, chuckling. "And I'll help Aunt Ivy with the show just as we'd planned. Her eyes glittered with excitement in the glow of the fire. "You guys will never guess who called to see if he could show his work here."

"I can't imagine," Ivy said, wondering if they could really pull it all off in time.

"Rowan Zachary," Poppy announced. "I had no idea he was an artist. But I looked him up online, and he's done a lot of work."

"Just keep him away from the pool." Ivy wondered what the actor was up to. She wasn't familiar with Rowan's art, but she wasn't surprised. Creative people were often creative in different fields.

"Then it's settled," Shelly said. "The Seabreeze Art Show is back on."

Chapter 12

"THIS IS INCREDIBLE," IVY CALLED out as she hoisted herself up into the attic. She sneezed against the dust she'd disturbed that now swirled against a slanting kaleidoscope of rainbow colors. The morning sun streamed through a small round, stained-glass window in the attic, casting prisms of color across the wooden floor.

"Amazing," she murmured, thinking about how she could render this on canvas. She reached into her pocket for her phone and snapped a photo for later reference. The day Reed had found the satchel had been gray and overcast, and she'd been preoccupied with Paisley.

"How's it look?" Shelly called up through the entry hole

in the ceiling.

Ivy peered down. "Come up. You have to see this." She tested the floor before walking across to the window.

At least this excursion into the attic would take Shelly's mind off Mitch for a little while, Ivy thought. He'd never appeared last night, even though Ivy, Shelly, Poppy, and Bennett had sat by the firepit talking until nearly midnight.

Shelly scaled the ladder, followed by Poppy. Bennett had been called away this morning on city business, but he promised to check in later.

"Wow, I hadn't noticed that window much from the outside," Shelly said. "I mean, I saw it, but from this side, it's gorgeous. Seems like a waste to have it in an attic where no one ever sees the sun shining through it."

Ivy ran her fingers over the vintage leaded glass, awestruck by the beauty and craftsmanship of the intricate design, which depicted a ship sailing across an open sea under crystalline skies.

Poppy flicked on her flashlight and craned her neck. "Who puts a chandelier like that in the attic?"

Ivy and Shelly looked at each other. "Are you thinking what I'm thinking?"

"That this was an attic room Amelia closed up?" Shelly flicked on the light from her phone. Above them, dusty faceted crystal glimmered faintly in the sunlight streaming through the stained glass.

"That chandelier has been raised," Ivy said. "Look at the

extra electrical cord looped over a hook up here. Originally, the chandelier was on a longer drop." She followed the line of the ceiling with a beam of light from a flashlight she'd pulled from her jeans pocket.

"Maybe that was the style back then," Shelly said.

"And the wallpaper," Ivy said. "It matches what I've seen behind the drawers in the closet cabinets."

Shelly made a face. "Who wallpapers an attic?"

Ivy swept the light over the attic floor. "This part up here might have been the upper half of the master bedroom. I bet the room had a raised ceiling. Maybe for a special piece of art."

"We can look at the plans," Shelly said. "We weren't looking for anything like that."

"So why would Amelia do that?" Poppy asked.

Shelly shrugged. "Maybe to make a hiding place for something."

"Or someone. This was done quickly, or they would have moved the chandelier, don't you think?" Ivy swung her beam toward a wall. "And the footprint is smaller than the bedroom. Let's see if something is behind that wall."

Shelly made her way across the floor and ran her fingers over the painted plasterboard. She tapped against it and turned around with a grin. "I think you're right. Sledgehammers again?"

Ivy swept her beam of light across the wall. "Maybe there's another way in."

Poppy walked around a corner. "There's a bunch of old furniture over here."

Ivy and Shelly joined her. A small table, chairs, a couple of wingback chairs. A mattress set covered in navy-and-white ticking leaned against a large bookcase.

"Nothing much here," Shelly said.

A prickly feeling tickled Ivy's neck. "Wait. Help me move this mattress."

"Are you crazy?" Shelly said.

"Crazy enough to think like Amelia." With Poppy's help, Ivy shoved the mattress to one side.

Shelly's eyes flared with understanding. "I'll get the bookcase."

As it turned out, the shelving unit was made of dark wood with an ornately carved base and sturdy shelves. "Looks like an old piece from Mexico or Spain. Must have taken two men to get this up here," Ivy said.

"With a crane," Shelly said, panting. "Wouldn't fit through that hole, so this stuff had to be moved up here before the ceiling was finished."

Ivy grinned at her sister. "Now, you're thinking. The question is *why?*"

The two sisters braced themselves against one side of the bookcase, shoving until the bookshelf creaked to one side.

Poppy cried out. "Aunties, look!"

Ivy dusted her hands and stepped around the massive bookcase. An entry the size of a tall doggie door was cut into the wall and sealed. As Poppy illuminated the area with her flashlight, Ivy said, "Looks like the entryway to the heating system. Maybe the ductwork was put in after the house was built."

Poppy raised her brow. "Just large enough for a person to crawl through."

Shelly knelt beside it and ran her fingers around it. "Seems like it has a little sliding door."

"Can you open it?" Ivy's pulse quickened.

"It's really tight," Shelly said. "Do we have anything I can use to dig in there to open it?"

"Here," Ivy said, fishing a Swiss army knife from her jeans.

Shelly looked surprised. "Since when did you start carrying a miniature tool kit around?"

"Since I had to start fixing lots of little things around here," Ivy retorted. "Thought we might need it up here." She flipped it open and folded out a short, flathead screwdriver blade. "Try this."

"I can't tell you how impressed I am with you, sis," Shelly said as she worked at dislodging the small panel. She shoved her weight against it until it sprang free.

Ivy and Poppy knelt to peer through the tiny doorway.

"Who's first?" Poppy asked.

Ivy and Shelly looked at each other. "You're the smallest, Poppy. Why don't you squeeze through?"

"Um, I'm not *that* much smaller than Shelly," Poppy

said, wincing.

"Ivy, you could easily fit," Shelly added.

Puffing out an exasperated breath, Ivy said, "What happened to everyone's sense of adventure?"

"I dunno," Shelly said. "Dark little enclosure. Possible rats—"

"We do *not* have rats," Ivy said, but neither Poppy nor Shelly seemed inclined to crawl through a tiny hole in the wall. "Fine. I'm going in."

Dropping to her hands and knees, she eased toward the opening.

"You have to slither through on your stomach," Shelly said, holding a flashlight for her.

"I have an idea." Ivy flipped over onto her back, grabbed the top edge of the opening, and slid herself through. An even mustier odor assaulted her nose, and complete darkness enveloped her. Only the outline of the small opening behind her offered any light.

"Need a light in here," Ivy called out, reaching a hand through the opening. With flashlight in hand, she arched the beam around the room.

"Oh, my goodness," she whispered, awestruck for the second time today.

On the other side of the opening, Shelly's voice rang out. "What is it?"

"You have to see this." The gravity of what Amelia must have faced in her life nearly overwhelmed Ivy. She flipped over and stood.

A scuffle sounded on the other side of the wall, and Shelly slid through, followed by Poppy.

"What? This looks like a dorm room," Poppy said, shining her flashlight over a stack of bunk beds.

"Seems Amelia was getting ready for an invasion," Shelly said.

"I think you're right." Ivy stepped toward the beds, each of which had neatly folded sheets, blankets, and pillows on them. She touched a dove-gray woolen blanket that was soft to the touch, not itchy as she'd expected.

"Not the upstairs maid's quarters?" Poppy asked.

Ivy shook her head. "Amelia took great effort to hide this. Think about it. World War II. Hawaii attacked. She must have built this to shelter people who'd be at great risk during the war. How many others would have had that foresight and acted on it?" Ivy's respect for Amelia grew as she considered this.

Shelly spun around in awe. "Wonder if it was ever used?"

Poppy shone her light on a table and chairs in the middle of the room. "Looks like you could sleep about eight in this room."

"And more on the floor," Shelly said. "Family-sized. Amelia must have lived through a lot in Europe in the first war." She opened a cupboard in a corner. "Oh, wow!"

Ivy looked over her shoulder. Tin cans with faded labels stared back at them.

Shelly picked up a torn piece of paper. "Jerky, raisins, crackers. This is someone's grocery list. I'd say she definitely housed people up here."

Ivy gazed at the old artifacts. "Submarines got close to the coast during the war, but never landed, except for one that ran ashore north of here." Ivy swung around. "Originally, there had to be another way in. While Bennett and I were looking for leaks in the ceiling, we never found another entry point from the house into the attic. So how would people get up here?"

"Look, there's another room beyond here. Poppy wedged herself through an opening beside the cupboard. "Beds are stacked in here, too."

Ivy and Shelly followed her into a series of rabbit-warren type rooms, all similarly outfitted. Simple artwork of still lifes and pastoral scenes adorned the walls, giving the dark spaces spots of cheer. None of the artwork was particularly valuable, Ivy thought, unlike what had been sealed in the lower level. She leaned in to look at a signature on a charcoal sketch, wondering if the artwork might have been created by an occupant.

"Looks like we have a lot more rooms to rent," Shelly said.

Poppy grimaced. "Guests wouldn't want to stay up here. I wonder how they, you know, tended to their personal business?"

"Chamber pots, I guess," Ivy said, opening a small door. "My guess is that this was not meant to be a closet."

The three women stared inside the small room, which was set up as a sort of indoor outhouse.

A wave of compassion overtook Ivy. Blinking, she said, "I can't imagine what the world would be like for people to need to hide in places like this."

"It happened," Shelly said quietly. "And it's still happening in many parts of the world."

Ivy heaved a great sigh. "Amelia must have been an amazing woman to put a plan like this in place. We know this home was used as a rehabilitation center during the war. This construction might have been done at that time, or maybe even before."

"Could've been around the time she sealed off the lower level," Shelly said thoughtfully. "If the coastline was attacked, people could hide up here. Others were interned, like Americans of Japanese heritage, right here in California and other states. It's pretty sobering."

Ivy rubbed her arms. "I think these rooms were havens of hope. I can't believe all this was up here, and we didn't know. Amelia was an expert in the art of concealment."

"Like a spy," Poppy said.

Ivy stared at her and wondered. "She *was* well connected."

"Paintings, jewelry, and now all this," Shelly said. "Maybe I was wrong. Maybe she wasn't a greedy old woman, after all."

They threaded their way back to the first room. Ivy paused. A door at one end stood slightly ajar. "Is that a closet?"

"I already looked in there," Poppy said.

Ivy opened the door and illuminated the floor area. "There's another hatch door in here."

"Bet it leads into the bedroom or bathroom," Poppy said.

Ivy knelt, lifted the hinged door, and peered inside. "This leads into the closet below." She sat back on her heels. "Just brilliant. This gave them access into the bathroom."

"Aunt Ivy, we should bring up the camping lanterns that we bought for our earthquake preparedness. That way, we can explore more. We won't have to use candles as they did."

"How do you know they used candles?" Ivy shut the hatch and stepped from the closet.

Poppy motioned toward a corner of the room. "There, on that little desk."

Ivy felt curiously drawn to the small wooden desk. It was a three-legged desk tucked into the corner just so, along with a diminutive chair. Ivy crossed the room. The little drawer was empty, except for a fountain pen. On the top of the desk, a slender candle stood in a darkly tarnished holder that was probably silver.

Reaching out, Ivy touched the waxy candle and burnt wick. Her fingers came away smudged with soot, and an odd sensation coursed through her. "Why is the candle *here*? Shouldn't it be in the center of the room on the table?"

"If you happened to be writing something there, you'd need light on it," Poppy ventured.

Ivy held up a finger. "Exactly." Bending over, she ran her hand under the desk until she touched a small ledge, similar to the one she'd found downstairs in the library under the built-in desk. She flicked on her light. "What have we here?"

Shelly and Poppy crowded around Ivy. A moment later, she slid out a small, leather-bound book.

"I'm almost afraid to open it," Ivy said softly, touching the cover with reverence. A frisson of excitement spiraled through her. Opening the dusty cover, a familiar, faint script stared up at her. "This might be..." She paused and looked up, smiling with anticipation. "Amelia's journal."

"Yes!" Shelly did a fist pump and high-fived Poppy, who was bouncing on her toes.

Chapter 13

BENNETT CRUISED THROUGH HIS OLD neighborhood on the ridge, observing the changes in the area. He recalled the freak, raging fire that had taken the homes of several neighbors, leaving other houses damaged and gaping into the night. But now, new foundations dotted the street.

He passed Imani, who was looking at a set of plans on the hood of a pickup truck. Easing his SUV to a stop, he saw a contractor he knew standing next to Imani.

"Hi, Mr. Mayor," Imani called out. Her canary-yellow sundress fluttered in the breeze, and she had a hand clamped to her head to keep her hat from blowing away. "Come see what we're planning. Boz will be here soon."

Bennett joined the pair, anxious to see what Imani had planned. "Hey Axe, how're you doing?" He clasped the other man's beefy hand. Axe was a well-known contractor in Summer Beach. He'd built and renovated many homes in the community, from Carol Reston's ridgetop villa to Jen and George's mid-century bungalow around the corner from Nailed It.

"Times are good," Axe said. "Still, my crew can start on your home next. Imani's is going to take some time."

"I'm taking care of the easy stuff," Bennett said. "When I get to the hard parts, I'll let you know. I want to see other folks back in their homes first."

A grin spread across Axe's weathered face. He was what people called rugged, but he had a heart as big as Montana, where he'd spent his childhood.

"I hear you're pretty comfortable at the Seabreeze Inn," Axe said. "You're in the old chauffeur's quarters?"

"He's got an entire apartment above the garages," Imani said. "I would've taken it, but Jamir wanted his own room. We've got connecting doors, so it's kind of homey. But this is my dream," she said, tapping on the architectural plans. "If only we can get the plans approved."

Axe nodded. "One way or another, we'll help everyone we can get back into their homes up here." He jerked a thumb just past Bennett's house. "Celia and Tyler can move back into their place soon."

Bennett was glad. His neighbors had sure had a rough go

of it, what with being separated for months. Tyler had finally woken up and realized he'd acted selfishly. To Celia's credit, she was making him earn a place in her heart again. Some men needed that. As smart as Tyler was, he could sure act childish at times. Tyler had called Bennett a few times for advice, and he'd sounded genuinely remorseful.

Bennett gestured toward the architectural drawings. "What's the problem with the plans?"

Imani turned toward the razed lot where her bungalow had once stood. "My house was the smallest one in the neighborhood, and it was on the smallest lot."

"Technically, she can't rebuild what she had under the current code for square footage and lot size. That's why Boz is coming up here."

At the mention of the city head of zoning and planning, Bennett looked up to see Boz pulling to the curb in his Jeep. Boz pulled a baseball cap over his thick silver hair and stepped out. They all greeted each other.

Imani shook Boz's hand. "Can't wait to show you what can be done on this tiny lot. Axe had some great ideas."

"Sure like to see them," Boz said. "You have a right to rebuild, but the building and zoning codes have changed since your original home was built."

They talked about the need for a shorter setback, and Imani's desire to build a second story.

"I'd like a retreat that's in the clouds," Imani said. "And wait until you see what I have planned for the landscaping.

Shelly's promised to help, so you know it's going to be incredible."

Axe pushed his cap back on his head. "Pretty talented lady, I hear. Is she dating anyone?"

Bennett and Imani traded looks. "Shelly just arrived back from New York," Bennett said, sidestepping the question. He wasn't sure if Axe and Mitch were friends. But then, maybe Shelly wasn't interested in either one of them.

"I might swing by the inn," Axe said, stroking his chin.

"Boz, will I need to go before the city council with this plan?" Imani asked, swiftly changing the subject.

"Let's stick to the formalities," Boz said, nodding. "We can get you on the agenda for the next meeting. Can you be ready for that?"

"She's ready now," Axe said.

Boz shook his head. "Can't break ground until you have approvals."

Axe turned his attention toward Bennett. "My crew can tackle your house in the interim. Won't take long to finish. How does that sound to you?"

"Anyone else on your waiting list?" As much as Bennett loved his home at the top of the hill, he was reticent about leaving the inn just yet. He'd grown accustomed to having coffee with Ivy in the morning. Seeing her around the old house and the grounds had become a favorite part of his daily routine.

"Another big job. Won't want to start that and leave it."

Axe cocked his head. "How about next Monday?"

Bennett had let other homeowners get in the contractor line before him, but his insurance company had been pressuring him to close the claim. He couldn't stay at the inn forever. "Unless there's anyone else who needs help first."

"We have to take care of our Mayor," Axe said.

"Constituents first," Bennett said, waving toward Imani, who was watching him with a little smile. She had him figured out, for sure. He felt his neck grow warm.

"Bennett, you're next on the list," Axe said, making a note on a small spiral notebook he tucked back in his pocket. "My crew will start work on your place on Monday morning."

This time, Bennett couldn't disagree. "Okay. Now, let's see how Imani's house would sit on the lot."

Axe pointed to stakes in the ground, anchoring the perimeter of the proposed house. While they walked the lot, Boz fell into step beside Bennett and slowed his pace.

"I hear you've got a nice apartment at the inn," Boz said. "Don't blame you for putting off your repairs."

"I'm comfortable." Why was everyone suddenly interested in his business? But then, this was Summer Beach. Word traveled as fast as the waves that hugged the shore.

"Uh-huh," Boz said. "Ivy's a pretty special woman."

"So now you're a fan?"

"Always was. It was her sleazy husband I didn't care for. Or that woman he was running around with. Say, did you know she's been nosing around?"

Bennett pressed his lips together and faced the breeze from the ocean. "Kind of hard to miss that news. Ivy said Paisley was looking for forgiveness."

"More than that, I think. Nan got friendly with one of the partner's assistants at the consulting firm where Paisley works. She helped the woman find accommodations for that partner named Dexter here in Summer Beach once."

"Paisley?

"No, Nan. She said Paisley might have another agenda now."

"Nan said that?"

"No, the assistant. Keep up, will you?" Boz elbowed him.

"I'm trying." Bennett's head was spinning. "Haven't we talked about the gossip problem in this town?"

"Come on, how else would you know what's really going on? You should talk to Nan and warn Ivy. Nan doesn't know how to approach her with this. It's pretty sensitive."

Bennett pressed a hand on Boz's muscular forearm. "Back up. Exactly what do I need to warn Ivy about?"

"Paisley just became engaged to this partner at her firm. Seems Dexter Hansen has been saying that Jeremy made certain promises to Paisley about the house that constitute a contract of sorts. He thinks she has a good case."

"For what? That's Ivy's property."

"Maybe not. Just giving you fair warning."

"When did this happen?"

"Yesterday. Just saying Ivy should know."

Ahead of them, Imani and Axe turned around to wait for them.

"The view from this angle is one of the best on the block," Axe called out, motioning to them.

Boz hurried ahead, and Bennett followed, trying to sort out what he'd just heard. They'd just gotten rid of Darla's lawsuit, and Ivy was concerned about her daughter Sunny. Plus, the two sisters were planning on putting on an art fair on the grounds of the inn, which could pull hundreds, if not thousands, of people into Summer Beach. Word around town was that Rowan Zachary was going to be there to show his paintings. *Who knew the guy could paint?* Bennett was still sore at him for trying to usurp Ivy's affections with a flashy convertible.

The last thing Ivy needed was a threat from Paisley—if the rumor was true. Sometimes he wondered who was really running this town. Maybe Nan should be the next mayor. He chuckled at the thought for a moment, but then decided that, with training, she might make a pretty good one.

For sure, Ivy had a lot on her mind. Now that Shelly was back, Bennett figured he might talk Ivy into getting away for a little relaxation before the art show. And he knew just the place.

After they'd finished walking the lot and discussing how to get approval for Imani's home by grandfathering her lot into the current code, Axe rolled up the plans.

"See you around the inn," Axe said. "As I recall, my

neighbor's son occasionally plays the violin there. The boy is part of Celia's music program at the school. He's pretty good."

"Well, isn't it a small world?" Imani commented, casting a glance at Bennett.

"So, I'll probably stop by to visit sometime," Axe said.

Imani raised her brow. "And meet Shelly?"

Axe only grinned. After he and Boz left, Imani whipped around to Bennett. "Your friend Mitch better figure out if he wants to date Shelly. Competition's heating up. And Axe is a good guy, too. Buys a lot of flowers from me for the ladies, but between you and me, his taste in women hasn't been too good lately. Shelly's in a different league, though."

"I'm not getting involved," Bennett said, holding up his hands. "Mitch and Shelly have some sort of agreement."

Imani put a hand on her hip. "Yeah, I heard. Just friends," she added, curling her fingers in the air for quotes. "Pfft. He's gonna lose out if he waits—and so will she. You should talk to him. He looks up to you like a father."

"Hey, I'm not that old."

"You're not getting any younger, but we're not talking about you right now. Though maybe we should be."

"You know what happens when people get involved in other people's business," Bennett said, catching Imani's hat as a gust of wind kicked up from the sea.

"I do," she said, snatching her hat back from him and planting it firmly on her head. "People get off their bloomin' arses and get together. Don't you want to see your friend happy?"

"It's not my place to interfere."

"It's not interfering, it's intervening to help a friend. Assisting. When it's your time—and that might be sooner than you think—I hope someone does a favor for you. Otherwise, Mr. Mayor, you might be missing out, too." Imani punctuated her words with a sharp nod before getting into her car.

Bennett rubbed his neck as he watched her drive away. *She might have a point.* He leaned against his SUV and pulled his phone from his pocket to make a call. A few moments later, he had his reservations. All he had to do was talk Ivy into taking some time away from the inn.

He grinned as he climbed into his vehicle. As he fired up the engine, he drummed his fingers on the steering wheel. Imani sure had a way of waking up people. Maybe he *was* being too patient.

When Bennett turned into the car court behind the inn, he could see Ivy, Shelly, and Poppy talking animatedly in the kitchen.

Curious, he parked his SUV and crossed the terrace. Several guests were lounging by the pool, and two children were splashing in the pool with their parents, who had grown up in Summer Beach. The family was having a reunion. With spouses and grandchildren, there wasn't enough room for all of them at their old home, so many family members were staying at the inn.

Waving at those he knew, Bennett smiled at the scene before him. This was precisely what he and Boz and the other council members who had voted for a zoning change had considered.

Summer Beach needed a place for friends and family to stay and feel at home, and the Seabreeze Inn provided that.

Bennett clenched his jaw. No way would Paisley Forsythe get her hands on the inn. *If* that rumor were true. Before he told Ivy, he needed to talk to Nan.

Bennett opened the rear door to the kitchen. "What's going on?"

"You won't believe what we found in the attic," Ivy said.

Shifting onto a stool next to Ivy at the kitchen counter, he spied an old leather-bound book on the tile. "That?"

"And more," Shelly said, her eyes bright with excitement.

"This is Amelia's journal," Ivy said with reverence, lightly touching the age-worn cover. "We put in a call to Megan. She'll be thrilled at this discovery, and she might be able to use it in the documentary."

"Find anything else up there?"

"Practically another inn," Poppy said.

Ivy's face brightened. "Behind a bookcase, we found a hidden entryway into a series of dormitory-style rooms that were clearly intended to hide people. We think Amelia must have had them built during the war, or just before. She must have been terribly afraid of what could happen."

"Unbelievable," Bennett said, amazed at the news. "I'd sure like to see that."

"We can go up again later," Ivy said. "After checkout. We have more guests arriving this afternoon, too, so we won't have much time."

Bennett looped his fingers with hers. Ivy's eyes sparkled with such brilliance that Bennett thought he could gaze into her deep-green eyes forever. *I should be so lucky,* he thought, recalling Imani's advice. "Now that Shelly is back, how about taking tomorrow afternoon off?"

"I don't know," Ivy said, frowning at her phone. "Sunny just texted to say she was boarding a flight. "I want to make sure she arrives okay."

"She'll be fine," Shelly said. "She's on a long flight to Boston, so there's nothing more you can do."

"I'm a mom," Ivy said. "I worry. That's my job. Still, Corrina found a decent itinerary for her. Sunny has a couple of connections and layovers, but the flights are shorter that way."

As they were talking, Ivy's phone buzzed with a notification.

While Shelly and Poppy talked about the attic, Bennett watched Ivy. She'd opened the message and was frowning at it. "What's wrong?" Bennett asked.

Slowly, Ivy turned her head to one side and back again. "This can't be right..." She scrunched her brow. "A *five-figure* charge from an airline? This must be a mistake."

Shelly splayed her hands on the counter. "Sunny?"

"I have to call on this right away," Ivy said. "But I'm calling Sunny first." She tapped her phone, then shook her head. "Straight to voice-mail."

"Let me see that," Shelly said. When Ivy spun the phone around, Shelly let out a yelp. "She didn't!"

Chapter 14

"THIS CAN'T BE RIGHT," IVY insisted, her head already pounding at the enormity of the credit card charge that had come through. *A five-figure fee from an airline? Impossible.*

"What?" Poppy asked, leaning in to look at Ivy's phone on the kitchen counter. "Uh-oh."

Bennett frowned at the notification. "Think that's for one flight?"

"Only if it's first-class," Shelly said, leaning on the counter across from her. Or if she's bringing all her friends with her."

"Maybe the card has been stolen," Ivy said, feeling adrenaline surging through her body. She didn't want to believe that Sunny would abuse her credit card like that. "I have to call right now."

After speaking to a representative, Ivy confirmed that Sunny had indeed purchased a ticket. She had even spoken to a representative at the credit company. Alternating between shock and anger and worry, Ivy drew her hands over her face. "Sunny was so upset on the phone. I have no idea what might have happened, but the cost of that flight was a big part of our money for the property tax bill."

"Can you reverse the charge?" Bennett asked.

"She's on that flight right now. So help me, when I talk to her…" Ivy pressed a fist to her mouth. *Why would Sunny spend a fortune on a flight?*

Poppy took out her phone. "I bet she sprang for wifi on the flight, too. I'll check to see if she's okay." Her fingers flew over the phone.

"At least she's on a flight home." Bennett swept his arm around Ivy, and she leaned into him. "We'll figure this out together. All of us."

"Here she is," Poppy said, wrinkling her brow. "She says, *Got tired of waiting. Tell Mom I don't do connections and layovers.* Want me to answer?"

"I'll deal with her," Ivy said, gritting her teeth.

"Pretty nervy of her," Shelly said, resting her chin in her hands. "Mom and Dad would've killed us if we'd ever pulled a stunt like that."

"Oh, my gosh, that's more than my car cost," Poppy said.

"*Way* more."

"And it's on my American Express card," Ivy said, the dire reality of the situation setting in. "I have to pay that in full when the statement arrives. Which means I can't pay the tax bill now. And the property goes to auction."

Everyone fell quiet, contemplating what that meant to all of them.

Poppy twisted her lips to one side. "We just found some new rooms to rent out. That would help." She snapped her fingers at an idea. "Maybe like an attic-level youth hostel. Seriously, I bet we could rent those at the right price."

"Complete with chamber pots," Shelly said, scrunching her nose.

"And an entry through my closet ceiling." Ivy let out a long moan. "At least Sunny will be back in Boston soon."

"Better warn Misty," Shelly said. "And you are *not* paying that Amex bill yet."

"But my credit—" Ivy stopped. Shelly was right. She might ruin her credit, but somehow, she had to hang onto the property. Though she disliked the alternative, she didn't have much choice. Her life was like a stand of dominoes, and Sunny had just kicked them off.

Outside the kitchen, a bell rang, signaling a guest at the front door. They were fully occupied this weekend.

"I'll get that," Shelly said. "Poppy, come with me." Shelly slid her arm around Ivy on her way out. "I'm really sorry about what's happening. But I'm glad I'm here to help."

"Me, too." At least Ivy didn't feel as alone as she had in Boston. Here she had friends and family. She might be broke once again, but as long as they could keep the inn running, they would have a roof over their heads.

Bennett turned to her. "Maybe I can help some," he began.

She shook her head. Bennett was a good friend—more than that if she were honest with herself—and she didn't want to jeopardize what they had with a potential financial disaster.

"We have the art show coming up," Ivy said. "I have some work I'd planned to sell. It won't bring in what we need, but it's a start. Maybe I can sell another chandelier."

Bennett took her hand. "Take the afternoon off with me tomorrow. You can think about all this on Monday. Nothing will change before then."

"I can't."

Bennett swept a strand of hair from her lashes, and Ivy's heart quickened at the gentle gesture. *An afternoon off.* She was tempted.

"You were working awfully hard while Shelly was gone. So, I've planned something special for us. I promise; it's a short drive to paradise."

Bennett slid his hand along her shoulder, rubbing her tense muscles. After everything that had happened this past week, she could use a respite. "You'll get me home at a reasonable hour?"

"Scout's honor," Bennett said, grinning. "As long as you

let me see that attic before we go."

"You're dying to see it, aren't you?"

"Can't believe I had this house listed and missed so much."

"Amelia Erickson was a woman of many secrets." Just how many, Ivy wondered, curious to read the old journal. She picked it up from the counter and ran her hand across the dusty cover. Sliding off the stool, she gave Bennett a wry smile. "Come up to see our new penthouse suites with me? Chamber pots included."

At the sound of his laughter, she already felt better. She wondered what he had planned for tomorrow.

***

When Ivy woke the next morning, Bennett was already outside, washing her car. After she'd greeted the morning guests, and Shelly surprised everyone by taking over the yoga class again, Ivy stepped outside with a cup of coffee.

"Good morning," Bennett said, shielding his eyes against the sun. The vintage, cherry-red Chevy gleamed in the sun. "Perfect day to put the top down and cruise the coast."

"Is that what you had in mind?" she asked.

Bennett grinned. "That and other things."

"Like what?" He still hadn't told her what they were doing today.

"Have some patience. Would I steer you wrong?"

"Maybe I'd better drive." She pursed her lips to sip her coffee.

After Bennett finished rinsing the car, he brought out a chamois to dry it. He tossed another chamois onto the trunk of the vehicle.

"Is that one for me?" Ivy asked.

"Mitch is on his way."

"Really?" Ivy arched an eyebrow. "That's good, I guess."

"He said Poppy called and said there's been a run on muffins. So, he's bringing more." He jerked a thumb toward the house. "Probably there now."

"Don't let me keep you two from talking. Besides, I have some reading to do."

Bennett looked at her with piqued interest. "Did you start reading the journal?"

"I stayed up way too late trying to decipher her handwriting. She used a fountain pen, and it's so faint now."

"Anything of interest yet?"

"Amelia wrote about their art acquisitions. Megan will probably find that interesting for her documentary."

"Megan and Tyler are coming down soon to look at another house to buy," Bennett said.

"I hope this deal goes through for them." They were outbid on a house in the village before, and Megan was quite disappointed. "It will be fun to work with her on this project."

"Did you tell her about the attic rooms?"

"I put in a call to her," Ivy said. "I want to hear the excitement in her voice."

"She'll be plenty excited."

Just then, the back door slammed, and Mitch ambled down the rear steps and across the terrace.

"Just in time, buddy," Bennett called out. "Sun's breaking through. There's your rag. Start wiping."

Dutifully, Mitch picked up the rag and began wiping in circular motions. "I think you've got a muffin thief."

"The Chihuahua again?"

"I don't know, but I sent over two dozen cranberry and blueberry muffins this morning, and you're already out."

Ivy made a mental note to ask Poppy what had happened to them. "Did you see Shelly?"

A small smile tugged at Mitch's lips. "She's teaching a class right now. It looked pretty intense. She was in some sort of pretzel position."

"So, hang around and say hello." Ivy threw a meaningful look at Bennett. "I'll leave you two. And thanks. The car looks brand new."

"Just wait till we open it up on the road," Bennett said, popping his chamois against a fender. "She'll be sweet."

Ivy paused. She still didn't know what he had planned. "What should I wear today?"

"Beach casual. Wear sandals you can walk in."

Ivy smiled. She couldn't wait to see where he was taking her this afternoon. "I'll be reading if guests need anything. And Poppy's at the front reception desk."

Ivy made her way upstairs. After several delays, her brother Forrest and his son Reed had called to say they would be over later this morning to begin prepping the ceiling. It was just as well that she was going out with Bennett, so she wouldn't have to be here for the construction work. She planned to ask Forrest about creating another attic access, too.

Gilda sauntered toward her in the hallway, clutching Pixie in her arms. "How are you and Pixie this morning?" Ivy asked.

"I'm fine, but I can't figure out what's wrong with my little sweetie."

Immediately, Ivy thought about the muffins. "Have you been down to breakfast this morning?"

Gilda shook her head. "Pixie was so lethargic this morning, I didn't want to leave her alone. Maybe she's depressed."

"Dogs get depressed?"

"Of course, they do. Pixie has been training hard to overcome her addictions."

"The kleptomania?"

"It's taxing," Gilda said. "I'll take her out to the beach later. She likes to ride in a stroller around the marina."

Ivy had seen Gilda pushing Pixie in a doggie stroller before. "That might be just the thing to perk her up."

"What are you doing today?" Gilda asked.

"A little reading, then Bennett and I are taking a day trip."

Gilda grinned. "You two make a nice pair."

"Oh, it's not really like that," Ivy said, feeling her cheeks color a little. "He wants to show me something."

Gilda raised her brow. "Pixie has to go out now, but tell the mayor I said hello."

Ivy made her way to her room. Reading would help her keep from obsessing over Sunny's actions, too.

Sunny would be touching down in Boston soon, and then she'd have to go through customs. Misty would likely meet her at the airport. Ivy was trying not to micromanage her daughters. After all, they were both in their twenties and fully capable of taking care of themselves. Misty more so than Sunny. Ivy hoped some of Misty's level-headedness would wear off on Sunny.

Ivy had also followed up with the credit card company and put a limit on Sunny's credit card. She'd thought about canceling it, but she didn't want to leave her stranded in case the plane had to make a detour.

Okay, that's too much worrying, Ivy acknowledged. Yet, her first duty was to her children, even when they misbehaved. Actually, Ivy was glad that Sunny was going to Boston. She almost didn't trust herself with her daughter right now. Sunny had not just crossed the line, but smashed through it, as Shelly said.

After bathing and putting on a navy-and-white sundress, Ivy sat down at the desk in her room in front of the window where the light was best. She brought out an antique magnifying glass and a pad of paper. Last night she'd discovered that Amelia hadn't written often, and her writing was hard to decipher. Amelia also referred to many people that Ivy didn't know. She decided to keep a list of pertinent details for Megan.

Ivy thought she might even find information that could be of value to Ari at the FBI as well. How she wished she could find more details on the provenance of the paintings they'd found. Or the reason the stolen jewelry had been stitched into a doll. And now, the barracks upstairs. Had people actually stayed there long?

Picking up the magnifying glass, Ivy began to read.

San Francisco. Gustav and I just returned from New York, where we had such a lovely respite visiting new galleries and meeting young American artists. We also visited dear Eleanor at her townhouse, which was overflowing with talented people. So many artists have fled their home countries, and we are alarmed over the state of affairs. Some people say that once He—and I hate to even write his name—is brought down that my country and its people will return to sanity. Until then, He is ravaging museums and private art dealers. My poor father!

Father did what he could to salvage work from his museum as well as others. Gustav agreed that we should wire funds, for this is an opportunity to acquire important works of art— regardless of the circumstance. However, we cannot

Cannot *what?* The passage ended abruptly as if Amelia had been called away. Ivy lowered the magnifying glass, not quite understanding Amelia's words. The Ericksons were *alarmed*, to use Amelia's word, but then she went on to write about acquiring artwork.

Regardless of circumstance.

Ivy studied the passage from a different perspective. Had Shelly been correct in her assessment? Ivy had so many questions, and she felt a little sick to her stomach. How could this woman have been so callused in her acquisitions? Was collecting artwork really the most important thing to her?

Overwhelmed, Ivy rose and paced the room, trying to piece together everything they'd found in the house. What she'd just read made her want to close the cover and forget about it all. Shelly was right. She preferred her version of the truth and painted the world the way she wanted to see it, not as it was. While that helped her maintain her equilibrium and sanity, it closed her off from the stark, disappointing reality.

Poppy tapped on the door. "How're you doing?"

"Just trying to work my way through this diary," Ivy said. "I've come across a passage that will make Shelly happy."

"What do you mean?"

"Maybe Amelia was an avaricious collector after all."

"Oh," Poppy said, her shoulders falling with disappointment. "I'd hoped she was one of the good ones."

"Me, too." Ivy stretched her arms overhead. "What did you want to talk about?"

Poppy's face flushed. "I thought I should tell you about the muffins."

"Did Pixie get into them?"

"What? No, it was me." Poppy lowered her gaze.

"*You* ate them?"

"I hid them."

Now Ivy understood. "So that Mitch would come over and bring more."

"Is that bad?" Poppy asked in a small voice.

"I don't know. We'll see."

"Shelly is deliberately not talking about him," Poppy said. "But I catch her staring off into the distance. I think she misses him. At supper on the beach, she kept looking at his chair."

"You noticed that, too?"

"Hard not to." Poppy still seemed embarrassed. "I'm not like Nan over at City Hall, who's always trying to match people up—she thinks Jamir and I should go out, did you hear?"

Ivy laughed. "He's a good kid."

"Yeah, a kid. He's barely eighteen."

"Shelly's older than Mitch."

"But they're already older," Poppy said. "Eighteen is still young, even if he is mature for his age."

"So, who do you like?" Ivy asked.

Poppy shook her head. "I've got plenty of time for that, Aunt Ivy. For now, I live vicariously through you and Shelly."

"You sure do," Ivy said. "You're one of the good ones, Poppy. Take your time."

"You won't say anything about the muffins?"

"No, but make sure Shelly doesn't find them, or she'll be on to you."

Poppy broke into a wide grin. "I'll take them to the beach and share. The kids will love them."

Just then, Forrest tapped on the door. "Hey, sis. We're early. Mind if we start?"

Ivy picked up the old journal. "Sure, come on in."

"Hi Poppy," Reed said. "Aunt Ivy." He deposited an armful of drop cloths for painting on the floor and began unfolding them. "Is there anything you want to get before I cover everything up?"

Ivy shook her head. "I'm going out this afternoon." As it turned out, she was happy to be leaving.

Forrest put down an armload of tools. "Going to take more than a day. Didn't I mention this would take about a week?"

"I don't recall that," Ivy said. "We're at full occupancy."

"I don't think you'll want to be sleeping in here." Forrest looked up. "That ceiling has got to be replaced."

"With Shelly back, there's hardly an inch of space left in our room," Poppy said.

Bennett poked his head inside the doorway. "Take my room. I'll sleep on the couch in the living room."

"Oh," Ivy said, feeling herself flush at the suggestion. But there weren't many options, except… "I could sleep upstairs in the attic."

Forrest frowned. "On the floor?"

"You have no idea what's up there," Ivy said. "For starters, I think this room had a high ceiling when it was built. We found a chandelier tied up in the attic."

"Probably so it wouldn't get away," Forrest said, winking at Reed, who laughed.

"Dad, stop with the corny jokes," Poppy said. "You can't stay up there, Aunt Ivy. Remember the chamber pot?"

"It's only for a week," Ivy said.

Poppy raised her brow. "Of shimmying up and down through the closet?"

"Plenty of bunk beds," Ivy said. "Or I could take a couch downstairs in the ballroom."

"How would that look to guests?" Poppy said.

Ivy sighed. She wasn't left with many alternatives. She turned to Bennett. "Would you mind if I slept on the couch in your living area?"

"Hey, what's this about chamber pots and bunk beds?" Forrest asked, looking between them all.

Ivy, Poppy, and Bennett told Forrest and Reed about what they'd found, and the two men immediately climbed the ladder to get a better look.

"This is incredible," Forrest said, calling down to her. "And this chandelier is a real beauty. Want us to bring it down? You've got a stunning stained-glass window, too."

"Leave the chandelier where it is for now," Ivy called out. "Poppy is coming up to give you a tour."

Forrest stuck his head through the hole in the ceiling. "We could open up the ceiling for you. Put in a spiral staircase, and you'd have a sweet little reading nook up here. At just the cost of supplies."

"That's a fine idea, but I really can't afford it now," Ivy said, thinking about Sunny's extravagance. "Maybe later. But could you enlarge the entry to the rooms? And we need attic access that's not through my bedroom. Poppy will show you what I have in mind." She had an idea about what they could do with the rooms, but first, they had to have a convenient entry.

"Leave it to me, sis," Forrest said, chuckling. "We've got this."

Bennett peered up into the attic. "Hey, Forrest. Do you mind if I take your sister on a drive?"

Laughter floated down. "No one's asked me that since high school," Forrest said. "I better get Flint over here, too. Maybe he could bring one of his sons. This job is larger than I thought."

Bennett leaned against the doorjamb and smiled at Ivy. "Forrest has everything under control. Do you need to bring some things in a bag?"

"It's not like I'm going far," Ivy said. "But that's probably a good idea. Are you sure you don't mind?"

"Do I look like I mind?"

"But you could be sleeping on the couch for days," Ivy said, trying to think of an alternative. She could sleep on the floor in the room Shelly and Poppy were sharing, but she had to laugh at herself. All this space and the three of them would be crammed into one room. "We can trade off."

Bennett shrugged. "I'm a guy, and I've got a good back. Come on, I can carry something. We'll throw your things up there before we take off for the beach."

Ivy let out a breath of relief. "You have no idea how good that sounds. We're going to this beach?"

"Not the one you think," Bennett said, his eyes twinkling. "A little farther down south."

Ivy gathered her toiletries in the bathroom and tucked her lingerie and a robe into a canvas bag that she used for the beach. Almost as an afterthought, she slipped in Amelia's journal. Though she'd lost a measure of interest after reading that last entry, she was still curious. As she zipped up the bag, she remembered something and called out. "Did Mitch see Shelly?"

"They're out by the pool right now."

Ivy peered from the window. Shelly and Mitch were sitting on a chaise lounge, deep in conversation. "How do you think it's going with them?"

"No way to tell," Bennett said. "None of my business anyway."

"Aren't you curious?"

Bennett grinned. "I have enough to occupy my mind."

He picked up her canvas beach bag and another larger bag that held jeans and T-shirts. Ivy looped a few sundresses over her arm and started off.

When Ivy walked into Bennett's apartment over the garages, she was surprised at how neat it was. Still, it was clearly a guy's place. His running shoes sat by the front door, along with a hoodie and cap that were slung over the coat hooks.

"I'll bring some sheets and towels in later," Ivy said. Flowers would look nice on the table, too. She peeked into the small kitchen. Again, it was clean and tidy, but then, she knew he hardly used it. They cooked together most nights in the kitchen or outside on the grill. She glanced away. Even though this was her house, she felt like she was invading his space. Which, technically, she was. He was still a paying guest.

"I'll put you in the bedroom," he said easily, leading her into the next room.

Even his bed was made, she noted. And he'd had no way of knowing earlier this morning that she'd be coming over. She hooked her hand through the hangars of the dresses she carried. "I'll hang these in the closet and unpack later."

"I've got that," Bennett said, taking her clothes and hanging them beside his shirts and jackets and slacks. He turned and hooked his thumb into a belt loop on his jeans. "Do you feel as awkward as I do?"

"Completely," she said, with a little laugh. "If it makes you feel any better, I can't possibly charge you for these nights when I've taken your bed."

"Don't worry about it. You have to sleep somewhere, and what kind of guy would I be if I didn't offer? Besides, my fire insurance is covering accommodations."

"Convenience and good manners it is, then." She tried hard to keep the question out of her mind.

Bennett hesitated before speaking. "You're welcome in my space, my home, wherever I am," he said, his voice deepening a notch. He reached out and twined his fingers with hers. "Shall we take the old Chevy? It's a good day for putting the top down and letting sea breezes blow through your mind. I'll drive."

"I'd like to change first, but I'd love that." Her daughter was still on her mind. Sunny would be touching down in Boston soon, and Misty would probably pick her up from the airport. Her children were adult women with mobile phones—they didn't need her hovering to make sure they connected. Or she would call a ride-share or take a taxi. Given Sunny's exorbitant charges, Ivy figured a little space would do them good. What sort of trouble could her daughter get into in a first-class cabin anyway?

Chapter 15

"LOOK WHAT'S STILL IN THE glovebox," Ivy said, slipping on a pair of 1950s cats-eye sunglasses as Bennett wheeled the vintage red Chevy onto the Pacific Coast Highway. In her haste to leave the inn in Shelly's care and take a much-needed break, she'd forgotten her sunglasses.

As she unfolded and slipped on the dark glasses, she laughed. "I feel like I've stepped back in time." In the open convertible, the breeze tousled her hair. She tipped her head back against the red-leather bench seat.

"Your eyes and sweet smile—just like that, there. Reminds me of Audrey Hepburn," Bennett said, glancing at her with evident admiration.

Ivy responded by lowering her sunglasses and arching an eyebrow with a laugh. "I loved her and her films." She slid her shades back up, bringing him into focus under the bright sun. "You look pretty snazzy, too."

"Snazzy, huh? Don't hear that one much."

Bennett had dressed casually, unintentionally matching the navy-and-white polka-dot sundress she wore. He paired a white shirt and navy chinos with a white windbreaker and navy deck shoes. With his sun-streaked hair, he could have passed for an actor on a beach or yacht set. She smiled to herself at the thought. A little gray speckled his hair at the temples, and he'd only become better looking with age. Pursing her lips, she made a little *moue* of approval.

"Maybe even Ava Gardner." Bennett laughed. "You've got that gutsy look."

"Is that how I come off?" No one had ever called her *gutsy* before. Although, as she thought about it, she liked it. A lot.

"Gutsy, yeah, in a good way," he said. "I like a woman who knows what she wants. It's attractive. Sure makes it easier for us guys, too." With one hand on the large steering wheel, Bennett reached to clasp her hand. "You never wavered in your dream to create an inn. I'll never forget your proposal and arguments before the city council. You're a force when you want something."

"That's because the zoning mattered," Ivy said. "It was a real necessity for long-term security."

"Your argument was impressive. You're determined and passionate about what you believe in."

"I can be," Ivy said. Once, Jeremy had accused her of not knowing what she wanted to do with her life, arguing that painting was not a real career. However, it could have been, she reflected, if she hadn't dedicated herself to taking care of his needs and those of their daughters. But hadn't she supported herself teaching art after his death? Not well, of course, but she'd just started.

Bennett glanced at her with a broad grin. "You strike me as someone who follows her dreams and is determined to reach them."

"Now I am." Though she'd been just as determined to have her children and be a good mother to them. "I like seeing my over-a-certain-age friends embarking on new careers. I've decided it's never too late to follow your dreams."

"Will we see any of your art at the art show?" Bennett asked.

Ivy beamed at him. "You sure will. I brought some pieces from Boston. I haven't had time to paint much—other than the art classes I'm giving—but I'll show what I have." Organizing the show with so many different vendors had been a lot of work, but Poppy had really stepped up to put the word out on the internet. Ivy hoped their first show would prove successful enough to become an annual event.

"What will you be showing?"

She'd been honing a rapid painting technique, but she

wasn't sure if she would show that work yet. Ivy gestured toward the ocean. "Mostly seascapes. I never tire of painting the ocean and the sky because they're never the same on any given day."

"Only an artist sees that." He slowed to a stoplight on their way out of Summer Beach.

Coconut suntan oil from the beach crowd wafted to Ivy's nose, and she gazed from the car. "I love all these little shops."

On one side, a surf store with a row of brightly colored surfboards blasted music. Next to that, a gardening center brimming with bougainvillea and jasmine and tiered stone fountains drew a lot of customers. A sushi bar sat next to a taco shop, and bright red umbrellas over tables dotted the sidewalk. On the other side of the street stood a beach fashion boutique with brightly colored clothing, an ice cream shop with a line of children and adults out the door, and an Italian restaurant where customers were enjoying wine. She loved this typical SoCal assortment.

Bennett nodded toward the shops. "It's important we support our local business owners. It's what makes Summer Beach unique." The light turned green, and he eased the car past the *Welcome to Summer Beach* sign.

"Where are we going?" Ivy asked.

Bennett's eyes gleamed. "It's a surprise, but I think you'll like it."

"Oh, come on," she said, teasing him. "Not even a hint?"

"It's sort of an island."

"Sort of? Either it is or it isn't."

"You're right, but you'll see."

"Not Catalina?"

"Nope."

"Balboa?"

"Wrong direction."

"Will I need a passport?"

"Not unless you plan to keep heading south." Bennett grinned. "Although that's a thought for another day."

As Ivy and Bennett cruised through other beach villages, they continued chatting about the art show and Ivy's plans for the inn for the rest of the summer. She was glad to stay off the subject of Sunny, although she couldn't help thinking about her.

Once her daughter was back on *terra firma* in Boston, Ivy would rest easier. And they would definitely have a talk with a capital T, as her mother used to say. Why couldn't Sunny accept responsibility and understand that her mother's financial position had changed? Sunny had seen her little rented room at the professor's home. Her daughter was testing her, punishing her for her father's death, and acting out like an angry, entitled child.

Ivy checked her phone, but there were no messages from either of her daughters. Maybe she should talk to a professional about Sunny—or arrange for her daughter to have a few sessions.

As Ivy was deciding that both would be a good idea, Bennett turned onto a soaring bridge that spanned the bay.

"Coronado Island. I haven't been here in years." She'd loved coming here as a little girl with her parents. It had one of the longest beaches in the area. "Sort of an island...now I remember. The Navy is on the other side that connects to the mainland."

"By a narrow strip. One of my old surfing buddies was the mayor here a while back."

"Is surfing a prerequisite for the position of mayor in SoCal communities?"

Bennett chuckled. "Doesn't hurt. Helps us understand the ocean and take care of our beaches."

Passing through the small town, Ivy took in the sights while people on the busy streets admired the old Chevy convertible, which fit right in here. She really appreciated what Bennett had done in getting the classic car running again.

He turned into a palm tree-lined driveway. "Welcome to the Del. Ever been here?"

"Never," she said.

Bennett raised his brow. "What kind of SoCal girl are you?"

"One that's been kicking around east coast beaches for years."

After the valet took their car, they walked inside. Ivy marveled at the architecture of the old hotel, which was reputed to be one of the largest wooden-structure hotels in the world.

"So, what are we doing here?"

"You'll see." Bennett took her hand and led her through a courtyard filled with tropical plants. Soon they came to the hotel spa.

Bennett stepped up to the front desk and gave his name.

The receptionist, a young, fresh-faced woman, smiled at Ivy. "He's booked our best massage for you."

Ivy squeezed Bennett's hand. "How did you know that's exactly what I need?"

"You once said you missed getting massages," he said. "And I know you've been under a lot of stress. Then we can relax by the pool or take a walk on the beach before dinner on the patio."

The receptionist slid two robes across the counter and directed them to opposite sides of the spa.

"You, too?" Ivy asked.

"Absolutely," he said.

The receptionist detailed the services and asked about others.

"Would you like a facial or visit to the hair salon?" Bennett asked. "I didn't want to presume."

"I'd rather hang out with you after our massages," Ivy said, meaning it.

He looked pleased. "Meet you afterward then," he said.

After being shown to a locker in the women's quarters, Ivy changed into the robe she'd been given. She spent a few minutes in the eucalyptus steam sauna and the whirlpool bath to loosen her muscles, which she hadn't realized were so tense.

She toweled dry, then put on her robe and relaxed in a waiting area while sipping warm mango-infused tea.

A massage therapist—a woman in her forties who looked kind and capable—appeared at the door. "Are you Ivy Bay?"

"That's me," Ivy said.

"What a lovely name," the woman said.

Ivy smiled as she cupped her fragrant tea. "My parents had a lot of fun with our names."

The therapist led her into a private cabana on the beach shrouded in canvas but open on one side to the sea. There, with a gentle sea breeze caressing her skin, Ivy relaxed thoroughly under the soothing touch of her therapist. The woman worked out the kinks in every muscle that Ivy had. As the stress of the last few days dissipated, Ivy drifted into a languorous, semi-dream state where she and Bennett were swimming through waves and playing with dolphins.

After the massage, Ivy felt a lightness in her step that she hadn't experienced in ages. She changed and stepped into the waiting area to meet Bennett, who was relaxing by a fireplace.

"How're you feeling?" he asked, standing to greet her.

"Like a bowlful of warm pudding," she said, smiling lazily. "Thank you for spoiling me."

"You've earned it." Hugging her, he inhaled. "Hmm, mango pudding?"

"The massage therapist used mango-vanilla massage oil." Ivy brushed her fingers along her arm. She loved the smell and feel of her softened skin.

As Bennett took her hand, she caught a whiff of the subtle woody oil his massage therapist had used. "Sandalwood?"

"Mixed with lavender," he said. "Up for a walk on the beach?"

"Sounds heavenly."

As they strolled along the water's edge hand in hand, Ivy couldn't remember when she'd felt so peaceful or fulfilled. He slid his arm around her, and they skipped through the lapping waves and back onto the sand again. Ivy felt as light-hearted as the children on the beach building sandcastles.

Bennett paused, holding her hands in front of him. "I'm awfully glad you landed in Summer Beach and came back into my life."

"It was a tough road, but it led me to a good new life. If only I can hang onto it."

"You will," he said. "I have faith in your ability."

Ivy tented her hand against the sun and smiled up at him. She couldn't remember ever hearing that from Jeremy. He'd taken for granted that she could juggle the house and kids like a circus act, but it lifted her spirits to actually hear those words from Bennett. She didn't feel so alone. Even with Shelly and Poppy pitching in, the final responsibility of making sure the taxes were paid and the inn was successful rested on her ability to manage everything.

Bennett paused at the water's edge and turned around to face the grand hotel. "Isn't that beautiful architecture?"

"I like to think that Amelia and Gustav and Julia Morgan

admired it, too," Ivy said, even though she was a little angry with Amelia right now. "Standing here just like this."

Squeezing her hand, he told her about the movies that had been filmed here. "Did you ever see *Some Like it Hot?*"

"I loved that film! With Marilyn Monroe, Tony Curtis, and Jack Lemmon in an all-girl band." She laughed. "I had no idea that was filmed here."

"Right over there," he said, pointing. "They have some photos inside the hotel. We can look at them later."

"I'd like that."

They walked back toward the hotel, watching other couples meandering along the beach. At the restaurant on the patio, Bennett pulled out a chair for her at the table, and Ivy felt shivers up her back. It was almost like they were on a date.

No, this was a date, she corrected herself, feeling slightly awed at the idea.

On the terraced patio, they dined on sweet steamed crab and a fresh summer salad of locally sourced bib lettuce, avocado, and strawberries. Afterward, Bennett led Ivy back into the grand hotel, where they paused to look at the old photographs that lined the hallways.

On the lower level corridor, Bennett paused by an old-fashioned ice cream parlor. "How about a scoop?"

"Mint chocolate chip for me," she said. The scent of warm waffle cones filled the air.

"Rocky Road and orange sherbet for me." He led her inside.

Once they had their ice cream, they carried it outside to enjoy in the sunshine. As they ate their dessert, they chatted about their childhoods and what they used to do with their families.

Ivy couldn't remember when she'd had such a good time on a real date. How many years had it been? Before Jeremy, of course. Shrugging off the thought, she glanced up at Bennett through her lashes. This was her new life, and, if she chose, Bennett might very well be a part of it.

"I love hearing about your family," Ivy said.

Bennett slid his arm across her shoulders. "There's still so much I'd like to know about you, too."

"Like what?"

He shrugged. "I don't know. Do you have any annoying little habits?"

"You want to know if I snore or something?"

"We'll find that out tonight, won't we?" His expression crinkled with playfulness.

Ivy jabbed him in the ribs. "I'll be listening through the door, too."

As they drove back to the inn, the sun was setting across the ocean, casting slanted rays in a palette of gold, rose, and orange.

"That's another reason we live at the beach," Bennett said, tilting his head toward the spectacular display of nature over the ocean. "Where else can you have dinner and a show every night of the week?"

After arriving at the inn, Ivy looked out over the property. A group of friends lounged by the fire pit, while a couple dangled their legs in the pool and toasted with champagne.

"Is that our police chief over there with Imani?" Ivy asked, nodding toward a pair sitting on chaise lounges.

Bennett grinned. "That's Clark."

Ivy was pleased to see them together, although it might be nothing at all, just two friends chatting. Still, she couldn't help thinking about how the chief often looked at Imani with admiration. She caught herself and chuckled. "Listen to me. Now I'm acting like a real Summer Beach resident, interested in everyone's business."

"Welcome to the crowd," he said, helping her from the car.

She followed him upstairs to his apartment over the garage, feeling a little self-conscious, but no one seemed to take any notice.

Bennett opened the door. "How about a glass of wine?"

"I'd like that." She crossed the living area and opened the door to the terrace that looked out over the car court and out toward the ocean. Leaning on the railing, she lifted her face to the cool evening breeze. Below, a taxi turned into the car court, and Ivy idly wondered who was arriving. The inn was full, and no new guests were expected. A guest had probably ordered the cab.

"Here you are. One of my favorite Cabernets from Napa Valley." Bennett handed her a crystal balloon-shaped glass, half full of silky red wine.

Ivy leaned into him and touched his glass with hers. "To tomorrow," she said. "And all that tomorrow may bring."

"I have a feeling tomorrow might surprise us."

"I love surprises."

Bennett swept his lips across her cheek, and Ivy thrilled to his touch. He encircled her with his arms, and she rested against him, enjoying his closeness. This was the perfect end to a perfect day. Melting into his arms, Ivy met his lips with hers.

Beneath them, a car door slammed, and a moment later, a loud gasp broke their reverie.

"Mom?" Sunny's indignant voice shot through the air. "What are you *doing*?"

Chapter 16

"SUNNY?" AS SOON AS IVY heard her younger daughter's voice, she instinctively stepped away from Bennett. In the next instant, torn between them, she felt like she was betraying him.

"I'll take that," Bennett said, reaching for her wine. "Go."

"I'll probably need it later." Ivy appreciated the understanding in his warm expression. "Be right down, honey," she called out.

As the driver unloaded a stack of Sunny's designer suitcases—a birthday gift from her father one year—Ivy clattered down the stairs. She was elated to see her daughter, even if she hadn't expected her. "Darling! I thought you were landing in

Boston."

Sunny whirled around. "Can you believe it took *three hours* to go through customs? And they didn't even have a place where I could plug in my phone. Or sit down. We *stood* in line the *entire* time. And children were screaming at the top of their lungs." She tossed her perfectly—and no doubt, expensively—blond-streaked chestnut hair over her shoulder. "Why can't parents control their little snot-nosed kids?"

"Sometimes adults are even worse," Ivy said softly, but the comment went right over Sunny's head. When Sunny was young, she'd been one of those barely-under-control children. And her daughter clearly hadn't grown out of her proclivity toward temper tantrums.

As relieved as Ivy was to see her, she was also irritated with Sunny's behavior. No, not irritated. Furious at her inconsiderate use of the credit card, especially after Corrina had found a last-minute ticket at a reasonable price. They would have *that* conversation later. "I'm happy to see you, sweetheart." She held her arms open for a hug.

Sunny made no movement toward her. Instead, she jerked up her chin. "Who's that?"

Ivy stalled for a moment, thinking about her response. "Who?"

Sunny made a face. "Kind of hard not to miss you in some guy's arms." She slung a large designer purse Ivy had never seen over her shoulder. "I need a bellhop for the bags," she said, not waiting for her mother's answer. "Where's my room?"

Ivy squelched the anger bubbling up inside of her. "No bellhops here. And we're fully occupied this weekend. But I'll find a place for you."

Sunny's mouth fell open. "You told me this was our *home*. I can't believe you rented out my room."

"You should have told me you were coming."

"Like I need a reservation for my own room? I wouldn't think I'd have to tell you that." She narrowed her eyes. "I *do* have a room?"

"I told you. We're full."

"I can't believe you rented a room that was supposed to be mine!" Sunny's voice echoed through the peaceful grounds. She flung up her arms. "You're always so concerned about money. You act like Dad didn't leave you a penny. At least this isn't as embarrassing as that room you rented in Boston."

Ivy took a step closer to her daughter. "We are *not* having a conversation about family finances here. You clearly need a place to sleep, and I'll find one for you. Now, you can wait in the kitchen—right through that door—while I make arrangements for you."

"Sunny?"

Ivy turned, relieved at the sound of Shelly's voice.

"Oh, Aunt Shelly, I'm so glad to see you," Sunny cried, falling into Shelly's arms. "You have no idea what I've been through." She cast a scornful look at her mother.

"I can imagine," Shelly said, hugging her lanky niece.

"Come on, let's chill by the pool."

"At least we have a pool," Sunny said. "Can I get a drink, Aunt Shelly?"

"I'll make a Sea Breeze for you." Shelly threw an apologetic glance at Ivy over Sunny's shoulder.

Sunny hesitated. "What about my luggage?" The cab driver had left Sunny's bags lined up in the driveway.

"I got it." Mitch sauntered toward them, running a hand through his spiky hair.

Sunny brightened when she saw him. "Well, finally. A real man who can help a girl out. I'm Sunny. What's your name?"

"Everyone around here calls me Mitch."

"Why is that?" Sunny cooed.

"Because that's his name," Ivy said, immediately detecting trouble. "You can put her bags in the kitchen for now. We're trying to find room for her."

Mitch chuckled and picked up a bag in each hand as Sunny followed Shelly toward a cluster of chaise lounges by the pool.

Ivy blew out an exasperated breath and looked up at the balcony over the garage. Bennett held up her glass of wine.

"Be right up." Ivy climbed the steps, and Bennett met her at the door.

"Wow," he said, raising his eyebrows. "She's a challenge, but I'm sure you're up to it." He opened the door to her.

Ivy picked up her wine glass. "I need this sooner rather

than later." She gulped an emergency swallow of wine. Regretfully, she deposited the glass on the coffee table in front of the red brick fireplace—where she'd been looking forward to relaxing this evening with Bennett. He had promised to tell her more about why he'd decided to run for mayor, but that would have to wait. *Maybe a long time.* "No more for me. I have to have a clear head."

A tap sounded at the door, and Bennett opened it.

Poppy stepped inside. "I heard the commotion, Aunt Ivy. Before I go see Sunny, I thought I'd tell you that she can sleep with Shelly and me."

Ivy was grateful to her niece for understanding. "Shelly can stay in the bedroom here with me."

Bennett nodded. "Sounds like a real slumber party. But do you think that's wise? I heard what Sunny said. I'm happy to sleep on Mitch's couch."

"I'm not kicking you out of your room," Ivy said, but she saw his point. Sunny was sure to question their relationship again.

"I have another idea," Poppy said. They all sat on the marine-blue, canvas-covered sofa Ivy had placed in front of the fireplace. Poppy went on. "Dad and Reed finished the ceiling access for the attic. They installed a folding staircase for now. We could take over that space."

"It's really dusty up there," Ivy began, shaking her head. "No light, no bathroom."

"Not anymore," Poppy said with pride, tucking her hair

behind her ears. "Uncle Flint came over with the boys, and I armed them with cleaning supplies. We even have lights and electricity up there. It's kind of cool, actually. Our own little cave. We wanted to surprise you, but I was thinking about relocating up there anyway. And we don't *have* to use the chamber pots," she added with a giggle. "We can use the downstairs bathroom by the kitchen."

"Then I could take your cot in Shelly's room," Ivy said, taking Poppy's hand. "I really appreciate what you've done. I can't wait to see how the attic looks."

"With all of us working, it didn't take long," Poppy said. "And in your bedroom, Dad left the windows open to give the ceiling time to dry. Then Reed will return to sand and paint it. The furniture is still covered."

"You should go," Bennett said, casting a firm look at Ivy, though she heard a trace of wistfulness in his voice. After such a perfect day, he'd clearly wanted it to end differently, too. "It's a good idea."

Poppy flicked a glance toward Bennett. "There'll be another time for a slumber party, right?"

"Poppy!" Ivy cringed. "Is that what everyone thinks?"

"I-I didn't mean it the way it sounded," Poppy said, her face coloring.

"We haven't reached that stage," Bennett said, grinning. "I've got all the time in the world for your aunt, but Sunny needs her attention right now."

Poppy beamed at Bennett.

"Might as well start with the accommodations," Ivy said, still imagining what Sunny might have thought, although Ivy had every right to have a relationship again if she wanted. "Sunny needs a good dose of reality."

"Those beds aren't exactly luxurious," Poppy said. "They're not bad, but not like the cushy mattresses you bought for the guestrooms. We washed the sheets, too."

Ivy hugged her niece. "You were awfully busy while we were gone. Thank you."

"Shelly did a lot, too," Poppy said. "She feels bad about abandoning us."

"Shelly is free to do what she wants, and we all need a break from time to time." Ivy was touched that Shelly felt that way. "How about you? Don't you want to take some time off with your friends?"

"Are you kidding?" Poppy laughed. "They all want to come to Summer Beach."

"Plenty of room upstairs now," Ivy said. She thought about her other niece, Honey's daughter, who lived in Los Angeles. "Ask Elena to come down. She could show her jewelry at the art show, and then you two could have a stay-cation. Isn't that what a vacation at home is called?"

"Elena would love that," Poppy said, nodding. "I'll let her know. And I'll go see Sunny and break the news that we're camping in the attic. Coming from me, it'll sound cool."

"Good luck with that," Ivy said. "I'll be right behind you. I need to move my things first. Sunny will have a fit if she sees me hauling my clothes out of here."

Poppy grinned and let herself out.

Bennett pushed up off the couch and pulled Ivy to her feet. "We could give her this apartment."

"You're a long-time guest, and you're the mayor of this city," Ivy said. "If you're too modest to pull rank, I'll do it for you. I think the attic will be perfect for Sunny right now."

"See? You're a gutsy mom, too," Bennett said.

Ivy managed a wry smile. "With the attitude Sunny rolled in with, I'm not surprised that the family in Europe fired her."

"Let's take your things back," Bennett said, heading toward the bedroom.

Ivy followed to help. She wondered what Sunny would do next. Was her daughter planning on staying in Summer Beach? Ivy passed a hand over her forehead, summoning all the patience she could.

***

Ivy woke to a blast of music. Groaning, she sat up on the cot, ready to spring up to find the guest who was disturbing everyone.

Then she remembered. *Sunny.* Ivy whipped the covers off and was halfway to the door, shoving her arms into the sleeves of her robe when the music cut off. Muffled voices floated above her.

"What was *that?*" Groggy, Shelly sat up in bed.

"Sunny must have been blaring music, but I think Poppy turned it off." Ivy paused by the door, waiting for the girls to quiet down. Otherwise, she'd have to deal with Sunny. And un-caffeinated, it wouldn't be pretty.

Shelly rolled over. "Sunny doesn't strike me as an early riser."

"She's not, but she's probably still on European time."

Ivy stared at the ceiling, willing Poppy to work magic on Sunny. The two girls had seen each other intermittently over the years and had played together when they were young, even though Poppy was closer to Misty's age. Ivy recalled that Sunny had always looked up to Poppy. Now, more than ever, she hoped Poppy could have a positive influence on her daughter.

When the voices subsided, Ivy sighed with relief.

Shelly sat up cross-legged in bed and patted a spot beside her. "Back in New York, I missed all the craziness out here."

"It's more fun with you around." Ivy crawled onto the bed beside her sister, just as they had done when they were kids, except it was usually little Shelly bouncing into her bed then. "At least we can laugh about it all. But how am I ever going to handle Sunny?"

"Sunny has to figure out how to handle her life," Shelly said. "And it has to be her idea. Remember how Mom and Dad couldn't tell us anything at that age?"

"We sure surprised them. Think Sunny will do the same?"

"If you're lucky." Shelly frowned in thought. "Sunny was flirting outrageously with Mitch last night by the pool—just because he happened to be around. I left to go into the house, and while I was gone, I think Poppy told her to back off."

"And did she?"

"A little. Or maybe Sunny thinks Mitch is even more of a challenge now." Shrugging, Shelly pulled up her knees and clasped her legs.

"Sunny really changed this summer." Ivy picked at a loose thread on the seafoam-green, cotton duvet cover. "And not for the better. I'm so sorry about Mitch."

"He was more embarrassed than anything," Shelly said thoughtfully. "But you know we decided to be just friends, right?"

"Still, you have to admit that would be awkward." Shelly was acting like Sunny's behavior toward Mitch didn't bother her. Suddenly it dawned on her. *Acting. That's exactly what Shelly is doing. She still cares for him.* Folding her arms behind her head and easing back onto the pillows, Ivy gazed up at the embossed ceiling. "Sunny and Mitch...that sure would close the door on any possible relationship."

Shelly sucked in her lower lip, then pressed her forehead onto her knees. Her hair tumbled over her face.

Ivy studied Shelly out of the corner of her eye. "Unless you still want to leave that door ajar..."

As if struck by a thought, Shelly whipped her hair back and scooted off the bed. She grabbed her yoga gear from the dresser. "I'm going to pick up the muffins at Java Beach this morning. Since Poppy's up, I'll ask her to cover for me in yoga."

"Go," Ivy said, grinning. "I'll tell Poppy. And I'll have a talk with Sunny. If I can catch her."

"Thanks," Shelly said, flashing her a smile.

After Shelly left, Ivy dressed quickly. As she dug through her canvas bag, her fingers rested on Amelia's journal. Even without Sunny there, she had a full schedule. Now was no time to indulge her curiosity. She texted Poppy about the yoga class and made her way into the dining room, where she greeted a few early risers. After a quick cup of coffee, she made her way into the foyer.

Catching a glimpse of Bennett through the front window, she drew aside the sheer drapery panel to watch him. He took off toward the surf at a leisurely pace. He'd treated her to such a wonderful day on Coronado Island yesterday, and she'd been looking forward to spending the rest of the evening together.

But Ivy was a mother first, and Sunny's needs were more important. Her daughter was floundering. While tough love had its place, Ivy would never forgive herself if she didn't try to crack through Sunny's crusty façade now.

Behind her, she could hear Poppy and Sunny coming down the stairs. Turning, she put on a pleasant expression. "Good morning, girls. Sleep well?"

Sunny scowled and rubbed her eyes. "Every board in this place creaks, did you know that? And the ocean roars constantly. I tried to drown out the noise with some music—"

"So we heard," Ivy said lightly. "A lot of guests come here

to relax and sleep in."

Poppy turned to Sunny. "Come to yoga with me. You're so good at it. I could use your help."

"Yeah, okay. Once I have some coffee." Sunny gazed past Ivy through the window. "That's the same guy as last night."

Every nerve in Ivy's body snapped to attention. "Bennett Dylan is the mayor of Summer Beach. Like some of our other guests, he's staying here until his house is repaired. This past spring, quite a few homes on the ridge above us sustained extensive fire damage."

"You'll meet them all," Poppy said, quickly diverting Sunny's focus on Bennett. "Imani, who has a flower stand, and her son Jamir, who's starting at the university next month. Then there's Gilda, who's a writer with an adorable Chihuahua, and Celia, who runs the youth music program in the school. The kids practice here in the music room."

"You guys *know* these people?" Sunny looked mildly horrified. "I thought this was a hotel. With privacy."

"It's an inn, and this is a small town," Ivy said. "If you stay, you'll get to know them, too."

"Hardly my type," Sunny mumbled.

"They're fun," Poppy said. "I'll introduce you at yoga."

"Maybe I'll go to the beach instead," Sunny said, threading her fingers through her hair.

"You can come with me on the beach walk then," Ivy said. "You'll meet Gilda, and Darla, our neighbor."

Sunny looked away. "I'll go to the pool instead."

"Celia swims in the morning," Ivy said. "You'll see her out there. Dark hair, great swimmer."

Sunny pressed her hands against her temples. "Can't I get any privacy here?"

"Of course," Ivy said. "In your room. But it's too nice a day to stay inside."

Sunny threw up her hands and stomped upstairs. Midway up, she stopped. "Can you send up some coffee? Extra cream and sugar."

"We don't have room service, honey," Ivy said. "You'll find all that in the communal dining room."

Sunny huffed and clomped back down toward the dining room.

Poppy twisted her lips to one side. "This should be interesting," she said softly.

Ivy stared after her daughter. "Did Sunny say why she came here instead of Boston?"

"She doesn't know where she wants to be, Aunt Ivy. She took the first flight she saw back to the states." With a little shrug, Poppy set off for yoga.

And wiped me out financially in the process. Ivy turned back to the window. She could reprimand Sunny—and she would—but the real challenges would be how to set Sunny on the right path and recoup the financial loss as fast as she could.

Ivy shivered and brushed her arms. In her locked drawer in the library was a demand letter from the tax authority. Probably the last one she would receive, Imani told her. Time was running out.

The art show had been meant as a service to the community. But Ivy could sell some of her artwork to offset some of the loss. Her new paintings had a different energy—a style that had surprised her when it emerged during one of the art classes she was teaching. *Let it flow,* she'd told her group one morning after Shelly's yoga class, demonstrating what she meant. With such raw emotion, Ivy was reticent to share these works in a show.

She thought about the neat, finished canvases she had—meticulous oil paintings of the rugged New England coastline she loved. One she'd painted on a foggy, atmospheric day in Marblehead near the craggy rocks around Castle Rock. Another was of the seals that barked on the beaches near the Merrimack River. Yet another was of the windswept dunes on the outer tip of Cape Cod near Provincetown. The style was realistic and precise.

Each painting held a memory of a holiday with Jeremy and the girls. Though she hated to part with the artwork, every brushstroke was sealed in her soul. She could paint them again if she liked, perhaps in a different light, or with the sheen of nostalgia.

She gazed at Bennett's now distant figure on the beach, gaining momentum. But why paint the past when the scene outside her door was so inviting? Ivy rubbed her arms. She was realistic enough to know that her paintings might not sell. Or generate enough to salvage her finances. If she were to ensure their future at the inn, she needed a solid, money-making plan. But what?

"Mom." Sunny's voice sliced through Ivy's solitude.

Startled, Ivy whirled around to face Sunny's stony glare.

"You're dating him, aren't you?"

"We're just, really just friends." Ivy stumbled over her words and felt her face warm with color. But yesterday, at the Del Coronado, had felt like a date. A proper date. And she'd enjoyed it.

Sunny smirked. "You always said we shouldn't lie, especially about things that matter." Sunny's voice held a bitter edge. "You can't replace Dad."

"I'm not trying to," Ivy said as evenly as she could while reining in her annoyance. She took in her daughter's combative stance and the blatant anger on her face. This was a new Sunny—with emotions that erupted like a volcano. Was Sunny still grieving her father, or was it something more? "I'm not as old as you think. Someday, I might meet someone."

"Like him?" Sunny shot a finger toward the beach.

"Your sister knows Bennett. He's kind, and he's—"

"No replacement for Dad. Eeww." Sunny thrust out her palms as if to block her mother's words. "This would destroy our family. You *can't* date him, Mom. Or anyone. You're too old for that."

Chapter 17

BENNETT STRUCK THE GAVEL ON its thick wooden base and called the meeting to order. "First order of business is a request for a zoning variance from Imani Williams," he said, settling into his chair.

Looking out across the room, Bennett saw that many residents who lived on the ridge were in the audience. These were his neighbors, too. Whether they were there in support of Imani's request—or against it—remained to be seen. Imani's neighbor had made an offer to buy her lot, but Imani steadfastly refused to sell.

However, Imani's small house would lower the comparative values of the area. Other residents wanted to gate the street and turn it into a private community, which could then assess homeowner fees. For retired residents on fixed incomes, this would be a burden.

A flurry of activity erupted in the back of the chamber, and Bennett saw Ivy and Shelly hurry in to sit down.

Imani passed out a package of material as she addressed the council. "Mr. Mayor, members of the council and zoning department. In the package I've given you is a rendering of the house I'd like to build to replace the one I lost in the fire." She'd also put a larger image on an easel and referred to it as she spoke.

Bennett kept his attention on Imani's proposal, though he couldn't help occasionally glancing at Ivy.

Although one neighbor spoke against the construction, others were overwhelmingly in support. Imani easily won her zoning approval with the full support of the council, unlike Ivy's request. After other business was discussed and voted on, Bennett adjourned the meeting.

He rose, but before he could make his way toward Ivy, Nan stopped him. "Boz said he told you about *you know who.*"

When Bennett looked perplexed, Nan shook her short red curls. "Paisley," she whispered, looking behind her at Ivy. "I don't want to say anything, but you might want to warn her. Boz told you, right?"

"He did," Bennett replied, nodding toward Boz. "But I don't like to worry people unnecessarily. Until something occurs, I don't see the point in upsetting her."

"Don't you think she'd want to be ready to fight back?"

"I'm sure Ivy could mobilize an army relatively fast."

Nan frowned, glancing at Ivy across the room. "If I were her, I'd want to know."

"If you feel strongly, you should tell her," Bennett said.

"I feel uncomfortable talking to her about *you know who.*"

"You know how I feel about gossip, Nan. This town has enough of it."

"This isn't gossip, it's a warning."

"Be careful that you don't hurt someone. Beyond that, I can't tell you what to do."

"That's why I want you to talk to her." Nan smiled up at him. "You always know how to handle people and situations."

"Then my advice is not to stir up trouble where there isn't any yet."

Nan rolled her eyes. "I ask for advice on what to do, and all you can say is do nothing?"

"That's often the hardest course of action," Bennett said, nodding with conviction.

After Bennett finished with Nan and others who wanted to speak to him, Ivy waggled her fingers at him. He was happy to join her.

"I have to run back to the inn," Ivy said. "I want to make sure we have a nice room ready for Megan and Josh today. But I wanted to thank you for approving the plans for Imani's home. It means so much to her and Jamir."

"Thank Boz and the council—they're the ones who worked with her and Axe to make sure she had a workable proposal." Bennett paused, appreciating the warmth in her eyes. Seeing her during the day gave his spirits an extra boost. "I'll meet Megan and Josh right after work to show them a new listing in the village."

"I'd love to see them settle here," Ivy said. "After you finish your business, why don't we all have dinner on the beach?"

"They'd probably like that." He smiled and grazed her fingers. "I know I would."

A shadow crossed her face. "I have to talk to you about Sunny."

"Let's include her, too."

Seeming distraught beneath her usual composure, Ivy shook her head. "I don't want to discuss this here, but we need to talk. Before you see Sunny again."

Tiny stress lines marked her brow. Bennett longed to take her in his arms and smooth them away, but the council chamber wasn't the place for that. "As soon as we can," he promised.

At his assurance, Ivy seemed to relax a little. "When Megan called to make their reservation at the inn, she told me they have a surprise," Ivy said. "Maybe they'll tell us at dinner tonight."

***

Later that day after work, Bennett met Megan and Josh in

made their way from room to room, envisioning where they would place furniture.

When they came back, Megan's eyes were glittering with excitement. "We've decided we want to make an offer." She squeezed Josh's hand.

"I think you're making a good decision," Bennett said. "Let's go back to the inn, and I'll prepare the contract. Join us for dinner, too."

After discussing their offer, Bennett followed Josh and Megan to the Seabreeze Inn to write up the paperwork. It was an attractive offer, and Bennett knew the older couple was eager to sell. Their boys lived with their families in different states, and neither of them wanted to keep the beach bungalow.

After Megan and Josh had signed the agreement, Bennett left them at the inn to visit the older couple, who lived in an apartment in an assisted living facility just a few blocks away. He shared the pertinent details of the offer, and they were pleased that a young couple would move in and enjoy the home as they had.

When Bennett returned to the Seabreeze Inn, he met Megan and Josh in the parlor. Giving them a thumbs-up sign, he said, "Looks like you two have a deal."

Elated, Megan and Josh fell into each other's arms. Josh said, "We have a lot to celebrate. Come have dinner with us at the Starfish Café."

"And I have a lot to tell Ivy about the documentary on

Amelia and Gustav Erickson, too," Megan said. "It's going to be much easier to work on it now that we'll be here. I think Ivy is in the music room. Let's tell her."

They made their way to the wine and tea gathering. Bennett paused at the doorway at the unlikely sight before him. Darla was chatting with Shelly, who looked genuinely interested in what her neighbor had to say. The two women who had been ready to tear each other apart a few months ago were now talking.

But where was Ivy? Bennett looked over the crowd that included well-dressed horse owners and trainers, along with a sweet honeymoon couple. He spotted Ivy outside on the veranda, where she was talking with Sunny. When he raised his hand in greeting to Ivy, Sunny swung around, then turned to stalk away.

While Megan and Josh greeted friends, Bennett checked in with Ivy. "How's it going with Sunny?"

Ivy stared after her daughter. "I don't know how to reach her anymore." Her voice held a note of sadness.

"Do you need to stay in this evening with her? Megan and Josh just signed a contract for a house in the village. They want to celebrate at the Starfish Café, and they'd love for you to join us."

"I'd like to go," Ivy said. "I'd been planning on getting together with them anyway. Poppy is taking Sunny out in Summer Beach tonight, and Shelly is staying in to mind the inn. I think she's expecting Mitch to stop by." She smiled at the last comment. "I'm free to join you."

"Full house again?"

"Fortunately."

When the four of them arrived at the café, the owner showed them to a table on a patio surrounded by roses. With the sun setting over the ocean, it was a magical evening. Josh ordered champagne, and as they toasted to the success of their offer, a flash of color behind Ivy caught Bennett's eye. A woman in a short, barely-there red dress swished down the steps to a table where a man sat waiting.

Paisley Forsythe. She eased into a chair next to the man that Bennett recognized as one of the firm's partners—the firm that Jeremy had been consulting to. *Dexter Hansen.* The man slid his arm across Paisley's shoulders and yanked her to him.

Bennett's senses sprang to high alert. He didn't want to spoil the evening, but Ivy should know that Paisley had returned. And after that stunt of checking into the Seabreeze Inn, he wouldn't put it past Paisley to approach Ivy again.

Still, as he watched Ivy in a spirited conversation with Megan and Josh, he couldn't bring himself to say anything. Why shouldn't Ivy enjoy the evening? He'd keep an eye on Paisley.

As Bennett cast an occasional glance toward Paisley, he thought about the scandalous gossip Boz and Nan had relayed to him. Seeing Paisley there with Dexter made him wonder if it might be true.

Chapter 18

LIFTING HER FACE TO THE balmy breeze off the water at the Starfish Café, Ivy sipped the champagne that Josh had ordered to celebrate their new home. She was enjoying the respite from Sunny's sour attitude.

Her daughter had been curt and dismissive, but more than that, Ivy was genuinely worried about her lack of direction and treatment of Bennett, which was unwarranted. She understood that Sunny resented him because he threatened to take a place in her mother's heart, but this wasn't a competition.

To his credit, Bennett wasn't forcing the issue. Stretching her fingers toward his, she touched his hand. This small gesture did not go unnoticed by Megan, who suppressed a slight grin.

"I can hardly believe that we'll be living here soon," Megan said. She clinked Ivy's flute with her goblet of sparkling water.

"Oh, you didn't get your champagne?" Bennett said. "I'll have a glass brought over."

Megan traded a look with Josh, and they burst out laughing. "Five months until I can toast with the bubbly again."

Ivy clasped Megan's hands. "I'm thrilled for both of you."

"So are we," Megan said, her eyes sparkling with happiness. "Between the move and the baby, our lives are about to change. Living here will be easier to blend work and family.

"Bringing kids up at the beach is fun," Ivy said. "We all loved it."

"We can still work together on the documentary," Megan said. "Even with a baby on my hip. You won't believe what I've discovered in my research."

Megan leaned across the table. "Amelia's father was a museum director in Berlin. He would have had access to many of the paintings that had been sealed up in the inn's lower level."

Ivy considered this new detail, meshing it with what she'd found. She told Megan about the downpour, the ceiling, and the satchel in the attic. "The album is a treasure trove of photographs of Amelia and Gustav and others. Some were taken at a museum."

Megan's face glowed. "We're going to unravel this mystery yet. It's going to be an incredible film about the Ericksons, and Amelia in particular."

Ivy appreciated her enthusiasm, though her own was more tempered now. "Ever since we found the paintings, I've been on Amelia's side, hoping this discovery would shed light on her altruistic acts." The FBI agents she'd been working with, Ari and Cecile, had a more realistic view. They were after facts, not the story she'd spun in her head. "But the truth is what's important."

"That's why I make documentaries," Megan said. "The truth is often more fascinating than fiction, or the stories made up to conceal the facts."

Bennett moved his chair closer to hers and slid his arm around her, almost protectively. Ivy noticed that he seemed more attentive this evening.

"Besides the photo album, has Ivy told you what else she found in the attic?" Bennett asked Megan.

When Megan raised her brow with interest, Ivy began the latest chapter in the Seabreeze saga. "We found a series of concealed rooms that were clearly designed to hide people. The only entry was through my closet."

Megan sat back, stunned. "Like a safehouse. Do you think the rooms were used?"

Ivy shrugged. "We're not sure. Maybe Amelia was frightened by the proximity of Pearl Harbor. You're welcome to explore up there. My daughter Sunny and Poppy are staying up there now."

Behind them on the hill, a group of people broke out in song. "Must be someone's birthday," Ivy said. "Maybe it's someone we know." She started to swivel in her chair.

Frowning, Bennett grabbed her arm. "Ivy, wait."

She laughed because he was acting so strangely, almost as if to warn her. About *Happy Birthday*? Her curiosity aroused, she swung around.

And found herself looking squarely at Paisley again. The other woman tilted her chin in Ivy's direction, looking more arrogant than when she'd met her before. Paisley held a highball tumbler in her hand and tossed back the remaining drink.

Shocked, Ivy turned back to the table. Her pulse was hammering, and she felt light-headed.

"I'm sorry," Bennett murmured.

A hot rush of resentment tore through her. "Will I ever be free of that woman?"

"Who is she?" Megan asked.

"It's not important," Bennett said.

"No need to cover for me." Ivy clutched his hand. "The whole town knows, and since you're moving here, you'll hear the gossip soon enough. That's Paisley Forsythe, my husband's mistress." And she was clearly drinking again. That is, if she'd ever stopped. Maybe her story of a twelve-step program had been part of her act. Anger coursed through Ivy, and she clenched a fist under the table.

Josh bobbled his champagne glass and began choking. Megan patted his back while he composed himself. He'd almost lost his straw hat.

"Wow, didn't see that one coming," Josh said, his face reddening with embarrassment.

Ivy went on. "She encouraged Jeremy to buy the inn. That's how everyone here knows her. She returned recently to stay there and ask for my forgiveness. To make amends."

"What nerve," Josh said. "I don't see that happening, am I right?"

Megan's lips parted in horror, and her gaze traveled up behind Ivy. "Don't turn around."

Ivy sighed. The icy chill she felt was a sure signal that trouble was nearby. A deep voice boomed behind her.

"Mayor Dylan."

Bennett slid his hand up her arm, and Ivy turned.

Wearing a tightly fitted cherry red dress, Paisley was hanging on the arm of a man who was about Jeremy's age, maybe a little older. He wore an impeccable suit with a starched shirt collar open and a jacket draped over his arm. Paisley's bare dress showed off toned arms, though they were smudged with purple bruises.

With a grim expression, Bennett nodded at the man. "Dexter."

The man looked down his nose at Ivy. "I hear your little Beach Inn at Las Brisas del Mar is quite the going concern."

Ivy gritted her teeth. "It's the Seabreeze Inn, and it's my establishment."

The edges of Dexter's mouth turned up in a faux smile.

"So, you're Mrs. Marin." He snaked an arm around Paisley. "Your husband made some promises about that property. Verbal contracts, see?"

Bennett rose to his feet. "That's enough, Dexter. We're not doing this here."

A chill raced through Ivy. "I have no idea what you're talking about," she said, wishing the glitzy pair would slither off to wherever they were going—which was hopefully back to Los Angeles.

Dexter crushed Paisley to his side, causing pain to crease her perfectly made-up face. "You will soon." With a chuckle, Dexter turned his back and led Paisley up the steps.

"Good riddance," Ivy said, pressing her fingers against a pulsing vein in her temple. *What did Dexter mean by verbal contracts?* Was this merely a threat, or was there any validity to it? She'd have to ask Imani.

Megan reached across the table for Ivy's hand. "What a creepy couple. I'm so sorry for you. What is *she* doing back here?"

"I can't imagine," Ivy said. Beside her, Bennett had sat down again, though he was shifting uncomfortably in his chair. *What does he know about this?* At once, the beautiful evening seemed to take on a grayish hue. Ivy struggled to maintain her composure through the rest of the dinner, which was a celebration for Megan and Josh for their expected baby and new home. However, she couldn't shake the feeling that Paisley was ushering in trouble, or that Bennett knew more than he was letting on.

Later that evening, after she'd made sure that Megan and Josh were comfortable in their guestroom, confirmed reservations for the next week, and answered a media question about the art show, Ivy closed her computer in the library and made her way upstairs to Shelly's room, where she was still sleeping on a cot. After changing into a nightgown, she slid under the covers, and Shelly turned off the light.

A soft ocean breeze from an open window rippled through the room. Outside, the constant lull of the sea was soothing and restorative. Waves breaking on the shore were a reminder of the good fortune she had of being in Summer Beach, in a home that was also providing a much-needed income.

As long as she could hang on to it.

Shelly called out softly in the dark. "Hey, Ives?"

"Yeah, Shells?"

"You know how you always figure out a way to get things done?"

Ivy tucked an arm under the goose-down pillow under her head. "You must've read my mind."

"From now on, we'll figure it out together. All of us. And this time, I won't run away."

Ivy let out a sigh. "Is that a threat?"

"You bet it is."

A decorative pillow plopped onto Ivy's legs. "Hey, you!"

"This will be the best art show anyone on this coast has

seen," Shelly said. "Well, the most fun, anyway."

They both fell quiet for a while. Finally, Ivy whispered, "Hey, Shells?"

"Yeah, Ives?"

"Even if things don't work out for us here, I'm really glad you came back."

"Ives, did anyone ever tell you you're full of it?"

"Hmm. Believe that was you."

Shelly laughed. "This is where we both belong."

"I think so, too." Despite the lawsuits and gossip, Ivy loved living here. Stretching her legs and wiggling her toes, she added, "Loves you."

Shelly let out a yawn. "Loves you, too."

***

The next morning at breakfast, Ivy invited Megan and Josh upstairs to see the attic. They climbed the folding staircase that Forrest and Reed had installed. Josh took special care to make sure Megan was okay on the stairs, though they were quite sturdy.

Pausing at the new door to the concealed rooms, Ivy knocked. She'd already alerted Sunny with a call and text that they were coming. Poppy was downstairs tending to breakfast in the dining room, but Sunny had slept in. As she always did.

The door eased open. Sunny still wore the T-shirt and flannel shorts she slept in, and her face was puffy and creased from sleep. "Hi, Mom," she said, holding open the door for them and shuffling to one side.

"Good morning, darling." Ivy introduced Megan and Josh. "This is the first room we discovered." Ivy stepped inside and introduced them to Sunny.

"Hi," Megan said brightly.

"Um, hi," Sunny replied. "I, uh, like your tattoo."

Megan swung her ponytail to one side and touched her neck. A delicate rose tattoo was etched behind her ear. "In memory of my grandmother."

"That's sweet," Sunny said.

Ivy was surprised. Sunny sounded almost human again. But then, the two young women were probably less than a decade apart. Megan seemed so much more mature. She had direction in her life, as well as skills and talent. That's what Sunny needed.

"Wow," Megan said, spinning around. "Look at the bunk beds. This place is full of secrets. Have you guys found anything else up here?"

"Besides the album, the old journal I called you about," Ivy said. "Though I haven't had time to read much."

"I can help," Megan said, her eyes sparkling with excitement.

"Let's look at it later." With Ivy leading the way, they set off to explore the series of rooms.

When they returned to the room that Sunny and Poppy were using, Ivy noticed that Sunny looked a little more alert. She held a round metal case in her hands.

"I don't know if this is anything," Sunny said with a shrug. "It was under the mattress of my bed." She shot a look at Ivy. "The mattresses are thin, so I could feel it."

"It looks like an old film canister." Megan reached for it. "Mind if I look at it?"

"Please." Ivy ignored Sunny's complaint and pulled out a chair for Megan at the small table.

Sunny placed the metal canister on the table. While Ivy looked on, Josh and Megan examined it. Finally, Josh managed to pry it open. Inside, film was wound around a reel.

"This is really old," Megan said. "And we need to be careful with it. The film could contain nitrate, which emits dangerous gases."

"Can we look at the film?" Ivy asked.

"I could take it to L.A. and have a film expert examine it," Megan said.

Ivy nodded. "Can they transfer it to a digital format?"

"Probably." Megan put the lid back on it. "Now, I really want to read that old journal."

Sunny narrowed her eyes at her mother. "What journal?"

With a start, Ivy realized how much Sunny had missed. But surely Misty or Poppy or Shelly had filled her in. "The woman who lived here before us—long before us. Amelia Erickson. She was an art collector, and rather eccentric. Why don't we talk about it over lunch?" This might be a good way to get Sunny talking again. To her, at least.

"Can't," Sunny mumbled. "Jamir's going to show me

some cool places on the beach."

"Another day then." Ivy missed talking to Sunny, who'd hardly said anything to her since she'd arrived. *At least Jamir's a good influence.* Ivy turned back to Megan. "I'll bring the journal to your room. There's a particular entry that maybe you can help me decipher."

Chapter 19

"LOOK AT THIS PASSAGE AND tell me what you can make out," Ivy said, pointing to a barely legible journal entry to Megan. They had moved to the parlor where the morning light spilling through the tall, arched Palladium windows was the brightest. Guests sauntered out of the dining room and milled about, curious about the old house. A couple visiting from Canada stepped into the ballroom, and Ivy could hear expressions of awe over the chandeliers and architecture.

Poppy was leading an informal tour, telling people about how the house was used as a center for physical therapy and rehabilitation during the Second World War. One person asked about the masterpiece paintings that had been discovered on the property, while another was curious about the jewelry. The media had covered these finds, but Ivy and Shelly preferred to keep their guests' privacy than enter a media circus.

Megan grinned at her. "Sounds like a popular tour."

"More and more people are asking about seeing the house," Ivy said. "Between the media coverage and Shelly's vlog, word has gotten around." She touched her chin in thought. With the crowd they hoped they'd attract for the art show on the grounds, maybe they could charge a nominal fee for house tours. People were curious about the Julia Morgan architecture, and she could use the funds to replace the deficit that Sunny's first-class splurge caused in her tax bill account. Plus, the more people who saw the house, the more likely they were to book events there. "Do you think art show patrons would pay a small donation for a house tour—including the lower level and the attic?"

"I sure would. I think that's a great idea." Megan leaned forward, squinting at the old handwriting in the journal. "I'm going to need a magnifying glass."

"I have one here." Ivy rummaged through her supplies on the table and located a large round magnifier. "This should help." She had brought out all the material she'd found for Megan to view for her documentary research. The vintage album and satchel, the journal she'd just discovered, and the few letters that she'd found earlier. She'd also brought a couple of yellow notepads and her laptop computer for research. "This house has harbored so many mysteries for so long. I'm determined to find answers."

"I'm betting a lot of other people will be interested, too," Megan said.

As they were deciphering the feathery writing, Shelly strolled in with an armful of white roses and green ferns.

"Fresh picks from the garden," Shelly said as she filled in a sparse bouquet on a round table in the center of the room with the roses and greenery. Tucking her gloves in the back pocket of her jeans, she peered over the work that Ivy and Megan were doing. "Any luck piecing together the old woman's story?"

"We're making some progress," Megan said, indicating her notes.

"I'll bet our friends Ari and Cecile at the FBI know more about the Ericksons than they let on," Shelly said thoughtfully.

"Possibly, though they had no idea about the paintings," Ivy said, slipping on her indigo blue readers. "Or the crown jewels. Only that they'd gone missing. But they had no idea how that stash ended up here. If they know anything else, they're not sharing it with us."

Megan rested her chin in her hand. "Why were those items here, I wonder? In the simplest terms, their presence really turns on profit or protection, doesn't it?"

"That's the big question." Ivy picked up her pencil, ready to make notes.

Shelly pulled up a chair. "The Ericksons were collectors. You bet they were in it for the money."

"Not necessarily," Ivy said. "According to some history that Nan and Arthur had, Gustav came to the marriage with old family money." Ivy brushed her hair over her shoulder. "And since Amelia's father—as we now know—was a museum director, she would have had a deep appreciation of artistry." She paused, recalling the journal passage she'd read. With a sigh, she turned a page and brought Megan's attention to the entry. "Read this."

Megan began reading. "Seems her father was in the middle of the campaign to rid the country of art deemed unfit. And here...she uses the word *agree*. That means both Amelia and Gustav were up for acquiring the banned works." Reading, she went on. "*This is an opportunity to acquire important works of art—regardless of the circumstance.*" Megan lowered the magnifier and pushed a hand through her hair. "Sounds kind of calculated."

"No, wait a minute." Shelly sat back in contemplation. "Now that I think about it from another point of view, maybe they *were* protecting the artwork. Naturally, they would have to acquire the pieces first."

Ivy stared at her sister. "Are we switching positions now?"

"Well, look at this," Megan said, pointing to another passage.

Before they could read it, the front door swung open.

Shelly glanced at Ivy. "More guests?"

Two people stepped inside, and as Ivy's eyes rose to the foyer, she sucked in a breath.

Paisley and Dexter.

"It's *her.* I'll take this." Ivy rose and started through the parlor while Shelly trailed her.

"Not alone, you're not," Shelly whispered.

Trying hard to suppress her anger, Ivy lifted her chin with purpose. As she strode forward, Paisley began whispering to Dexter. Ivy's heels clicked sharply on the wooden floor, matching the pounding of her heart. What on earth could this distasteful pair want?

Since there were other guests around, Ivy tried to force a pleasant look on her face, but she failed. The best she could do was to refrain from lunging for Paisley's throat. "Hello, Paisley," she said, opting for a flat, strained conversational approach. "You look like you're feeling better. What can we do for you?" She could just imagine what was going through Shelly's mind. Darla hadn't been anywhere near as threatening as this pair.

Paisley angled her head toward the man who stood beside her. With his impeccably tailored sport coat and slacks, he reminded Ivy of how Jeremy had dressed. "This is Dexter, my *fiancé,*" she said, stressing the last word. An eye-popping diamond glittered on her left hand.

"I see. Congratulations." They couldn't possibly want to stay here, Ivy thought with a shock. "If you're looking for a guest room, we're fully booked."

Paisley curved up a corner of her bee-stung lips. "I wouldn't expect you to have any vacancies for me."

Dexter cleared his throat. "May we speak somewhere in private?"

Ivy glanced at Shelly. "I think we can say what we need to here." The last thing she wanted was a re-enactment of the scene in the library with Paisley.

Dexter shrugged and thrust out an envelope in a neatly manicured hand. "Inside, you'll find Paisley's sworn statement and a copy of a letter from Jeremy Marin promising her a 49% share in Las Brisas del Mar. Or we could acquire it cheap at the tax auction."

Shock seized Ivy, and an icy clamminess surged through her. Squaring her shoulders, Ivy said, "The estate has been settled. I am the sole heir of Las Brisas del Mar—the Seabreeze Inn. And there's not going to be an auction for this property." From the corner of Ivy's eye, she could see Poppy and Sunny on the staircase.

"We'll see." A smooth laugh erupted from Dexter as he tossed the packet on the foyer table. "That should make interesting reading then." He glanced around the foyer and into the ballroom. "Paisley said you'd fixed up the property. Quaint, isn't it? However, we plan to break ground on a high-rise resort within the year."

"You can't do that," Shelly shot back. "This has a historic designation."

Standing behind Dexter, Paisley was trying to say something. Her mouth was moving, but Ivy couldn't hear her. Ivy's attention was riveted on Dexter anyway. *What he said…it couldn't be true. Could it?*

Dexter shook his head. "We'll prove in court that the historic status was illegally obtained, no doubt, through your improper relationship with the mayor."

"That's it." Ivy's anger ratcheted up another notch. "I will not stand for your allegations or insinuations. Please leave before I call the police. If you have anything to say to me, you can talk to my attorney, Imani Williams."

Ivy turned on Paisley. "Is *this* your way of making amends? What an act that was."

"No, I-I," Paisley stammered. Beneath her painted-on bravado, she looked stricken.

Dexter smoothly cut in. "I have no idea what you're talking about. But we intend to go forward with this, so I suggest you contact your attorney so that you can begin to refund your guests' money." He raised his voice on his last words.

"Out," Ivy said, thrusting her arm toward the door, which Shelly sprang across the foyer to open. "You'll never see the inside of this inn again, or step foot on this property."

Beyond them, guests had frozen in place, watching as the scene unfolded. A nearly uncontrollable shiver raced through her, making her limbs shake with pent-up fury. She could not lose control in front of their guests.

With a chuckle, Dexter sauntered out, his hands in his pockets in a cocky display of confidence. Behind his back,

Paisley threw an odd look of apology toward Ivy and mouthed something again that Ivy couldn't make out. Ivy was so fraught with anger that she could hardly focus.

"How could you?" Ivy spat out. "All that talk about your *program*—it was just another lie, wasn't it?"

"No, no," Paisley said in a pleading whisper. Tears threatened to spill from her perfectly contoured smoky eyes. "I'm so ashamed."

Ivy could smell alcohol on Paisley's breath. "Then, don't do this," she said, lowering her voice. "You have a choice. What kind of hold does that man have on you?"

"I love him…"

"His type doesn't love anyone. You could be better. You just have to believe it in here," Ivy said, striking her heart with her fist.

Shelly jabbed a finger at Paisley. "Are we done here?"

"I'm so, so sorry." Paisley backed out, then hurried out after Dexter.

Shelly slammed the door behind her. "Show's over, folks," she said to the guests who were lingering around.

The fury that Ivy had been holding back burst forth, and she gritted her teeth. "I need air," she said, tugging on Shelly's sleeve. "Get me out of here." She hated to leave Megan, but she was shaking uncontrollably. Confronting Paisley and Dexter in their impromptu visit was just too much.

"Come on," Shelly said, leading her past the library and music room and out the kitchen to the far end of the pool area. Thankfully, they were alone.

Ivy blinked against the bright sun and sank onto the edge of a cushioned chaise lounge facing the pool. She buried her face in her hands.

Shelly rubbed her shoulders. "Heck of a performance back there, Ives. You're a lot tougher than I thought. Guess my New York attitude rubbed off on you."

Ivy managed a weak grin. "And look at me now, completely falling apart."

"That pair staged a dirty sneak attack." Shelly frowned. "You're strong in the moment, that's what counts. So, let's see those documents."

Ivy realized she'd snatched the envelope that Dexter had left and crumpled it in her fist. She promptly dropped it into Shelly's hands as if it were aflame. "I can't right now."

"I've got this." Shelly took the envelope from her and drew out the crinkled papers.

Just then, Sunny and Poppy burst through the door and raced across to them.

Sunny's eyes were bulging. "Mom, what's going *on*? Are you *losing* this place?"

Ivy sent up a desperate plea for strength. Sunny had arrived in Summer Beach at the worst time, and she wished her daughter didn't have to witness this. But then, maybe Sunny was spoiled precisely because Ivy had kept too many of life's messy realities from her.

"I plan to fight with everything I have to keep it." Ivy

drew her hands over her face. She didn't need another Paisley complication.

Sunny charged forward and knelt by her mother. "What was that about a *tax* sale?"

Ivy scrubbed her cheeks with the palms of her hands. "Your father didn't pay the property taxes owed before he died because he drained his retirement accounts to buy the house. I've been saving to pay the bill before the forced sale."

"I don't understand. You *have* money." Sunny scrunched up her face. "Why don't you just pay it?"

Ivy had been over this with her daughters right after Jeremy's death, but Sunny had refused to believe it. "Your father left more debts than cash. This house sat on the market for almost a year before Shelly and I moved in to make a go of it as an inn. I had no other choice."

Sunny swung around to Shelly, who nodded in agreement. "That's the truth. And I love you, kid, but your five-figure, first-class ticket didn't help your mother."

Sunny shot a glance at Poppy, who was standing behind her. "Then it's *my* fault, isn't it?" she wailed.

"No, no—" Ivy caught herself. Her natural response with her daughters was to gloss over hardships and make them feel safe. Misty had seen through Ivy's defenses, and she was old enough to understand. Sunny was, too. "All right. It's true. The airline tickets you bought I couldn't afford. Now I have a credit card bill I can't pay."

For the first time that Ivy could remember in many,

many months, Sunny closed her mouth in contemplation. Poppy stood beside her and held out her arms to her cousin.

As Sunny fell into Poppy's arms, tears trickled down her cheeks. "I'm not stupid, but I guess I've been acting that way. Poppy told me everything that's been going on here." She shook her head. "I wanted to think that Dad had left us a lot of money and that nothing in our lives would change. When you told me that I couldn't finish at the university, I flipped out. I mean, all my friends were there. I didn't want to be the only one on financial aid or working part-time at a burger joint. I mean, I'm *vegan*."

Ivy rose and put her hand on Sunny's shoulder. For once, her daughter didn't shrug her off. "It didn't have to be a burger joint, and student loans are nothing to be ashamed about." Ivy had paid off those she'd incurred years ago. "I know you miss your father, Sunny. We all do. But things have changed." She opened her arms, and after a moment of hesitation, her daughter came to her. As Ivy wrapped her arms around her, Sunny relaxed against her as she had as a child. Ivy closed her eyes and swayed slightly. Somehow, they would figure a way out of this mess.

"I'm so sorry for the way I've treated you, Mom." Sunny sniffed against Ivy's shoulder. "I'm such an idiot."

"No, you're not," Ivy said, smoothing her hand over Sunny's trembling back.

"You sure *acted* that way," Shelly said. "But we know you can do better. No more running up your mom's credit card, okay?"

Ivy would have to learn to trust her daughter, too. Now that Sunny was asking questions, she had to be truthful with her.

Sunny turned her face to Ivy. "So, who was that couple that was just here, and why did they say that Dad promised that woman the property?"

Ivy stiffened. *Give me strength*, she thought. "That woman…was someone who…" She hesitated. This would ruin Sunny's image of her father. *Was it worth it?*

"What, Mom?" Sunny stood and shot a glance between Poppy, who lowered her eyes, and Shelly, who was focusing on the wrinkled envelope. "Is anyone going to answer me?"

Ivy shivered at a gust of wind off the ocean. "Your father might have promised Paisley something because they…" She couldn't bring herself to utter the words, but from the hurt look on Sunny's face, she didn't need to.

Sunny whirled around and caught Shelly by the arm. "Tell me. Was that Dad's…*girlfriend?*"

Ivy cut in. "Leave Aunt Shelly alone." She sat down again and patted a spot beside her on the tufted recliner. "I'm sorry. I didn't know anything about her until I moved here."

Sunny stared at Ivy, her eyes flashing with anger. "You're not going to just let her walk in and take what she wants, are you?"

"Ha! You clearly don't know your mother very well," Shelly said, taking a step toward Sunny. "She's been fighting to keep this place ever since we got here." Jerking a thumb in the direction of the house, she added. "Your mom's a badass lioness. She could eat those two idiots for breakfast and still have an appetite."

Ivy couldn't help laughing through the tears that welled in her eyes. She could always count on Shelly to serve up the attitude.

Across the terrace, Celia stepped outside and waved. She pointed inside.

"I think we're needed," Ivy said, preparing to tuck away their private dramas to tend to business.

Poppy acknowledged Celia. "I'll see to it, Aunt Ivy." She hurried away.

Deflated, Sunny plopped down beside Ivy. "I can't believe Dad would do that. Why? Did you guys argue about something?"

Ivy shook her head with sorrow. "I don't know how to explain your father's actions because I don't understand them myself." The details of a marriage were complicated, but that was the truth that Sunny needed to know. "I'll deal with this situation."

"Uh-oh." Shelly thrust out the papers that Dexter had left. She'd been scanning them while they talked. "You need to see this."

With Sunny looking over her shoulder, Ivy read the first document, which was a sworn statement from Paisley confirming that Jeremy had promised a nearly equal share of Las

Brisas del Mar to her in a partnership between them. Did Paisley actually expect to be a partner with *her* now? The thought was at once both ludicrous and horrifying.

As Ivy turned to the next document, Jeremy's handwriting leapt from the photocopied page, bringing back a fresh wave of memories of when they were newly married. *Of the notes he used to leave tucked into my lingerie drawer, along with a new negligee.* She skipped over his term of endearment for Paisley. In the short letter, he wrote about his vision—the two of them building their future together in Summer Beach, along with the most luxurious new high-rise resort on the west coast.

Ivy's heart sustained the direct blow, pumping even more blood to her heated face, while Sunny moaned in anguish beside her. *How could Jeremy have done this to us?*

Still, the fine hairs of the back of Ivy's neck bristled with warning, and she lowered the wrinkled pages. "Something isn't right about this." Not wanting to hold the papers for a moment longer, she shoved them back into Shelly's hands.

Her sister took the documents and folded them back into the envelope. "Do you think that's his handwriting?"

"It is." Ivy sighed and brought her arm around Sunny as her daughter nestled against her. This was uncharted territory for her, and Ivy could only imagine the therapy Sunny would have to undergo to put all this into perspective. It was a lot for Ivy to grasp, yet her daughter's matinee-idol image of her father was now forever damaged.

Ivy pressed her hand to her forehead. The scene in the foyer with Paisley and Dexter reeled through her mind. Despite what Paisley had put forth in her sworn statement, she had acted strangely. *Reluctant. Embarrassed. Repentant.* As if her actions were Dexter's idea. And judging from his grip on Paisley and the rock on her finger, Dexter was probably counting the Seabreeze Inn as his after they married.

That was it.

"Dexter is using Paisley to get this property," Ivy said.

Shelly nodded. "Probably. But I don't feel sorry for her."

Ivy blinked against the sunlight. There was more, though. *What am I missing?* Then she remembered. "After Dexter stormed out, Paisley was trying to say something. Mouthing the words. Did anyone catch it?"

Sunny looked up glumly. "Seemed like she said *the letter.*"

The letter. Ivy passed a hand over her face. "I threw it out. I've really blown it."

"No, you haven't." Shelly knelt beside her. "I would have done the same. And we're all in this with you."

Ivy shook her head. "I know what Paisley was trying to do. The letter she gave me probably disproves *that* note because it was written afterward—when Jeremy wanted to break up with her and focus on our family. Or so she told me."

Sunny blinked. "Really?"

Shelly brightened. "That's it. All you need to do is produce the letter. Give it to Imani. She'll know what to do."

Ivy grimaced. "But I couldn't stand to look at it, so I threw it away." And probably tossed away her last chance to save this property. She thought about the financial resources that Dexter clearly had at his disposal—and the high-priced attorneys he'd probably already engaged.

Even now, Ivy's head was throbbing at the magnitude of the problem. "Dexter knows what this property is worth, especially as a tear-down. It would take a team of lawyers to fight him, and the cost of a legal defense would be staggering. As much as I adore Imani, I don't think she could handle this case. She has a business to run and a son to put through medical school. I can't pay her."

Shelly kicked the ground, sending up a fine spray of sand that settled on the pavement surrounding the pool.

Ivy had to be honest with herself, too. She looked up at the house standing majestically against the clear blue sky, the sound of the waves crashing just beyond the property line. This home had stood for a hundred years, yet it still might take Amelia's secrets to its grave beneath a wrecking ball. Blinking at that thought, Ivy gulped in the fresh sea breezes she loved. This house, this beach, this community—all of it had swept into her heart. How could the dream die now? But the choice wasn't solely hers to make. "I hate to say it, but this might be the end of our beachside adventure."

Shelly and Sunny fell silent, taking in the magnitude of what this meant. While Sunny looked stunned, Shelly crossed her arms with defiance.

"Look at what we've done here," Shelly said, thrusting out her hands. "It's an amazing house, but it's just a house. We can do this again if we have to. Another inn, another place."

Shelly was right. Ivy brushed away her tears and hugged Shelly and Sunny close to her. Through it all, she had her family. Her real treasure. She and Shelly could create another future for themselves. It might not be in a grand house on the sandy shores of Summer Beach, but they could find another old home suitable for an inn somewhere. They'd figure it out. As she thought of Bennett, she bit back a sob. How close they'd come... but she had to play the hand that life was serving.

And so, with renewed resolve, Ivy rose from the chaise lounge and pushed her hair back from her hot forehead. "If we have to lose this place, let's throw a party to remember. Let's make this art show the most amazing event Summer Beach has ever seen." And she knew just where to start.

Chapter 20

BENNETT RUSHED THROUGH THE REAR kitchen door at the inn, where he found Ivy perched on a stool looking shaken. He'd been at the office working on his speech for the annual bonfire tonight, but as soon as Nan told him what had happened at the inn, he'd hurried back, consumed with worry over Ivy.

"I heard you had a visit from that scheming pair," he said, holding his arms open to her.

She came to him, letting him fold her into his arms. "Is anything a secret in this town?" she murmured against his neck.

"Gilda overheard your argument with Dexter and Paisley,

and she was sharing that with Imani at the flower stand, which is where Nan overhead it."

"If only I could mobilize the town like a good piece of gossip does." Ivy pulled back and arranged a brave smile on her face. "This art show might be our last event here, so we're going all out."

Bennett frowned. "What are you talking about? What happened?"

"Jeremy wrote a note to Paisley that effectively gives her a part of the inn. Dexter is backing her to challenge the estate so they can build that high-rise resort."

"Aw, no, no, no!" Bennett pushed his hands through his hair in frustration. The city had spent a fortune defending against Jeremy. But Jeremy had only been a consultant to Dexter, who was a partner in the technology firm and had more money than Bennett would ever see in ten lifetimes. *Private plane money. Floating-palace yacht money.* Dexter was the kind of guy that unless he got his way, he would bankrupt Summer Beach just for the fun of it.

And leave Ivy and Shelly out in the cold. He slammed his fist into his palm. "Why can't they leave us alone?"

"Dexter will ruin whoever gets in his way." Ivy gave him the saddest look he'd ever seen. "I'm so sorry Jeremy ever found this place."

Bennett took her hand. "I'm not sorry, Ivy. The day we reconnected was one of the best days of my life."

"You're just trying to make me feel better." A faint light

shone in Ivy's eyes. "I remember that day. You couldn't wait to get rid of Shelly and me. In fact, you were so anxious that you raced off in your SUV with our luggage still in the back."

"What can I say?" He kissed her lightly and squeezed her hand. "You grew on me."

Just then, the kitchen door swung open, and Imani marched in. "What's this I hear about Dexter and Paisley coming here and threatening you?"

Ivy handed her the crinkled documents than Shelly had left in the kitchen.

As Imani studied Paisley's statement and Jeremy's letter, she sank onto a stool, then handed them to Bennett. "Dexter Hansen is one mean guy. He stops at nothing. You know, he had his eye on this place before Jeremy bought it."

Ivy nodded. "Paisley told me the partners were doing a feasibility study on this property when she talked Jeremy into buying it out from under them." She stretched her hand across the counter to Imani. "I know this case is too large for you to handle alone, so I won't even ask."

"I'd have to refer it out, but you'd need big money to fight it." Imani shook her head. "Could you offer to sell it to him at a great price? At least you'd walk away with something."

Ivy shrugged at the idea. "Dexter seemed like he's going to take great delight in buying the place at the tax sale, or forcing Paisley on me and challenging the historic designation. Said it was fraudulent because of my relationship with the mayor."

"He could probably spin that." Imani shook her head sadly.

Ivy blinked back tears. "His plan is to tear down this lovely place."

Bennett's gut churned at the thought of losing the historic landmark, but more so at the prospect of Ivy's loss—and losing Ivy. "The community doesn't have the money to defend against him. He'll argue job creation and higher taxes paid in, and he'll eventually wear everyone down and win."

The three of them grew solemn at the thought. In the time that Bennett had been mayor, he'd managed to maintain and enhance the unique spirit of Summer Beach—of relaxed lifestyles by the sea and neighborly affection toward each other—which had changed little in decades. Bennett knew Dexter Hansen's track record. Dexter would buy up surrounding property at generous prices for parking lots and wider streets to manage an increased flow of traffic and tourists. He'd buy up small shops and then sell out to chain stores and restaurants for top dollar as he had in another beach community up the coast. Dexter Hansen would have his way.

But Bennett wasn't giving up yet. "There's a wealthy—though reclusive—group in this community that could be mobilized to fight back. You throw your big event next weekend, and I'll help spread the word."

"Along with Nan," Imani said, grinning. "She and Gilda and Darla should form a PR firm."

"That's not a bad idea," Bennett said with a wry laugh.

The kitchen door flung open again, and Megan rushed in. "Shelly filled me in on what's going on."

Ivy held a hand out to her. "I'm so sorry about your documentary. We were so close to discovering Amelia's motivations and real intentions, too."

"And we will," Megan said. "The documentary will go on. I'll start shooting film footage inside the house and on the grounds so that we'll have it. Nothing is going to deter us from finishing that film."

"That's the spirit," Bennett said, giving Megan a high-five. Though it would be a bittersweet film—a swansong to the historic home that had served the community well through the years and the couple behind it. "What else can the community do to help you with this art show?"

"I'll give you a list," Ivy replied. "Here's what I'm thinking so far. Carol Reston loved singing here at her daughter's wedding. She said it was a special place in her heart, so I thought she might like to come back and give a mini-concert—maybe make a donation to the local schools or animal shelter. People would love that."

Bennett nodded. "You're pretty savvy."

As Ivy outlined the plans, Bennett found himself staring into her bright green eyes, but hardly hearing what she was saying. Over the past few months, getting to know Ivy had been a gift that had awakened his damaged heart. No matter what fate awaited the inn, he wouldn't let her go so easily.

Even though Sunny disliked him, he knew time could heal broken hearts—and Sunny was definitely grieving for her father. But would Bennett have enough time? If Ivy had to move from Summer Beach, their relationship might never grow beyond what it was unless he put forth the effort.

"So, what do you think?" Ivy asked.

Bennett had been lost in her eyes and mesmerized by her voice. "I'll let people know," he managed to say, pulling himself from the rush of emotions that surged through him every time he was near her.

"Hey, Mr. Mayor." Imani tapped on the counter. "You should pay Megan to shoot some film of the art show. The city could use a new promotional video, and this will be a spectacular event."

A shadow crossed Ivy's face. "The show might not be here next year."

"*You* will be," Imani said firmly. "You'd just change the venue. Hold it at the park or the marina. Bet the city would give permission for a successful event that brings in tourist business. Right, Mr. Mayor?"

"I'll talk to the Visitor's Bureau and see if it's in their budget." Bennett grinned. "Carol Reston might even make a donation to cover it."

Megan's eyes lit with enthusiasm. "And they should give her permission to use it. Carol Reston has millions of followers. That's a win-win all around."

Imani jabbed Bennett's arm. "We're not such a bad PR

team ourselves."

"I appreciate your help," Ivy said with a slight catch in her voice. "I'll call Carol right away."

"I have to relieve Jamir at the flower stand," Imani said. "I'll see you all at the bonfire tonight."

"Josh and I will be there," Megan said. "I need to go remind him."

As Imani and Megan left, the two women were already sharing ideas about the art show. Bennett was glad that Ivy had supportive friends and family, especially now, after such a tough day.

"Hey," he said, running his fingers along her arm. "Is there anything else you need? I'm open for shoulder massages. Complimentary wine, too."

Ivy rubbed her neck. "Can you hold a place for me?"

"Sure." He circled her with his arms, and she leaned into him. "How about later tonight? After the bonfire."

"I'd like that. Today has been pretty sobering."

Her words cut through him. "I wish I could do more."

"You do an awful lot for me." As she rested her head against his chest, her lips curved. "Strong heartbeat."

"Always for you." He ran a hand over her tousled hair. Gently, he lifted errant strands from her face. Furrowing his brow, he felt the pressure of longing filling him. Bennett had already asked Ivy to go with him to the annual bonfire on Main Beach, but that was before Sunny had returned. "Still want to go to the bonfire?"

"I promised Sunny I'd take her," Ivy said. "Or she might go with Poppy."

"Let me know. I can meet you on the beach. Most of the locals will be there."

"Or we can all walk there together," Ivy suggested. "Might be good for Sunny. You know, before you arrived, we had a talk about the airline ticket."

"And?"

"It was the first honest conversation we'd had since she returned," Ivy said. "Sunny understands the situation now. I think we made progress."

He traced the slope of her shoulder and dragged his thumb along her neck, applying gentle pressure along a tense muscle. "I'm glad to hear it. You need each other right now."

She rotated her neck. "Hmm, that feels good. I'll give you a month to stop that."

"How about a lifetime?" he murmured, longing to kiss her sweet lips again.

She closed her eyes. "We'll see," she said softly.

Bennett shifted her hair and gave her a parting kiss on her neck. If only he could be so lucky.

***

Later that afternoon, Bennett surveyed the crowd that had already gathered on the beach. The Summer Beach bonfire was one of the town's most popular events, honoring members of the community for involvement efforts. He breathed in the smell of barbecue and suntan lotion and warm sand mixed with the briny scent of the sea. This was the Summer Beach he loved.

He spotted a couple of city fire engines lining the nearby street and stopped to greet Chief Paula and her team standing by. "Hello, Chief. Did you have a look around?"

"Good afternoon, Mayor," Paula replied, touching the brim of her hat. "We've already inspected the area, and volunteers helped clear excess debris. The winds are forecast as calm, so as long as folks behave themselves, I expect we'll have a noneventful evening. Should be fun for everyone today."

"Good to hear." After the Ridgetop Fire that had damaged and claimed so many homes in Summer Beach—and filled Ivy's Seabreeze Inn—the firefighting crew and residents were extra vigilant. Most of the homes had already been repaired, although those who had suffered total losses, including Imani and Gilda, were still in temporary housing.

"Thanks for keeping an eye on the revelers," Bennett said, chatting with the firefighters before he moved on. Threading through the gathering crowd and the accompanying array of beach chairs and coolers—or as Arthur called them, *chilly bins*—Bennett nodded and waved at the locals and visitors. Ahead of him, he spied a duo of pink and royal-blue hair sparkling in the sunlight. Gilda and Darla were bending toward each other in animated conversation.

Bennett greeted them and asked Gilda, "Where's Pixie today?"

Gilda beamed up at him. "She's at a doggie spa getting

groomed and pampered while Mama has fun. And look who I managed to get out."

"Darla, it's good to see you out. And Debra, welcome back to Summer Beach. Hope you ladies enjoy the bonfire." Bennett was pleased to see Darla, who appeared rested and engaged. Change was often tough on their older residents, but Darla seemed to be adjusting. "You're looking well, Darla. Doing okay?"

"Feeling much better now that I'm in yoga," Darla said. "Shelly is such a good teacher. She and Debra push me outside my comfort zone all the time. But in a good way." She linked arms with her sister and Gilda, and the three women laughed.

Change is good, Bennett mused.

Bennett moved on and caught sight of Shelly and Mitch, who had staked out an area for their friends. Sunny and Poppy were catching late afternoon rays in lounge chairs, while Jen and George from Nailed It were chatting with Nan and Arthur.

Waving at Shelly, Bennett picked his way across the beach to them. "Is Ivy here yet?"

"She's still at the inn," Shelly said, swinging her hair back and pulling on a straw hat that matched Mitch's. "We had a late arrival."

"Any sign of your earlier unwanted visitors?" Bennett glanced across the crowd. The bonfire didn't seem like the sort of scene that Paisley and Dexter would like, but you never knew. They had a knack for popping up unexpectedly.

Shelly tracked his gaze. "None, but I'll let you know if I see them."

Nearby, the bonfire committee was getting ready to light the logs, a custom that had been going on since Bennett had been a boy and came here with his family. Across the crowd, he saw his sister and her family heading toward them.

Mitch nodded toward them. "I told Kendra we'd be over here. I figured you'd join us."

"Thanks." Bennett meandered toward Poppy and Sunny. He heard them talking about when the bonfire would be lit. "Hi Poppy, Sunny. The bonfire will start right after the sun sets. It's an amazing sight."

Poppy's eyes flashed with excitement. "I can't wait to see it."

Sunny shot him a cold look, which surprised him because Ivy had told him they'd had a good talk. Not about him, though, he guessed. "It's quite a sight. We've got music and dancing, and a whole lot of toasted marshmallows."

"I won't eat them," Sunny snapped. "They're not organic."

Here we go, Bennett thought. "I can appreciate that."

"Can you?" Sunny whipped toward him. "Do you know what all those chemicals do to a person? I can tell just by looking at someone if they abuse their body or not. Like you."

Bennett held up his hands, trying to diffuse Sunny's verbal attack. "I agree with you. I can probably pay more attention to my health. We all can."

Sunny crossed her arms. "Everyone here is going to be so sick tomorrow."

"A couple of marshmallows won't hurt you," Poppy said, poking her cousin. "Besides, you're really not vegan. But Beach Burger was so worth it, right? Named Best Beach Burger in SoCal for years. Next time we'll get their Green Burger. It's good, too, and totally vegan."

"That's not the point," Sunny said, waving her off.

Sunny was clearly trying to create friction with whatever argument she could manufacture. The last thing Bennett wanted to do was engage in a dietary conversation with her. Changing the subject, he asked, "Have you seen Jamir?"

Poppy quickly followed his lead. "He's meeting us here. Jamir has been showing some friends from out of town the campus before school starts."

"And he's been trying to talk me into registering," Sunny said with a huff. "Which I'm not."

Okay, next subject. Is anything safe around Sunny? "I'll head off. You two have fun." He started off.

Glowering, Sunny called after him. "If you're looking for Mom, I doubt she'll be here. She had kind of a rough day, not that you care."

Bennett stopped, flexing his jaw. How could he possibly respond to her in a way that wouldn't set her off?

Poppy elbowed Sunny again. "Cut it out. Bennett's on our team."

"I'm just saying. He's the *mayor*. He should be able to

stop that couple from taking my mom's property."

Now he realized what was going on in Sunny's mind. She was angry and taking it out on him. For a college-educated young woman who was close to getting her degree, she didn't seem to understand how the world worked—or want to learn.

He turned back to Sunny. "It's a complicated issue. If you'd like to come to my office next week at City Hall, I'll be happy to take the time to explain it." Nan would relish the chance to educate Sunny. "I can give you a tour and explain how the city functions. Both of you," he added, indicating Poppy.

Sunny raised a shoulder and let it drop. "Not interested."

Bennett pressed on. "But you're interested in how legal affairs and zoning issues affect you and your family, right?"

"Well, sure, but..." Sunny looked exasperated.

He saw his opening. "Next Monday. Call the city, and Nan will set up a good time for you."

"We should go," Poppy said. "I'd like to learn more about how the city operates."

"Why? We're not *staying* here." Sunny seemed shocked at the mere idea.

"I might," Poppy said. "And city government is probably pretty similar wherever you go."

Shrugging, Bennett smiled at Poppy's efforts at appeasement. "Pretty close."

Sunny rose. "I need some water." She drew close to Bennett. "And I need you to stay away from my mother. Although without the big house on the beach for much longer, I figure you'll take off anyway. I've seen guys like you."

"Sunny!"

They all turned at the sound of Ivy's voice.

"That's incredibly ugly talk," Ivy said firmly. "I thought I'd raised you to have some semblance of manners. Apologize at once."

Sunny's face flushed, but she simply turned and stalked away.

"I'm so sorry," Ivy said, stretching a hand to Bennett. "Mortified, really."

Bennett shifted his attention to Ivy, who had changed into a vivid orange sundress that complemented the golden strands in her sun-streaked chestnut hair. She wore a stack of brightly painted bangles on her wrist. "I thought you two had a good talk earlier."

"We did, but I can see it's going to take more than one talk, especially where you're concerned," Ivy said. "How did all this start?"

"Marshmallows," Poppy said with a shrug. "Sunny's aching to pick a fight with Bennett. Any chance she gets."

"Is that what she says?" Ivy asked.

Poppy shrugged. "She doesn't mean it. Sunny's mad at herself."

"You're smart to see that." Bennett admired Poppy's capacity for insight. He kissed Ivy on the forehead. "I'll see you later. You need to be with your daughter."

Ivy shook her head. "Just when I thought we had turned a corner in our relationship."

Bennett twisted his lips to one side. "Clearly not this corner."

After leaving Ivy, Bennett spoke to a few more people, then it was time to start the presentation. When he climbed up onto a stone picnic table, some older kids in the crowd whistled. "Nice legs, Mr. Mayor," called one of the high school seniors.

Bennett laughed. He'd worn a pair of long shorts and a Summer Beach T-shirt. "Come with me for morning runs on the beach, Austin. You'll be as buff as I am in no time."

Laughter rippled across the beach. Everyone—except Sunny—was laughing.

"Hasn't it been an amazing summer here at the beach?" Bennett opened his arms wide while people yelled and whooped. "Before we kick off the bonfire, we want to recognize people who help keep Summer Beach a great place to live and visit. Starting with our junior high and high school students who help with beach clean-up, let's give them a round of applause."

As the sun drew close to the horizon, Bennett read off the names of the community's top swim and sailing teams. He recognized lifeguards and others who helped keep the beach safe and clean. Everyone received a ribbon for their efforts before posing for a group photo for the local newspaper.

"Next up, our business awards, which most everyone here

probably voted on." Nan gave Bennett a list of winners for funny achievements, and he read through them all, drawing rousing cheers from the locals. "And the winner for Best Place for Local Gossip is...Java Beach."

Mitch stood to take a bow, while Arthur and George and the rest of the regular clientele clapped and exchanged sheepish grins.

Bennett chuckled before going on. "And finally, the business voted Most Likely to Erupt into a Party is...the Seabreeze Inn."

Above the crowd, Bennett could hear Shelly yell out, "Woo-hoo!" Poppy waved her arms, while Ivy laughed and Sunny watched it all with a look of confusion and irritation.

Bennett laughed, but inside he was incensed over the latest threat against the Seabreeze Inn. How could this community lose such a magnificent treasure, which was only recently revived to become a favorite meeting place full of quirky people, laughter, and a stash of old secrets? It didn't seem fair that it should all end this way—at the greedy, rapacious hands of Dexter Hansen and Paisley Forsythe.

Bennett could hardly bear to see the anguish in her face, though she concealed her feelings with a smile as she accepted the award from him.

Ivy held up a hand to the crowd. "Thank you, and I'd like to invite all of you to the upcoming art show over the Labor Day weekend. We'll have quite a few big surprises in store. We'll have fabulous artwork from talented artists, including

Rowan Zachary and jeweler-to-the-stars, Elena Eaton from Beverly Hills. And we'll also conduct house tours and have a mini-concert from our very own Carol Reston."

Cheers went up through the crowd, and Bennett applauded her. "Let's hear it for Ivy Bay, folks. Now, it looks like we have just a minute before the sun disappears and the revelry begins."

"Woo-hoo!" Shelly called out again, waving her hat. Beside her, Mitch joined in.

The crowd fell quiet as people turned to watch the sun slip beneath the horizon. As the ocean extinguished the last sliver of light, a cheer rippled across the gathering.

Ivy was waiting for him, so Bennett hopped off the picnic table. "Ready for this bonfire to begin?" he asked.

"Looks like fun, though I might not last too much longer," Ivy said. "It's been a grueling day."

He took her hand in his and lowered his voice. "It's not over yet. You're an amazing woman, and you still have a few weeks to pull off a miracle. If anyone can do it, you can."

"I don't give up easily," Ivy said. "But sometimes, you have to be pragmatic."

"Or wildly crazy." As he spoke, the bonfire team gathered and, in unison, tossed matches onto the mound of tinder and logs. The fire started slowly at first, and then with a great whoosh, the flames caught and leapt into the air amid a rising cheer. Bags of marshmallows became airborne as people tossed them to the front.

"Wildly crazy…" Ivy inclined her head, and a little smile touched her lips. "Funny you should say that."

A crackling surge of electricity to rival the bonfire passed between them. Bennett wondered what Ivy had in mind. She had been full of surprises since the day she'd arrived in Summer Beach.

And he couldn't bear to lose her now.

Chapter 21

"EVERYONE IS SO EXCITED TO hear you sing at the art festival," Ivy said into the phone as she sat on her bed in her newly ceilinged bedroom. She was thrilled that Carol Reston had agreed so quickly to give a mini-concert. Ivy had made the announcement right away at the bonfire.

Carol's rich, commanding voice floated over the connection. "Darling, guests are still talking about Victoria's wedding at the inn—and on such short notice after the fire. What you're doing for this community is marvelous. I don't know why we haven't had an art festival long before now. Superb idea. And I'm so glad Rowan will be showing his artwork there." She dropped her voice a notch. "I rather think he fancies you, too. But I've heard you and our sexy mayor are getting along well, yes?"

"Just good friends, Carol." Ivy laughed. Even Carol was on the Summer Beach news loop. "Please let me know whatever you need for the show."

"Darling, all I need is electrical power for a microphone. My team does the rest."

Since Carol had been confirmed to sing, more artists had called to commit to space. Poppy told her they were almost booked up now.

After Carol hung up, Ivy clasped her hands over her shins, thinking about the final days of summer that stretched before her.

In preparation for the show, Ivy had been painting, too. After Forrest and Reed finished repairing the ceiling, she'd moved back into her bedroom and set up an easel by the window overlooking the ocean. Early in the morning, while the house slept and threads of light illuminated her room, she experimented with a new technique full of vitality and verve and brilliant colors of the sea.

Ivy sensed an energy in this room that she didn't feel anywhere else in the house. Not in her studio where she taught her art classes. Not on the veranda. It was almost as if Amelia were beside her—an international connoisseur of art—saying *yes, that's it,* or *no, not there.* A crazy thought perhaps, but she felt a different energy here that drew her in and brought out what she believed were her best efforts.

She wouldn't have time to frame her work before the show, but she was determined to show it. People might love it or hate it, but her new work represented her authentic self.

Ivy made a mental note to contact local galleries to see if they'd take some of her work. Or maybe she could find an agent. With Dexter forging ahead with his plan to acquire the property—his attorney had already served up a flurry of documents—Ivy needed to have alternate arrangements. Still, she wasn't going down without a fight.

Shoving off the bed to examine one of her paintings in the brighter light of day, she thought about what lay ahead. Legal battles took time, and at the very least, she was determined that Dexter and Paisley would not seize control of her property through a tax sale. She hadn't come this far to be unceremoniously dumped out the front door—if she could avert it.

Barring torrential rains or gale-force winds or waterspouts, the art show should be a success. She was looking forward to the day she could write checks to both the tax department and the credit card that Sunny had maxed out. Ivy ran a finger along the edge of the vibrant canvas. This new work of hers might allow her to do just that.

Feeling a swift swoosh of air, Ivy shivered. *There it is again.* She glanced around, but the sheers over her windows hadn't moved.

Lifting her arms overhead to stretch, Ivy felt energized. Over the past few months, she had pulled herself out of a pro-

fessor's dingy extra bedroom in Boston and embarked on one
of the craziest ideas she'd had in years. She'd never run an inn,
but here she was, the proprietor of an inn voted by residents as
the business Most Likely to Erupt into a Party. She chuckled
to herself. Bennett had told her it was a vote of love.

That was true about the parties or social gatherings, she
supposed. Their afternoon wine and tea hours often moved to
the terrace or the fire pit, sometimes to the pool, and still other times down to the beach. Occasionally, a karaoke session
might break out in the music room. Shelly was often the instigator, but so was Imani. And then, when they all got together—watch out. Ivy still thought about the night she and Shelly
took axes and hammers to the brick wall to the lower level—
and Bennett and Mitch saw the shadows and thought they
were being attacked. She laughed at the memories.

Ivy shifted the sheer curtain at the window and gazed out
over the calm sea. The inn was also a restorative place for the
soul. It certainly had been for her. In the quiet slices between
chaos, she could almost grasp her *raison d'etre,* her reason for
existing. More than her *métier,* her life's work—she caught
glimpses of her life's meaning.

Swiveling back to the room, Ivy looked around the bedroom full of antique furniture. This house had a meaning, too,
though she had yet to fully understand it. Still, it had brought
Bennett back into her life, and for that she was grateful. If only Sunny weren't attacking Bennett every chance she got.
What would happen if her relationship with Bennett deep-

ened? Could they live with the stress of Sunny's vitriolic outbreaks? She could condemn her daughter's actions, but Ivy couldn't help feeling that Sunny's outbursts were cries for help.

Ivy's phone buzzed, and she glanced at the text from Poppy. *Megan just arrived, and she's really excited to show you something.*

Be right down. Ivy brushed her hair back and secured it into a ponytail. She added large gold hoop earrings and gold bangles to accent her flowing white shirt and white jeans, slid her feet into gold sandals, and hurried downstairs.

Ivy greeted Megan with a hug. "How's the new house?"

"Boxes everywhere." Megan ruffled her short hair. "We're crazy for moving in before we renovate, but we couldn't wait to get in."

When Megan and Josh had offered cash for the house, their offer was immediately accepted, just as Bennett had predicted.

"What's got you so excited?" Ivy asked. Though Ivy and Megan had both read through the journal, they didn't find anything that explained how or why Amelia had acquired the paintings and jewelry—or what she planned to do with them. Amelia wrote quite a lot about their vacations in Summer Beach, but nothing much of deeper substance.

Megan's eyes sparkled. "Remember that canister of film we found in the attic?"

"Did you manage to see it?" Ivy asked.

Ivy kept watching as Amelia moved from one piece to another, discussing each one. In the end, Amelia seemed to summarize her thoughts, but none of them could make out what she was saying.

"Wait," Ivy said. "I think she's talking about Berlin."

"That's where she grew up," Megan said. "And we know that her father was a museum director. Tough time to be there, for everyone. For some more than others."

They grew silent in contemplation.

After they watched the old film footage, Megan closed the file and tapped the keyboard. "I just sent you a copy. You can do whatever you want with it."

As she thought of the film, Ivy frowned. "Besides knowing how Amelia came by all these priceless works of art and jewelry, we really need to know what her motivation was for hiding it all. This could blow up on us if it was revealed that her motives were dishonorable."

Megan traded looks with Shelly. "Controversy sells. If she was a greedy old woman, then that would get people talking, too."

"I wouldn't want to be associated with that," Ivy said, pursing her lips.

Shelly snapped her fingers. "News flash. You already are. As long as you're here. And it was Amelia who bricked up the walls. We found the stash, so we're the good guys."

"This is important history." Megan spread her hands in an earnest appeal. "Either way, people will be intrigued."

"They already are." Ivy steepled her hands in thought, tapping her fingertips together. "Shelly and I have been planning a tour of the public areas of the house for the art show." She rose and paced the length of the library, examining the idea in her mind.

Turning back to the group, she said, "Wouldn't it be interesting if we could project this film onto the wall in the lower level? I'll bet people would love to see this, especially since it includes images of the paintings that were concealed there for so many years."

"That's brilliant," Shelly said, leaping from her chair. "Maybe we can decorate the place like an old-fashioned movie theater with drapes on the wall and a popcorn maker."

"And actually serve popcorn?" Poppy frowned. "That would be a lot of cleaning afterward."

"Okay, nix the popcorn," Shelly said. "But Megan, you could chat up your documentary."

"I'm sure I can line up some press for this," Poppy said.

Seeing the enthusiasm on their faces, Ivy grew excited about the prospect of sharing this old film. "This is going to be so much fun. But I still wish we knew more."

Ivy pressed her hand against the library's smooth wood-paneled wall. To her, the house seemed alive with secrets, releasing them in its own time and way. But with Dexter determined to destroy the house, if these walls held any more confidences, the time to reveal them might be running out.

Chapter 22

"SIGNAGE AND CHECK-IN TABLE FOR tours, check and check," Ivy said, skimming the lifeline of a list she clutched in her hand. The art festival was tomorrow, and she was trying not to panic. She stood outside in the car court with Shelly and Poppy, conducting a final check before the show tomorrow. But as they walked the property, Ivy still noticed a lot of little things that needed attention. She ran down her list. "Are the food trucks confirmed?"

"Except for French Crepes & Beignets truck," Poppy said. "I'll double back with them. But the Beach Burger Mobile, Big Island Shave Ice, Tacos Baja, and Vegan Schmegan trucks are all confirmed. And the Rollin' Sushi truck."

"We should put up cones tonight to save their parking spots." Shelly circled the task on her list.

"Do we have any of those orange cones?" Ivy asked.

"Uh, nope, so I'll call Jen and see if she has any," Poppy said. "Food trucks mean trash and leftovers. Do we need any more trash cans for waste?"

"Everything from the shed is already out," Shelly said, patting her pockets. "And I need something to cover the electrical cords, so people don't trip. Where's my pencil?"

Ivy reached up and slid a pencil out of Shelly's haphazard topknot, letting her sister's hair fall down her back.

"Oh, thanks," Shelly said, tucking her hair behind her ear. She chewed on the end before making a note.

"Back to Jen again." Ivy was relieved that Jen and George were running a tab for them at Nailed It, but she'd make sure they were the first ones paid after the event.

"I'll put up the step-and-repeat in the morning," Poppy said.

Ivy glanced at Shelly. "Do you have any idea what she just said?"

Shelly laughed. "You know what that is."

"I absolutely do not." Ivy blew wisps of hair from her face. "Enlighten me."

"It's the backdrop celebrities stand in front of to take photos." Poppy stretched out her arms, indicating height. "A large backing that has logos on it. The lights bounce off the backdrop for photography."

Ivy looked up from her list. "We need lights, too?"

"We'll make do with the sun," Poppy said.

Shelly brightened. "I have a light ring on a tripod I use to shoot my videos. That will help the vloggers."

"So, what about that step thing?" Ivy asked.

Poppy checked her phone. "Looks like the package is two stops away."

"You're tracking the delivery?" Ivy leaned over Poppy's shoulder.

Poppy grinned. "I'll download the app for you."

"Why do I feel ancient?" Ivy made another note.

"Just wait until this is over," Shelly said. "We'll all need a massage and a hot tub."

"Does that go on the list?" Poppy asked.

"Absolutely," Ivy and Shelly said in unison.

If only that was in the budget. Ivy recalled the day Bennett had treated her to a massage on Coronado Island. *Blissful.* If enough people took the tour, or she sold some art pieces, maybe they could. Her team deserved a little pampering. Ivy scribbled a note. "Carol's people will set up her stage tonight."

Above the garages, a door slammed. Bennett, dressed in casual trousers and a sunny-yellow knit shirt for work, descended the stairs.

"Good morning, ladies," he said, flashing a warm smile and pausing by Ivy. "Ready for the big event?"

"Um, yeah, almost ready," Ivy said, feeling her heartbeat kick up a notch. He'd just finished his beach run and show-ered. His hair was still slightly damp, and his face was freshly shaven. She wondered what it would have been like, sharing his apartment over the garage for a few days, seeing him emerge from the bathroom. Could she have trusted herself?

Just as her thoughts were racing down that blissful path, Ivy caught herself and reeled in her imagination. Sunny was here, and Ivy didn't want to take any time from her. She stole another glance at Bennett. Why this man still had such an effect on her after so many years was beyond her, but there it was. Bennett made her feel like she was eighteen again.

"Thank goodness the guests are excited about the show," Shelly said, drawing her hand across her forehead.

Bennett chuckled. "Sounds like you've put half of them to work for you."

Ivy loved the sound of his laughter. "Gilda and Poppy are selling tours. Megan is shooting photos and videos, as well as running the projection on the lower level. I'm leading tours, and Jamir is assisting the artists. But we're still short-handed. Are you available?"

"Poppy put me on sound," he said. "What about Sunny?"

"She might not want to help." Ivy knew her daughter. "Sunny plans to stay in her room and watch movies on her tablet. We need someone on guest relations, for emergencies and such. Definitely not Sunny."

"Why not?" Bennett looked surprised. "I thought this was a family effort."

"I don't want to push her." In truth, Ivy didn't think that

Sunny would want to be around Bennett. As mayor, he was hosting a ribbon-cutting ceremony, so it would be hard to miss him. Tomorrow, of all days, Ivy dreaded one of Sunny's tantrums.

With a half-smile, Bennett said, "We'll see." He stepped into his SUV and pulled out of the driveway.

Watching him leave, Ivy wondered what he meant by that.

"Earth to Ivy," Shelly said, teasing her.

Frowning, Ivy tucked her notepad under her arm and clapped her hands. "That's it. Let's get to work."

Shelly locked arms with Poppy. "Yes, ma'am. We're off to Nailed It. And Ivy?"

"Yes?"

"Relax and try to have fun." Shelly winked at her. "I've done a zillion of these events, and hardly anything ever goes wrong."

"What?" Ivy called after the pair, who were laughing and racing toward the old Jeep. "That doesn't help, you know."

She shook her head. Maybe Shelly was right. Whether or not they managed to save the inn, she might as well have a good time while it was still hers, because this would be an event to remember. That was living in the moment. And at Summer Beach, that's what residents did. She turned toward the breaking surf.

From where she was standing, she was only steps from the beach. Spindly-legged children played nearby, intent on shoveling wet sand into buckets to build sandcastles that all too quickly would be swallowed up by the sea. As she watched the industrious kids, she wondered…was her home like that? About to be swallowed up by a force too great for her to battle?

No, she thought, admonishing herself. Somehow…she would prevail. But precisely how, at this moment, she had no idea. All she could do was work toward her goal—just as she had been doing since she'd arrived in Summer Beach—and pray that a previously unseen door would swing open for her.

Turning her gaze toward the other side of the point, a handful of surfers were riding small waves, but most of them were paddling and laughing, waiting for the big waves. Closing her eyes, Ivy reeled back the years, recalling the sound of the water lapping against her board, her legs dangling in the depths, the waves bobbing her and her friends in a gentle rhythm until waves swept them up and sent them surfing toward the shore. Ivy remembered the exhilarating rush, the breeze that cooled her sunburned limbs, the salty taste on her tongue.

That was living in the moment. She'd had that ability at sixteen, and now, three decades later, here she was trying to recapture that feeling.

Footsteps sounded behind her. "Well, hello, gorgeous."

Ivy whirled around. "Rowan, you're early."

His magnetic eyes twinkling in the morning light, he leaned in to kiss her—first on one cheek and then the other. "I couldn't wait to see the angel who saved me from the murky depths." He followed her line of sight and spied the surfers. "Freelancing, are you?"

"A lifeguard is watching them," she said, laughing. When Rowan Zachary, star of stage and screen, had fallen into her pool at his son's wedding to Carol Reston's daughter, Ivy didn't hesitate to dive in.

"I feel much safer by the sea with you nearby," he said, tilting his designer sunglasses to gaze into her eyes.

"Please don't venture in," Ivy said. "I might not be watching so closely tomorrow."

"Pity," Rowan said in a forlorn voice. "I finally find the woman of my dreams, and she hardly looks at me. Won't accept my gifts. What am I to do?"

"You'll be too busy tomorrow to think about it, what with all your fans crowding around." To her, Rowan was still as attractive as he had been as a teenage heartthrob, though he'd mellowed in a debonair, Cary Grant sort of style. He was smooth and sexy, but he simply wasn't *her* style.

Ivy shaded her eyes with her hand. "What can I help you with, Rowan?"

He held his arms open wide and knelt on one knee. "I've come to whisk you away to a land far, far—well, not that far away. I've reserved a table for two on the terrace in La Jolla. And then, who knows?" He clasped her hands.

The kitchen door banged behind them.

Ivy turned and sucked in a breath. Sunny was standing

with her arms folded.

"Mom, I need to talk to you. Can you spare a minute from *whatever?*"

Shifting away from Rowan, Ivy said, "Sure, honey. Be right there."

Sunny rolled her eyes and went back inside the kitchen.

A smile played on Rowan's lips. "An angel of a daughter, too."

"Hardly," Ivy said. "And you stay away from her."

Looking wounded, Rowan pressed a hand against his heart. "I'm appalled you would think that. I see her only with my artist's eye. I was thinking of painting her."

"Uh-huh."

"You can't believe the tabloids, my dear. I've reformed. No more martinis." He patted his trim torso. "The doctor said they were catching up with my liver."

"I'm impressed. But I have to go. I have a thousand things to do today." Living in the moment would have to wait until after the art show. "I'm sure you can find another angel to take to lunch." She followed his gaze toward the kitchen. "Just not my daughter."

"Until tomorrow, my darling." Bestowing two more kisses on her cheeks, Rowan released her.

Ivy was still chuckling to herself when she went inside the kitchen. Rowan made her laugh, but then, so did Bennett. As she shut the door, she could hear one of the old refrigerators making noises. Gert seemed to be wheezing.

Sunny was leaning against the counter, a sullen expression on her face. "Mom, I can't believe you. First, the mayor, and now an old actor."

Ivy drew herself up and tilted her chin. "Rowan Zachary is my age, dear. And your mother isn't old. Now, what's so important that it couldn't wait?"

"Someone wants to check in. Not that I'd know how to do that. I just hang out upstairs in my dark room, being bored."

Or sunning on the beach and flirting with lifeguards. Ivy peered at her daughter. "Do you want to learn?" Maybe Bennett saw something she'd missed in Sunny.

Averting her scrutiny, Sunny gave her an elaborate shrug. "Only so I could help Poppy."

"Come on, then." As Ivy made her way toward the door, she paused by the vintage refrigerator, gave it a thump on the side, and the whirring noise ceased. "Back to work, Gert."

Sunny looked surprised and strangely impressed.

By noon, the official check-in time for artists to begin their set-up, Ivy and her crew were ready. Fortunately, most of the artists were regulars on the art show circuit—from Carmel to Beverly Hills to Laguna Beach—and knew more than Ivy did about setting up their booths on the grounds of the Seabreeze Inn.

"Excuse me, ma'am."

Ivy looked up from her clipboard into the face of an earnest young woman. Clad in a black T-shirt and jeans, she was loading plastic cartons on a hand dolly. "Welcome to the show. How can I help you?"

"I'm setting up for Rowan Zachary. I'm Emily, and I manage his art sales." She motioned to a van and a tower of stacked cartons that were branded Rowan Zachary Artworks. "Which way is his booth?"

Ivy didn't have to check the site plan. She'd made sure to place Rowan in a high-traffic area far away from her own booth, which was in a rear, leftover spot. Her parents had reserved the space next to Rowan's to show pieces they'd discovered overseas.

"Right there," Ivy said. "We gave him a prime location. And be sure to join us in the library for wine and tea at five. If you need anything—tape, electrical—let me or one of the others in bright orange shirts know." Poppy had ordered matching tank tops and ironed on their Seabreeze Inn logo so they'd be easy to find.

"Cool," Emily said, flashing an eager smile. "I've done this before, so I have everything I need. Mr. Zachary might be in later today, but tomorrow morning for sure."

After his long lunch, Ivy thought with a smile.

Across Shelly's manicured lawn and gardens down to the beach, white canopies sprouted like giant mushrooms. Crews and artists pitched the lightweight tents and displays in record time. Only one or two new artists needed assistance.

Best of all, they had sold out the booths.

Satisfied that everything was under control, Ivy climbed

the stone steps to the house just as she had that first day she'd arrived with Shelly. She rested her hand on the railing, recalling how they'd waited while Bennett had fumbled with the keys. Although she and Shelly and Poppy had only lived here a few months, it was home. She would miss it if Dexter and Paisley had their way.

What a tangled mess Jeremy had left her. Receipts from this show—after expenses—might just cover the tax bill. She'd sorted out the lawsuit with Darla, who was volunteering at the show tomorrow, but this last hurdle with Dexter and Paisley might prove insurmountable.

What if a judge or jury or mediator deems Paisley my partner?

Blanching at the thought, Ivy stopped at the door. She couldn't think about that. Not today, not tomorrow. Not until this show was over.

Stepping into the house, Ivy saw Poppy and Sunny at the front desk, where Poppy was training Sunny on guest relations. Ivy had shown Sunny how to check in guests, and to her surprise, her daughter seemed genuinely interested. Ivy wondered what had changed. Maybe it was Poppy's influence. Whatever the reason, Sunny was beginning to engage. Ivy was guardedly relieved.

Ivy gave the public areas a cursory glance. Tomorrow she would begin the tours at several designated times during the day. Mentally she rehearsed the points she wanted to make about each room. After making a loop through the ballroom, music room, and library, she returned to the front parlor, where Megan sat going through the old photograph album and journal that Ivy had left there for her.

"How's the research going?" Ivy asked.

"Pretty good," Megan said, taking a break to stretch. "Reading Amelia's journal has been revealing. What's surprising is that she was in debt."

"I thought they were wealthy?"

Megan turned a page in the journal. "Maybe they lost a lot in the stock market crash of 1929."

"That sounds plausible." Ivy grinned. "Or they spent too much on art."

"That, too."

"What's that?" Ivy asked, indicating an array of sticky notes attached to the journal and photo album pages.

"I'm cross-referencing names that I find in her journal with corresponding photos in the album. She didn't attach names to photos often, but enough to start figuring it out. And I have some online sources to verify, too. Many of their guests were prominent in their day."

Ivy ran her hand over the old photo album cover, which crinkled under her touch. It seemed like the interior padding had broken down over time. She smoothed down a loose piece. "We have to be careful. This artifact is coming apart. Maybe I can glue this."

"It is old." Megan turned a page in the journal. "There are several entries I don't understand. I know you're busy, but could you look over them when you have time?"

"Sure, after the show is better." The entire edge of the photo album cover was coming loose. Ivy pressed it down, but when she did, the other end lifted. "The cover probably shrank over time. Too much padding now. I can fix this right now. I'll be right back."

Ivy made her way to the library, and then she returned with a letter opener and glue. "This will keep it from further damage." She slid the tool under the edge to remove the old padding. When she withdrew it, folded pieces of paper slid out after it. "What's this?"

Megan's eyes grew wide. "Open them. Let's see."

Unfolding a paper that had darkened with age, Ivy scanned the document. "It's a list," she said, growing excited.

"Of what?"

"I think...it's of the paintings. The name, the artists. The owners..." Ivy could hardly believe what she was looking at.

Megan leaned over to look. "Why would she stuff that in there?"

"So that it wouldn't be found, I guess."

"But why?"

That struck her as odd, too. Ivy ran her finger down the neat, handwritten list. "Names of museums and individuals. Some are probably dealers. This is similar to what Ari and Cecile at the FBI had compiled. In fact, we should probably let Ari know about this."

"So that's part of the provenance, but just the most recent

owner?"

"That's right."

"But why hide it?"

A cold feeling came over Ivy. "So that the list wouldn't implicate her."

Megan frowned. "Not necessarily."

"This will add to the provenance of the art works." Ivy chewed her lip in thought. "Or, so she would remember who the paintings had belonged to. There were a lot of paintings."

"She had to do that."

Ivy leaned back in her chair and rubbed her neck. "I feel like we're not asking the right questions. If we were, the answer would be obvious."

"We're still missing a piece of the puzzle."

Ivy unfolded another piece of paper, which was a similar list. She slid the letter opener under the cover again, and more papers emerged.

Megan helped her open them. "More of the same."

"We have to think of explanations for Amelia's actions and back into the questions," Ivy said. "We need to know her motivation."

Megan chuckled. "Now you sound like an actor."

"She might have been motivated as a collector, an investor, or a preservationist. If she were in debt, maybe she was motivated by the potential for investment after the war."

"And yet, she didn't sell them," Megan pointed out. "The entries in the journal span years. It seems she would remember to write something and add it. But mostly she didn't, especially after the war."

"Her memory might have been declining then," Ivy said, tapping a paper. "I still wonder *how* she got the paintings. And the jewels. I wish I could spend more time on this, but I still have a lot to do before the show. Will you join us in the music room later?"

"Absolutely," Megan replied. "I'll put this away for now. I have to set up the projection for Amelia's video downstairs and arrange some seating. I've also invited some industry friends from L.A. who're interested in the documentary."

By *industry*, Ivy knew Megan meant the entertainment industry. That's what everyone called it in Los Angeles. "Do you need any help?" Ivy asked.

Megan assured her that she had everything she needed, which Ivy appreciated.

After Ivy left the parlor, she wondered about the details they'd found. Unless the house held any more secrets, they probably had all the clues they were going to find. Still, she had the strange feeling that they were overlooking something.

Chapter 23

BENNETT GLANCED AROUND the transformed grounds of the Seabreeze Inn, tenting his hand over his eyes against the morning sun. A riot of color stretched before him, shielded under canopies. Hand-blown glass, paintings, pottery, sculptures, multimedia. The energy of creativity, as well as anticipation from the crowd, was nearly palpable. Residents and tourists had turned out in support of Ivy and the community's first art show. His sister Kendra and her family stood nearby.

Entrusted with the job of timekeeper, Kendra began the countdown. "Ten, nine, eight..." Other people around them quickly joined in.

Bennett hefted a large pair of ceremonial scissors to a red

ribbon stretched across the entrance to the property.

Ivy stood next to him in an orange tank top and a skirt the same aquamarine shade as the shimmering ocean behind them. A necklace of turquoise and coral graced her neck, and her face was lit with the glow of excitement and anticipation. He was proud of her never-give-up efforts and pleased to play whatever part he could in her success.

"Ready," Ivy said, holding the ribbon taut.

Kendra held up her fingers. "Three, two, one!"

Amid cheers from the crowd, Bennett clipped the ribbon. "Welcome to the inaugural Summer Beach Art Festival at Seabreeze Inn. This was made possible by Ivy and Shelly Bay, along with Poppy Eaton and a host of volunteers from Summer Beach."

Summer Beach residents and neighbors applauded and congratulated Ivy and Shelly and Poppy on their efforts. The Bay family had turned out in force, too. Carlotta and Sterling had rented a booth to show their international artists' works, and Flint and Forrest and their families had come to spend a day at the show.

Bennett chuckled as he watched the Bay family children—all young adults now—laughing and jostling for positions in line at the food trucks. He scanned the crowd. The only person missing from their group of friends was Mitch, who was busy at Java Beach with customers on their way to the art show.

"I'll catch the first wave," Mitch had told him yesterday.

This morning, he'd texted Bennett: *Big crowd waiting for the show to open. We're slammed! Hope you're ready over there.*

Bennett noticed Sunny was perched on the front steps, her chin cupped in her hand, watching her mother and aunt with an expression of genuine interest. Her chip-on-the-shoulder attitude had dissipated. Perhaps it was the presence of her grandparents and cousins, or maybe she was beginning to feel like she fit in.

Selfishly, he hoped Sunny would give her mother the room to date, without automatically hating the man. Not that he wanted to see Ivy date anyone else. But if Ivy wanted to, he'd have to deal with that. After all, he'd had years to look around after his wife's death.

But no one compared to Ivy.

And he'd make sure no one compared to him.

As Ivy stood on her tiptoes and looked out at the crowd waiting to get in, her lips parted in surprise. Entry to the exterior booths on the ground was free, but people were lining up to pay for the interior house tour. "I didn't expect this much interest in the tour."

"This house is a landmark, and it has a special place in people's hearts," Bennett replied.

"I'd better help Poppy and Gilda," Ivy said, watching the line grow. "Will you stay for a while?"

He smiled. How could Ivy think he'd abandon her? "I thought I'd make a day of it," he said easily. "If there's anything you need, I'm here. After all, I do live on the property."

Though for how much longer, he wasn't sure. He'd seen his contractor, Axe, in the line.

"I wouldn't blame you if you wanted to escape and hide," Ivy said. "There's such a crowd."

"That's because the art show was a great idea. Go on, I'll help work the line." He trailed her to the front table, where people were lined up to buy tickets for the historic house tour.

Poppy and Gilda—with Pixie beside her—were taking payment and stamping hands as fast as they could. Ivy took a seat and began making change for people.

"Thanks, Ivy." Poppy smiled with relief. "But what about your booth?"

"Mom and Dad can watch it," Ivy said.

"I'll get a line count," Bennett said. As he walked the line, he greeted locals and visitors. When he came to Axe, his friend reached out and clasped his hand.

"Almost finished on the house, Ben. You'll be back in no time." Axe grinned. "I told the crew to get it done for our mayor."

"Thanks, Axe. Sure appreciate that." Bennett had mixed feelings about moving back. He moved on to finish the count.

Returning to the table, Bennett knelt beside Ivy, he asked, "How many tours are you giving?"

"Two today, and two tomorrow."

"You might want to double that. At least. Do you have anyone else helping with the tour?"

Ivy twisted her lips to one side. "I can ask Shelly, but

she's pretty busy."

"How about I step in? My sound job is fairly simple. One of Flint's or Forrest's kids could fill in to make announcements or change music as needed. There's Reed now." He waved toward him. "Hey, buddy. Can you come here?"

"Would you?" Ivy's voice held a note of relief as she made change for a couple.

Bennett laughed. "Relax, Ivy. You're surrounded by helpers. Anything special you want to say about the house?"

"I think you know most of it. Megan's running Amelia's video on the lower level." She quickly made change for another person.

"Just tell me the route." Bennett noticed Nan and Arthur standing in line and waved at them.

Ivy smiled and lifted her chin at them while she worked. "They've done so much for us," she whispered. "I can't charge them. Or Jen and George back there. Or Boz, or Darla. Would you tell them to come around and we'll stamp their hands?"

Bennett leaned close to her, detecting a subtle floral scent on her neck and hair. "They want to help you stay here. Don't take that away from them. Let them. Besides, they all brought friends."

Ivy pressed her lips together and blinked several times. "You don't know how much I appreciate that."

He drew his arm around her. "You've got this, Ivy. You always have." And he would do whatever he could to help her stay right here where she belonged. Summer Beach would never be the same without her.

Nor would he.

Bennett grabbed a chair from a vacant booth and plunked it down beside Ivy. "Let's get this line moving. Tours on the hour?"

Ivy grinned and nodded. "Let's do this."

Bennett let out a whistle and motioned for people to split the line, which they did.

Working together, it didn't take long for the four of them to check in the tour guests. Finally, Poppy turned toward them. "Thanks for helping. Isn't it great how many people paid for the tour?"

"And that's just today," Ivy said.

"I'm at your disposal," Bennett said. "Add on as many tours as you need to. I'll fill in."

"I can, too," Poppy said. "Gilda can manage the front table."

"Except for when I have to tend to Pixie's business," Gilda added. As she reached down to pet her, she cried out. "Pixie, where'd you get that?" She tugged something from beneath the little Chihuahua and held it up. "I wonder who's missing a coin purse?"

Pixie stood and began yapping, straining against her leash, which was secured on Gilda's chair. Pixie attempted to leap toward a nearby woman who was considering an exceptional beach landscape rendered in watercolors.

"There, there," Gilda said, comforting Pixie. "I think Pixie wants to return it. See? She's gone from thief to borrower." She picked up the little dog. "We've made such progress through this awful fire trauma, haven't we, sweetie? It won't be long until you have your own home again." She scratched Pixie behind the ears and turned back to Bennett. "She'll settle down then, I'm sure."

"Any word when your new house will be ready?" Bennett asked. Like Imani, Gilda was also rebuilding on her lot after losing her home.

"Not before spring," Gilda said. "Your house should be ready soon, though."

"Soon," Bennett repeated, nodding. When it was time for him to move back into his home, he'd miss the Seabreeze Inn—and sharing morning coffee with Ivy, barbecuing on the terrace, and sharing evening walks on the beach. Yet he couldn't put off the repairs much longer because the insurance company was pressuring the construction company to finish the work.

Gilda put Pixie down. Sure enough, the little dog led her right to the woman by the watercolor landscapes, who cried out with joy at the darling Chihuahua who found the coin purse she was sure she must have dropped.

Overhearing this, Bennett and Ivy suppressed their laughter. Despite her training, Pixie was still an expert thief.

Ivy gave Poppy the cash box and turned to Bennett. "Want to come with me for a last check inside? I can show you what I'd planned to point out on the tours."

"Sure," Bennett said, welcoming time with her.

They threaded their way through the artist booths on the way to the house. He watched as Ivy took in every piece, occasionally stopping to welcome an artist and introduce herself to those she hadn't met.

Ivy paused at a jeweler's booth. "Have you met my niece, Elena Eaton? She's the daughter of my older sister, Honey, who lives in Sydney with her husband."

Elena extended her hand. "I've heard a lot of good things about you." She had short dark hair, and a tiny blue diamond sparkled on the side of her nose—matching her eyes. And her work was stunning.

Bennett grinned. "Really?" He swung toward Ivy and arched an eyebrow.

"Mostly from Poppy," Elena said with a laugh. "Word gets around in the Bay family."

"Kind of like Summer Beach," Ivy shot back with a broad smile.

They chatted with Elena before continuing. People gravitated toward the warmth of Ivy's smile, which was a reflection, Bennett knew, of her inner grace, strength, and beauty. He stood by her side, but she had the lead. And he'd never dream of taking that from her at her event or in her business.

Bennett had seen some men try to dominate conversations when their wives were speaking at events or being honored—as if those men had to prove their worth, too. Not him.

He was happy to watch Ivy take charge and excel.

Ahead of them was Rowan Zachary, wearing a beret at a jaunty angle and holding court before adoring fans at his booth. When Rowan saw them, he opened his arms. "Ivy, my love. The woman who saved my life when I took an untimely dip in her pool—fully clothed at my son's wedding, I might add."

As the people surrounding them laughed at the story, which no doubt had become even more theatrical, Ivy gave Rowan a quick hug. Bennett extended his hand and Rowan shook it vigorously. "Good to see you, sport."

Leaning in, Rowan added in a whisper, "Gave it my best shot, but she's only got eyes for you, mate."

Bennett grinned, wondering if Ivy heard that.

"We're excited to have Rowan and his exquisite work," Ivy said to Rowan's fans, who were crowding under Rowan's canopy to look at his paintings of fellow Hollywood actors. Several begged to pose with him for photos.

Rowan gave Ivy a thumbs-up sign and happily succumbed to the crowd, clearly in his element.

"I'm so relieved the show is off to a good start." Ivy paused, almost imperceptibly, at the door as Bennett opened it for her. He'd noticed that she'd just started doing that. Was it deliberate, or was it a habit from her marriage that had surfaced? Whatever it was, he enjoyed doing that for her—along with being there for her, even though she didn't exactly *need* him. But this made him feel like they were growing closer.

Like a couple.

"The festival is going well because you planned well." He'd watched Ivy make lists and double-check everything. For a woman who claimed to have little experience in business, she sure knew how to manage and execute with a common-sense approach.

Inside, they wove their way through the downstairs—the ballroom, music room, library, dining room, and parlor.

"How about the kitchen?" Bennett asked.

Ivy's eyes sparkled. "And introduce them to Gert and Gertie?"

"They'd like that," he said. "People always gravitate to the kitchen. And they don't see too many vintage turquoise fridges."

"Okay, as long as the dishes are clean." After looking in to make sure the dishes were washed and put away, Ivy led him upstairs.

"Only those who feel capable of climbing the folding stairs should go up to the attic," Ivy said, walking toward the attic entry. "Poppy enlarged photos so everyone could see it."

Near the entry stood several easels with photographs of the rooms that Amelia had built and enclosed. "These are a good addition," Bennett said, impressed.

"Poppy and Sunny like camping up there," Ivy said, motioning through the opening in the ceiling. "We're talking about hosting groups of kids up there for sleepovers and beach parties." She turned and met his gaze.

Bennett sensed an undercurrent of concern in her eyes. "That would be fun on Halloween. And parents could check in downstairs."

She frowned. "Halloween. As long as we're here—"

Wrapping his arm around her, he murmured, "You will be. You'll find a way, and Summer Beach is behind you."

She brushed her lips against his cheek, which sent a feeling of warmth and longing through him. A smile bloomed on her face. "Yes, we will," she replied, tilting her chin with renewed confidence.

Taking his hand, she said, "Let's go downstairs. You've got to see the old film we found. Megan transferred it to a digital format."

Bennett had been looking forward to seeing Amelia Erickson on screen. "Let's go."

They took the service stairs down a level, and then another to the lower level, where Megan and Josh were setting up the projection. Several other people stood nearby.

Megan and Josh greeted them. "I'd like you to meet my friends from L.A.," Megan said, introducing them as fellow documentary producers. "Dermott and I went to film school together. And his wife, Elsa."

They all chatted a little, and Bennett realized Elsa was Deaf. He had a cousin who worked at a school for the Deaf.

"And now, let's meet Amelia," Megan said. "I want to do a practice run before the first group arrives."

"You have about half an hour," Ivy said. "We're starting

each tour on the hour."

The group sat on chairs arranged for the viewing. Bennett noticed plenty of standing room in the back, too. He knew Poppy and Jamir had tidied the lower level, and now boxes were neatly stacked and organized. They'd swept and rolled out rugs and arranged the extra furniture into groupings in the spacious area. The overhead lights were working, and Shelly had dug out part of the mounded earth outside to reveal a row of high windows that let in filtered light. However, Megan and Josh had draped these for the projection.

The projector flicked to life. Soon, the screen was filled with the commanding presence of Amelia Erickson, surrounded by the masterpiece paintings—all in grainy, black-and-white images. The room fell silent in awe. Seeing Amelia on the screen, Bennett was moved. Next to him, Ivy was also overcome with emotion. He took her hand, and they exchanged a smile.

Megan stood beside the screen she'd set up and cleared her throat. "The film we found was from the 1930s and 1940s. Different footage had been professionally edited and spliced together as if Amelia Erickson wanted to document her story. Since she'd concealed the film, we can only guess that she wasn't ready to share it—for whatever reason."

The video of the old film flickered in silence. Amelia was showing the paintings to another person on screen. However, without a voice track, their words were lost to time.

The attractive couple seated next to Ivy leaned forward

with intense interest. Elsa began signing to Dermott, and he nodded with enthusiasm.

"Excuse me," Dermott said. "My wife is reading some of the conversation."

Elsa stood. "Would you like to know what Amelia is saying?"

Chapter 24

WITH THE VINTAGE FILM OF Amelia Erickson flickering in the half-light of the lower level, Ivy whirled on an old chair to face Dermott and Elsa. A frisson of excitement spiraled through her. "You can follow the conversation?" she asked Elsa.

"I'm also a forensic speech reader," Elsa said, pitching forward in her chair next to her. "I've been Deaf from birth, so I grew up reading lips."

Ivy pressed a hand to her heart. This was beyond what she had imagined possible. Was it too much to even hope for?

Dermott put his arm around Elsa with pride. "If anyone can tell what they're saying, Elsa can. She consults for the police in analyzing security footage of crimes or other instances where the audio is unavailable."

"That would be incredible." Ivy clutched Bennett's hand with enthusiasm.

Megan hurried to join them. "When can you start?"

"Right away," Elsa said. "This is so interesting."

Beaming, Megan hugged her. "I'll send you the digital files."

"I can't wait to tell Shelly and Poppy," Ivy said. "Or maybe I'll surprise them." After all, Amelia's words might reveal nothing, yet a glimmer of hope burned within her. This could be the break they'd hoped for to discover Amelia's intentions.

"Here's some extra footage we found toward the back," Megan said. "We just added it to the video. I think you'll like it."

As the video continued, Ivy gasped in surprise. "Is that who I think it is?" A popular actress from the Golden Age of Hollywood flashed onto the screen.

"Marlene Dietrich," Megan said. "They were both from Berlin. Perhaps that's how they knew each other."

In the next frame that cut to another location, Ivy nearly came out of her seat. "Oh, my gosh, look what Amelia has in her hand!" It was the tiara that Pixie had nicked and hidden.

"This is the most recent footage," Megan said. "Probably the last, in fact."

Ivy leaned forward, watching intently for any clues.

Again, Amelia was showing this piece to another person. Ivy could hardly contain herself, and she kept squeezing Bennett's hand.

Absolutely priceless.

After the short film ended, Ivy rose and clapped. "Astounding," Ivy said, her heart full of gratitude and excitement. "If this is a preview of your documentary about Amelia Erickson, I can't wait to see the rest of it."

"It's going to be amazing," Megan said. "And I'm so glad we're neighbors now. Josh and I just love this community."

"You'll meet a lot of locals at the show this weekend," Bennett said.

"That's what I'm looking forward to," Megan replied.

Ivy hugged Megan before she and Bennett left. Although it had only been a few months since she and Shelly had arrived, Ivy felt an affinity with Summer Beach and the people who lived here. More people than she'd imagined had turned out in support of their art festival, and for this, she was grateful.

Before meeting the first tour group, Ivy hurried upstairs to check on her mother and father. Reed was already broadcasting, announcing the tour in ten minutes. Bennett went to check on him, while Ivy cut through the throng of art lovers to the Bay Arts & Crafts booth.

"Hey, Mom. Hi Dad. How is the show going for you?" Her parents already had a booth full of visitors.

Carlotta turned to Ivy with a hug and kisses on both

cheeks, her turquoise and silver bracelets and earrings jangling in the light sea breeze as she moved. "You've been so busy, *mija*. We didn't want to take you from your work."

Ivy's father hugged her. "Looks like quite a crowd. Are you doing well?"

"We all are," Ivy said. "Couldn't have done it without Shelly and Poppy. Even Sunny is helping." Laughter bubbled across the crowd. "I'm so pleased—and relieved—that people are having a good time."

Ivy was so pleased to see her parents. They looked fit and well rested, too. Carlotta and Sterling were preparing for their round-the-world sailing adventure in early spring. In fact, Ivy had never seen them happier. She would miss them, but she knew they'd have a wonderful time. She noticed her artwork in the booth. "Thanks for looking after my paintings."

"We brought them all over," Sterling said. "Figured you have enough to do." He slid his arm across his wife's shoulder and winked at her. The two of them glanced off to the side, looking as if they were bursting with a secret.

"What is it?" Ivy followed their gaze. She spied one of her recent paintings that she'd been experimenting with using bold, rapid strokes. A tag on the edge read *Sold*. Ivy squealed with joy. "You actually sold one of my paintings?"

"Don't act surprised," her mother said. "You're talented."

Her father grinned with obvious pride. "Glad to see you putting your work out there now."

"Thank you. This means a lot to me." For years Ivy had

downplayed her skills because Jeremy had always referred to her painting as a hobby. A disturbing thought crossed her mind. "Don't tell me Rowan Zachary bought it."

"It was another art connoisseur, but wouldn't a Rowan Zachary purchase make great press?" Carlotta said, her eyes flashing at the idea.

"Mom, please don't." Ivy shook her head, but inside she was bursting with joy. Between this sale and the sell-out tours and booths, her financial goal for the art show was that much closer now. "Are you staying for Carol Reston's show tonight? She said it might run late."

"We wouldn't miss it," Sterling replied with a grin. "We can still stay up past our bedtime."

"Oh, Dad," Ivy said. "I didn't mean for it to sound like that. You two are in better shape than I am."

After leaving her parents, Ivy rushed to meet the first group who'd gathered for the tour. Leading them through the house, she shared stories of the original Las Brisas del Mar, when Amelia and Gustav Erickson were in residence during the off-season in San Francisco. The artwork, the parties, the visiting dignitaries... And later, after Gustav's death, when Amelia re-opened the summer house for members of the military who were recovering and undergoing physical therapy.

Ivy answered questions along the way. Some people had attended charity events at the house in years past. When she led the group into the attic, they were enthralled about the concealed spaces in the attic and lower level, as well as the treasures that had been found there.

Besides enlarging photos of the attic, Poppy had also displayed other images around the house to show what had been found in each location—paintings, jewelry, journals, and letters. Ivy told them about the old Chevrolet in the garage, and the vintage doll they'd found. The people on her tour loved the story of the crown jewels stitched inside the doll. Ivy ended the tour in the kitchen, where everyone laughed about Gert and Gertie, who were still running strong.

Ivy and Bennett alternated the tours between them, giving each other a break. As people marveled at the house, Ivy realized what a vital part of Summer Beach it was. After listening to people's memories—some had parents and grandparents who'd known the Ericksons or worked for them—she renewed her resolve to protect the house from the grasp of Dexter and Paisley.

As Ivy returned with one group, and Bennett took off with another, Ivy recalled the strange, protective feeling she'd had about the house the first time she'd seen it. Perhaps this is why she'd been drawn here—to shelter the home from the wrecking ball of progress and preserve a link to the past. And to find artistic treasures thought lost to the world.

Somehow, maybe Amelia *had* guided her.

As the sun crossed the sky, Ivy hardly noticed the time. As she completed the last tour, Shelly waved her down.

"Hey, Ives," Shelly called out.

"Yeah?" After such a long day, Ivy wondered how her sister's hair and makeup was still perfect.

"Carol goes on stage soon."

"Already?" Ivy blew wisps of hair from her face.

Shelly laughed. "Freshen up. Carol wants us in front."

"We can watch from the veranda in back. Guests should be in front, not us."

"What part of 'Carol wants us in front' did you not understand?" Shelly palmed her forehead. "That's *Carol Reston* up there. What she wants, she gets. Now, come on. You need to fix your hair if you're going to be on camera."

"What? Oh, no, no, no. You go ahead. Take Poppy or Sunny. My feet are killing me."

"They're already there." Shelly glanced down. "And your feet won't be on camera."

"Whew, it's hot." Bennett sauntered up behind them. "Who wants a shave ice?'

"Oh, you two," Shelly said, shaking her head. "Afterward, please. Carol goes on soon. And we're filming the event."

Bennett snapped his fingers. "Almost forgot. We've got to go."

"What's this for?" Ivy asked.

"For the preservation of Las Brisas del Mar, now known as the Seabreeze Inn." Bennett grinned. "Megan's videoing, and Carol is going to let the Summer Beach tourist bureau use footage on the website. So, let's go."

"Okay, but I have to fix my hair," Ivy said, grabbing Shelly's hand. "You'd better help me."

They piled into the spacious, old-fashioned bathroom next to the ballroom, where countless women over the years had probably done exactly what they were doing. In the anteroom, Ivy sat on a tufted stool in front of a gilded mirror. At once, Ivy and Shelly were giggling and acting like kids again.

Ivy reapplied her lipstick before threading her fingers through her hair. "This will do," she said, pulling her hair back into a low ponytail.

"No way." Shelly made a face. "Higher up on the crown of your head is more youthful."

"I'll look like I'm twelve."

"Better than a hundred."

Carlotta burst into the powder room. "What are you two doing? Carol's show is about to start." She put her hands on her hips. "Fixing your hair? Oh, for heaven's sake, wear it down, *mija*." Carlotta pulled the band out of Ivy's hair and mussed her layered cut.

"Hey," Ivy protested, but she was no match for her mother.

"Tousled, like that," Carlotta said. "It's sexy. And you need sexy, especially with that handsome man saving you a seat."

Ivy and Shelly looked at their mother, surprised for a moment, then they burst out laughing.

"When your own mother tells you to look sexier," Shelly said, trying to catch her breath, "you know you have a problem."

Ivy fluffed her hair, then swatted her sister.

"Oh, you two." Carlotta picked up a bottle of hairspray, wielding it like a pro over Ivy's hair. She finished and held out her arms. "There, *mija*. You're fabulous. Let's go."

Carlotta took each of her daughters by the hand, chastising them. "Haven't you two grown up by now?"

The three women emerged from the powder room, still laughing, partly because the day was over, and they could now relax and have fun. Sterling was waiting for them, and they rushed to the front seats by the stage that Carol's team had erected.

Bennett was waiting for them—with Mitch.

Shelly let out a cry. "I'm so glad you made it."

"Missed you," Mitch said, flinging his arms around her. "And you didn't think I'd miss this, did you?"

Shelly smothered his face with kisses, while Carlotta and Sterling chuckled behind them.

As pleased as Ivy was to see Mitch, she was also surprised at Shelly's reaction. When her sister turned her way, Ivy mouthed, *Just friends?*

Shelly blushed and shrugged. "Things have changed," she whispered. "For the better."

"As long as you're happy," Ivy said softly.

"Oh, I am," Shelly murmured. "I really am."

Ivy slid into a seat beside Bennett, who tucked his hand into hers and looked at her with an approving smile.

"You look...*wow*," Bennett said.

"Thanks." Ivy tossed her hair over her shoulder. Feeling color rise in her cheeks, she turned in her seat and saw that she was surrounded by family.

Besides her mom and dad, Ivy saw Flint and Tabitha with their kids, Skyler, Blue, Jewel, and Sierra. Forrest and Angela were there with their children, Poppy, Reed, Coral, Summer, and Rocky. Sunny was sitting next to Poppy with Jamir. And all around them were the new friends they'd made in Summer Beach. Ivy smiled as she saw that Tyler was back with Celia, and Imani was sitting awfully close next to Chief Clarkson.

"Everyone is having a great time," Bennett said, squeezing her hand.

And that was enough for Ivy. *To know that people are having a great time.* She nudged Shelly and grinned.

Her sister winked. "Sisters forever."

"Don't threaten me like that," Ivy said.

Poking her in the side, Shelly said, "Hey, that's my line."

"Got you."

Next to Ivy, Bennett chuckled and leaned over. "Only one of us is missing. Want to send a photo to Misty?"

"Great idea." Ivy gave Bennett her phone, and he snapped several photos of the family. She texted them to Misty. "She'll appreciate this."

Just then, the stage lights blazed, and people leapt to their feet, cheering for Carol. The music cranked up, and Megan zoomed in on the front rows with a camera.

"Woo-hoo!" Shelly yelled, throwing her hands up in the

air.

Bennett pulled Ivy to her feet, and together they shouted, "Woo-hoo!"

When Carol finally strutted onto the stage in a glittery top with thigh-high boots and her signature red hair flowing around her shoulders, everybody went wild. They were cheering on not only a musical legend, but also a neighbor who was very much a part of their community. Against the roar of the ocean and the seagulls soaring overhead, Carol belted out the songs that had made her famous—hit after hit after hit.

Never in her life had Ivy imagined she'd be in the front row at a Carol Reston concert in her own backyard. Or have Carol's number in her phone. Ivy couldn't have dreamed such a fantasy—or the man next to her who was holding her hand.

"Just roll with me," Carol was singing from her top hit, and the crowd was singing right along with her.

Clapping with the rhythm, Ivy grinned. *Sometimes you just have to roll with whatever life serves.*

She fervently hoped life would follow up with a perfect serve.

Or this would be the end of one of the best times of her life.

 Chapter 25

"I CAN'T BELIEVE IT'S OVER," Ivy said, groaning and elevating her feet on the kitchen stool next to her. "Having fun is exhausting."

Outside, artists were packing their canopies, the food trucks had motored off, and teams of volunteers had made countless runs to the recycling center.

The art festival had been a splendid success.

"This group looks in dire need of refreshment." Shelly placed a pitcher of mixed juice—her Sea Breeze juice cocktail, vodka optional—on the kitchen counter.

Ivy poured the cranberry and grapefruit juice mixture over ice cubes in a tall glass. She lifted her glass to Shelly and

Poppy and Sunny. "Cheers—we made it."

Shelly clinked her glass. "And next year, the show will be even bigger and better. My aching feet should have recovered by then."

Ivy turned to Poppy and Sunny, who still looked quite energetic. "You two don't get to complain. Not for another ten years, at least."

The two younger cousins laughed.

With half-lidded eyes, Ivy scrutinized Sunny. She hadn't seen her daughter look this relaxed in a long time. She stretched out her hands to Sunny and Poppy. "Glad you two had fun. You were an enormous help, too."

Shelly poured juice cocktails for the girls and slid the two glasses across the table. "We're going to miss you when you go, Sunny."

Ivy watched her daughter, who seemed uncharacteristically quiet.

Sunny ran a finger around the rim of her glass in sync with the low whirr of the refrigerators. "Um, Mom?"

"Yes, Sunny?"

Ivy glanced up and saw Bennett leaning against the doorway behind Sunny. He put his fingers to his lips.

"I don't have to go back to Boston. What if I stayed on a while?" Sunny sipped on her drink with nonchalance. "Jamir said I could enroll at the university. Maybe even finish this year, depending on how many of my credits are accepted. I could apply for financial aid. You know, a loan, like Poppy did."

Ivy was so flabbergasted, she choked on her drink. She managed to nod through her coughs.

Poppy pushed up her sunglasses over her hair. "I have some marketing clients in L.A. who are going to need more help, so Sunny could take my place some days."

"Don't expect me to stay forever," Sunny said with a grin.

Ivy caught her breath. "Of course not." She flung her arms around Sunny. This is all she'd ever wanted for her daughter—to have a sense of direction and a goal to work toward, without Ivy pushing her. "Welcome home, baby girl."

Sunny winced. "Mom, never call me that again."

"Okay, but you'll always be my baby girl in here," Ivy said, pressing a hand against her heart.

Sunny hugged her mother. "I still love you, Mom. And I'm truly sorry for being such a brat. I don't know where my head was."

"We've both learned a lot," Ivy said. Having Sunny stay here was more than she'd hoped for. This would be good for both of them.

"Jamir promised to help with clean-up after everyone left," Sunny said, gulping her juice. "Mind if I go?"

"I'm delighted." Ivy smiled at this new, happier version of her daughter. "And I appreciate all you did, Sunny."

"We all do," Shelly added. "Love having you on the team."

Beaming, Sunny jumped up and turned around. "Oh,

hey, Bennett." She spun back to her mother and jerked her thumb toward Bennett. "And you can even go out with this guy if you want. Because I heard he's not so bad." She grinned and ducked around him.

"Bye, Sunny," Bennett called after her. "And, thanks for that."

With her long hair streaming behind her, Sunny waved back at them before she raced out of sight.

Slowly, Ivy wagged her head in amazement. "Can you believe the transformation? I can't imagine what changed in her mind."

Poppy folded her arms on the counter and leaned over, resting her chin on her arms. "Sunny saw that everyone here is doing something they like. No one is trying to impress anyone. From what she said, her friends in Boston are nothing like that. She told me she feels happier here than she can remember."

As Ivy was letting that sink in, Bennett ambled toward them.

"Could be the negative ions in the air," Bennett said, sliding onto a stool next to Ivy. "Between the mountains and the ocean, the negative ions they produce lift the level of serotonin in the brain. More serotonin, less depression, happier people. Why do you think I stay here?"

Shelly sipped her drink. "He's right, you know."

"Maybe that's it," Ivy said. She was too tired to argue, though she knew that was a valid point. She'd never felt better than she did living here. Perhaps it was the negative ions, or maybe it was another strange new chemical firing in her brain. She stretched a hand toward Bennett.

With a glimmer in his eye, he took her hand and kissed it. "I came to tell you I'll see the rest of the artists off. You stay here and relax."

"Thanks," she said, staring after him and thinking about what Sunny had said. But she had other critical matters to tend to first.

"He's definitely a keeper," Shelly said after Bennett was out of earshot. "So, sis, think we reached our goal?"

Ivy looked up. This weekend, she'd been running the numbers to track their progress. "With revenue from the booths, the tours, and the paintings Mom and Dad sold for me, I'd say…we made it." She broke into a broad smile and gave a high-five to Shelly and Poppy. "I can write that check to the tax collector now. And Amex."

"Way to go," Shelly said, giving her a hug.

Yet keeping the inn would be another matter entirely. Ivy clucked her tongue. "Now I have to fight Paisley and Dexter."

"Wish you hadn't mentioned them," Shelly said, making a face. She gazed from the window over grounds, which were almost deserted again. "Everyone had such a good time this weekend, but I'm so angry about what those two are trying to do. After all your hard work—and all of ours—how can you lose it to them? It's just not fair." She took Ivy's hand. "We're here for you, Ives."

"No regrets," Ivy said. "We did our best—and it's not over yet." A miracle, that's what they'd need. She tilted her head back, thinking about Sunny and her decision to stay here for school.

Poppy took their hands, forming a circle between the three women. "You and Shelly gave me an amazing opportunity here, and you did everything you could to make the inn a success. You can't have any regrets, either."

Ivy gave her niece and her sister a sad smile. "Only one." Looking back, Ivy wouldn't change much in her life. Even Jeremy. Still, Ivy had to be honest with herself. If she hadn't let pride and anger overwhelm her, she could have averted this latest dilemma with Paisley and Dexter. Looking toward the sea, Ivy bit her lip as she watched the waves that lapped the shore.

Poppy frowned. "What's that?"

Ivy spoke softly, struggling to keep her emotions in check. "I wish I'd kept Jeremy's letter that Paisley left with me."

Shelly reached across the counter and clutched Ivy's hand in support. "You didn't know."

Staring at her, Poppy asked, "Why would you want that now?"

"Doesn't matter. It's gone. No regrets, right?" With a heavy heart, Ivy slid off the stool and shuffled toward the door. A walk on the beach would help cleanse her mind of Dexter and Paisley. Maybe those negative ions would work their magic on her. She tucked her feet into a pair of flip-flops by the door.

"But you were right, Aunt Ivy." Poppy shifted on her stool. "I should've burned it," she mumbled.

Had she heard correctly? Ivy paused. "Do what?"

Poppy averted her gaze. "You were right to throw out that letter. And Paisley should have burned them."

"No. I wasn't."

Shelly perked up. "That's not what you said before."

Poppy flicked a guilty look at Shelly. "I saw how much Paisley hurt her." She shrugged self-consciously. "I don't know why I did it, only that Paisley seemed so insistent that day in the library. I'm sorry, Aunt Ivy. That's what I regret doing."

Her mouth opening in shock, Shelly rose from her stool. "Exactly what, Poppy?"

A tickle skittered across the back of Ivy's neck, and she stopped by the door. "Poppy, do you *have* that letter?" She threw a look at Shelly; her eyes were as wide as she'd ever seen.

Poppy's lower lip trembled. "I'll get rid of it."

With adrenaline coursing through her veins, Ivy took a step toward Poppy. "Do you have Jeremy's letter?"

Poppy nodded shamefully. "But I didn't read it."

Ivy flung her arms around Poppy. "You have it! Where is it?"

Poppy sat up in surprise. "Upstairs. I swear I was going to tell you."

"Yes!" Shelly shot a fist into the air.

"Oh, you dear, sweet girl!" Ecstatic, Ivy grabbed Poppy's hands, guarded joy welling up inside of her. "That letter might be the answer to everything. Let's go get it."

Ivy tugged Poppy along beside her, anxious to see what her niece had saved. As they raced through the house, Shelly followed, jogging to keep up with Ivy's manic pace.

"Why didn't you give that letter to Ivy?" Shelly cried.

Poppy looked confused. "I didn't know it was important."

Ivy gripped Shelly's hand. "She wasn't there when we were talking about what that letter meant. Only Sunny was. Remember? Celia needed help."

"Oh, that's right!" Shelly shrieked with joy and flung her arms around Poppy. "I love you forever and ever and ever and ever, you crazy, fastidious, obsessive girl!"

"That's good?" Poppy looked stunned.

Ivy cupped Poppy's face in her hands. "Paisley was trying to signal to me that day that she and Dexter showed up here. That letter might be the key to us keeping the house. Evidently, he wrote to her, saying that he had changed his mind and was breaking up with her. He was returning home. To me. That's why she wanted me to read it the first time she came here. That's how Paisley thought she would make amends."

Poppy's eyes lit. "Then, this is a good thing?"

"Possibly a very good thing." Ivy could hardly contain her emotions. "Find Bennett and Imani," she said to Shelly. "And meet us in the kitchen."

Ivy and Poppy tore upstairs, while Shelly took off to find Bennett and Imani. After climbing the folding stairs into the attic, Poppy opened the bottom drawer of a built-in dresser and lifted out an envelope. "I hope what you need is in here."

At once both repelled and drawn to Jeremy's letter, Ivy stared at it. "I need my glasses."

Poppy followed Ivy to her bedroom. After snatching her readers from the table beside her bed, Ivy stood by the open window, welcoming the ocean breeze on her flushed face. Poppy sank onto the edge of the bed and waited. Ivy slipped the stationery from its envelope and unfolded it.

Recognizing Jeremy's handwriting, Ivy sucked in a breath, immediately sobered. She ran her fingers across the page.

My dear Paisley, the note began. As much as the words sliced through her, she kept on reading.

I should never have succumbed to your charms. You were relentless, and I was flattered. As you should recall, I was honest with you in the beginning. I have always loved my wife, and I understand this more now than ever. I never meant to harm either of you. You are a bright young woman who should never have become involved with a married man. Therefore, I cannot, in good conscience, continue our relationship.

In my excitement over the vision for Las Brisas del Mar you shared—and my own greed that precipitated and spurred my action—I made promises to you that I cannot keep. By legal rights, Las Brisas del Mar was never mine to share with you as it was purchased with funds that also belong to my wife. I must do the right thing, so I shall put the house up for sale immediately and return the funds to our retirement account. She might never know of this transgression, but if she does, I will have to tell her everything.

I must end our relationship at once and return to my wife and my family. I have been complacent in my marriage, yet I know where I belong. Someday when you are married with a family of your own, you will understand my actions and the shame I feel.

Ivy took off her glasses, lowered the letter, and bowed her head, adding her tears to those that already stained the ink on the page. She sobbed softly, hearing his voice uttering those words in her mind. Her husband—and Paisley—had made a dreadful mistake.

But in the end, Jeremy had returned to Ivy in his heart.

Ivy lifted her face to the breeze. She could continue to harbor the hatred and anger and disappointment that left her sleepless in the wee hours, or she could release these emotions to the wind and let the tide carry them out to sea. Pressing the stationery to her chest, she willed all the twisted, ugly feelings she had for Jeremy from her heart, casting them onto the white-capped waves beyond.

"Aunt Ivy, are you okay?"

Wiping her tears, Ivy turned around and held a hand out to Poppy. "I am now. Thank you, my darling girl. You're a treasure. You saved a very important letter." Taking Poppy's hand, she led her downstairs. "Let's see if Imani is here."

As Ivy came into the kitchen, Bennett rushed in the rear door with Shelly right behind him.

"Poppy had the letter," Ivy cried out. A note she'd never wanted to read, but now thanked heaven still existed. Was it enough to save the home and life she'd grown to love?

There, in the middle of the kitchen, Ivy flung her arms around Bennett and began crying, her deepest emotions finally bursting through her dam of self-control.

Chapter 26

"CAN WE USE THIS LETTER?" Ivy perched on a stool at the kitchen counter next to Imani, who was reading Jeremy's last note to Paisley. Despite her anguish, Ivy tried to focus. Having Bennett beside her helped.

"This is most unusual." Imani removed her bright pink sun hat and shook her sisterlocks around her shoulders.

"The letter?" Shelly asked, taking juice from the refrigerator.

"The entire story," Imani said. "Dexter is trying to bully his way into this property. He's angry with Paisley for showing it to Jeremy, who bought it out from under him. So now he's stooping to intimidation and using Paisley with promises of insta-millions and marriage. Those are her weaknesses."

"Doubt if she'll get either one out of old Dex," Shelly said. "Or he'll marry her and toss her aside once he convinces her to transfer the property into a company he owns." After mixing the juices into her Sea Breeze concoction, she added a generous shot of vodka. When Ivy raised a brow, Shelly made a face. "If you don't need a drink after reading that letter, I'll do it for you."

"I need a clear mind." Ivy leaned against Bennett, grateful for his emotional support.

"I'm so sorry I brought this up today," Poppy said, pacing the kitchen. "We had such a great show this weekend, and I had to go and spoil it with that mess." She flung her hand out at the letter that Jeremy had written to Paisley.

Ivy placed her hand over the envelope. "This isn't pleasant, but you have no idea how grateful I am that you fished this out of the trash can. How did you think to do that?"

"I overheard Paisley begging you to read it. Maybe I was eavesdropping a little." Poppy tucked her hair behind an ear and turned up her palms. "That day in the library, she seemed genuine about making amends to the people she'd harmed. Strange as it seems, she thought that if you read Jeremey's words and understood why he was leaving her, it would help you."

Shelly shook her head. "Paisley's a serial liar. I know her type. She'll say or do anything to get ahead."

"Dexter is coercing her," Ivy said. "Making promises…like Jeremy did."

Imani ran her hand thoughtfully over the page. "Do you think Paisley is in love with Dexter?"

"I don't think she knows what that means." Ivy rested her head against Bennett's chest. He stood behind her with one arm encircling her.

Imani tapped her nails on the counter. "So, figure out how to get Paisley away from Dexter, and the claim falls apart. She's not strong enough to pursue the case without him." Imani paused. "This is a long shot, but do you think Dexter is abusing her in any way?"

Closing her eyes and passing a hand over her forehead, Ivy tried to recall what Paisley had said. Was Dexter intimidating her? "When we saw Ivy that night at the Starfish Café, she had on a skimpy red dress. I couldn't help but notice the purple bruises on her arms. And Dexter grabbed her with such force that he must have left another one. If Paisley had been one of my friends, I would have warned her or helped her get away from him. She told me she's living with him now."

Shelly nodded begrudgingly. "Still…"

"I was there," Bennett said. "Ivy's right."

"Maybe this is the answer." Ivy splayed her hands on the cold tile to steady her nerves. "I can't believe I'm even suggesting this, but I could call Paisley. Suggest she gets help to distance herself from Dexter. She was going to A.A. meetings, so she's reaching out. And she didn't say anything about wanting the property when she came here alone."

"She wouldn't," Shelly said, folding her arms. "She was setting you up."

"I don't think so," Ivy said.

Imani reached into her bag for her phone. "I can give you some numbers in L.A. for battered women's centers. They'll give her a place to stay and help her make a break from him."

"Aunt Ivy, I'll call her if you want," Poppy said.

Ivy shook her head. "Paisley showed a lot of courage coming here to face me. She's not my favorite person, but she needs help. If she can extricate herself from this mess, she'll have a chance to change. So, I'll call her."

Though it was tempting to wallow in hatred and anger, Ivy couldn't let her pain keep her from doing what she must. This property supported and sheltered her and family.

Bennett rubbed her shoulders. "That's a gutsy move."

"And the smart one." Imani curved up a corner of her mouth. "Dexter will never see this coming. He thinks he's got you two divided, and why shouldn't you be? Your ability to rise above the conflict will blow his egregious, asinine case away. Without Paisley, he has no claim." Imani held up the letter again. "You have all the proof you need. I'll sit with you when you make that call. I'll even meet her in L.A."

"Would you?" Ivy asked.

Imani chuckled. "Heck, I'll take my sister along. She's bigger than Dexter. Everyone in the family is scared of her."

"Operation Rescue Paisley." Ivy couldn't believe that it would take saving her late husband's mistress to salvage her life. "I'm sure a therapist would relish the layers of irony here. But let's do this."

Ivy reached up and kissed Bennett on the cheek. "I need to do this alone. Imani, can you coach me before I make that call?"

"Sure, hon. Library?"

The two women made their way to the library to form their strategy.

"Make sure she's alone first," Imani said, pulling her chair to the round table where Ivy was seated.

They talked a little more, and then Ivy picked up her phone. Poppy had taken Paisley's number when she'd checked her into the inn.

Paisley picked up on the first ring.

"Hi, Paisley, it's me. Ivy. If you're alone, I'd like to talk to you. Just us girls."

"Oh. Hi." Paisley's strangled voice floated to her over the phone.

There was a long stretch of silence as Paisley sniffed and caught her breath. "I-I can meet you," she whispered into the phone.

"Okay." This wasn't what she'd expected. "Where and when?"

"Ten minutes."

"Are you still in Summer—" *Click.* Ivy lowered the phone. "I think she's coming here."

Imani arched a brow. "Now?"

Ivy nodded. This hadn't been the way she'd thought this day would end. "I'd better tell the others." She got up and opened the door.

Shelly, Poppy, and Bennett were waiting in the hallway.

"Well?" Shelly asked.

"Paisley is coming here," Ivy said. "Ten minutes."

Shelly's eyes bulged. "What? She can't come here."

Ivy waved a hand. "She's stayed here before, so why not. Now, all of you scatter. This is between us. And our livelihood depends on this."

"Ivy's right," Bennett said. "Come on, let's wait in the kitchen."

Imani frowned. "Dexter could follow her, you know.

"I'll call Clark and have him send a police car over on standby," Bennett said.

After they left, Ivy blew out a breath to calm her nerves. She waited in the foyer with Imani, glancing out the tall Palladium windows. After a few minutes, she spied a slim figure in a hoodie running toward the door. "She's here." Ivy swung open the door.

Paisley was shivering, even though the night was warm. "I-I can't stay long. He doesn't know I left."

"That's good," Ivy said, surprised at Paisley's appearance. With a face devoid of makeup, she didn't look much older than Sunny. Though a part of Ivy still wanted to hate this young woman, her heart went out to her. Paisley had made several grave mistakes, and the payment for these was high.

Ivy introduced Imani and got right to the point. "Paisley, it was hard for me to face you when you came here, but I'm glad you did. I remember what you said about the letter. I have it, and—"

"I'm so glad," Paisley cut in. "Dex means business, he really does. I'm scared, and I'm so sorry." Tears trickled from her eyes. "I never meant for it to turn out like this. I don't know what I was thinking…"

Outside the window, Ivy saw a Summer Beach police car cruise by, and she relaxed a little. With compassion edging out her pain, she took Paisley's hand, which felt cold and small in hers. "You want out, don't you?"

Unable to speak, Paisley nodded.

"Has Dexter hurt you?" Imani asked.

Casting her gaze down in shame, Paisley pushed up the sleeve of her hoodie. Her wrist was swollen and bruised.

Imani pursed her lips. "Then we have a proposition for you. Let's sit down."

"You don't have to be afraid of Dexter anymore," Ivy said. "We can help you get out, and all of this will go away."

"I'll help you get a restraining order," Imani added. "You can start fresh. Some other town if you want."

At this thread of hope, Paisley gulped and crushed her palm to her wet eyes. "For real?"

"Right now," Ivy said.

Paisley's gaze shot toward the door. "But what about Dex? He might have followed me."

"There's a police car outside," Imani said, jutting her chin toward the window. "That's my friend, the chief of police. We want you to be safe from Dexter."

"I don't know if I'll ever be," Paisley wailed, and then her words tumbled out. "I was doing so good, going to my A.A. meetings. And do you know what he did? After I moved in with him, he spiked my drink, and I slid all the way down. But I'm trying again."

"Listen to us." Ivy reached out and grasped Paisley's hands. "This is your chance. Right now. Tonight. You'll never have to see him again. Just say yes, and we'll do the rest."

Paisley gulped and nodded.

Imani rose. "I'll take you to a shelter where you'll be safe. You'll be with others, mostly women and their children, who are going through what you are. And my friend in the police car will follow us."

"What about all my stuff?" Paisley asked.

Imani shook her head. "Maybe a friend can get it for you. But it's just stuff, believe me. I lost everything I owned in a fire. As long as you have your precious life, you can start over."

Ivy hugged the thin, quivering young woman. "You can do this, Paisley. I believe in you."

"You do? No one has ever…" Paisley broke down, unable to finish.

Ivy was appalled. Had Paisley never had anyone to believe in her? Ivy didn't know Paisley's background, but that would explain a lot. "You've done well," Ivy said. "You made full amends with me."

"I did?" Paisley's eyes welled with tears. When Ivy nodded, she said. "Oh, thank you, thank you for that."

Ivy rubbed Paisley's back. "Now go, and start your life over. We can all have a second chance if we're brave enough to take it." She took her lightweight, tan raincoat and flung it over Paisley's shoulders, and placed a broad-brimmed sunhat on Paisley's head to cover her hair. "Wear this. Just in case Dexter is out there. We care about you."

Paisley kissed Ivy's cheek in gratitude, then let Imani guide her away. As the door closed behind them, Ivy sank onto the bench by the door, overwhelmed with emotion.

Ivy had done what she'd never thought she could. Helped the woman who'd hurt her so deeply. She raised her face to the warm, shimmering light from the chandelier above. A new life awaited them both.

Chapter 27

SEATED AT THE ANTIQUE TABLE in the parlor and surrounded by those who'd stood by her, Ivy held her pen aloft, then pressed the tip to the check's signature line. This was the moment she'd worked so hard to achieve, through countless challenges that had pushed her to become more than she'd ever dreamed she could be. It was worthy of commemoration with those she loved.

Shelly had passed around glasses of champagne, and everyone stood ready for Ivy to write her signature.

"Paid in full. Sweet words, indeed." Ivy signed her name with a flourish and held up the check for all to see. "We're officially out of debt. And tomorrow morning, I'll hand carry this check to the Tax Collector's office." She had also paid Sunny's American Express charge and told her daughter earlier in private. Sunny had cried and promised never again.

"Woo-hoo! Let the celebration begin," Shelly called out, clinking her glass of champagne with Ivy's.

Ivy laughed and hugged her sister. "Thank you for staying with me through this crazy mess." She mussed Shelly's already tousled hair. "Well, most of it."

"Hey, I came back, didn't I?" Shelly smiled up at Mitch, who wrapped his arms around her and grinned. "Thanks to this guy."

Ivy loved seeing Shelly and Mitch together. They were right for each other, just as they were now. Ivy had learned the necessity of living in the moment. The future she'd once so carefully constructed had crashed around her. But today was different.

Today was hers.

"Hold the check high, and everyone pile in," Bennett said, snapping photos.

Ivy pushed back from the table. Poppy swung her long hair over her shoulder and smiled, while Sunny gave a thumbs-up. Even Pixie scurried to jump into the picture.

"Come on, Gilda and Imani," Ivy said. "Celia and Darla, you, too. We couldn't have done it without you." Everyone hurried in for the photo op.

Just then, the front door burst open. "Am I too late?" Megan called out.

"Never," Ivy said, enjoying the celebration. Now the property truly belonged to her—and the operation of the inn to her and her sister. As they'd agreed, they would run the inn together. The Seabreeze Inn would be their home, sheltering her girls when they needed it, and pampering anyone who wanted to chill in Summer Beach.

"Get in there," Bennett said to Megan. "I'm setting a timer." Quickly, he wedged in behind Ivy. "Three, two, one!" The flash went off, and everyone cheered.

"I have a surprise, too," Megan said, holding up several folded pages.

Ivy pressed a hand to her chest. She'd been asking Megan about Elsa's speech transcription of Amelia's film. "Is that the audio text?"

Megan nodded, her eyes sparkling with delight. "Wait until you hear this."

After Bennett snapped a few more photos, Ivy and Megan huddled together on a sofa, while everyone gathered around. Bennett rested his arms on the back of the couch behind Ivy. She looked up at him with excitement.

Unfolding the pages, Megan began. "My friend Dermott's wife, Elsa, is an expert speechreader. It didn't take her long to understand what Amelia was saying. She couldn't understand everything, because Amelia wasn't always facing the camera or speaking clearly, but she got enough. Here's the script. Ivy, if you want to read it, I'll run the corresponding scenes on my tablet." Megan flicked on her screen device and brought up the video.

"Let's do this." Excitement bubbled through Ivy. Who's got reading glasses?"

"Here, try these." Gilda unclipped an emerald-green pair of readers she wore around her neck and handed them to Ivy.

"Just my color," Ivy said, slipping them on and scanning the page. As the words came into view, she said, "These will work." Snippets of conversation with corresponding video time marks lined the page. "Now, let's see…" She ran her finger down the paper.

"Out loud, please," Shelly said, nudging her.

"Okay, here goes. In Amelia's words." Ivy cleared her throat and began to read Elsa's transcription as Megan played the video.

"Though I am an American now, in my heart… always a Berliner, always a European… I mourn the destruction of my country, my people… Every religion, every ethnicity. Every human."

"Wow, that's pretty sobering," Shelly murmured. "Explains the shelter she built in the attic."

"There's more." Ivy continued.

"I vowed to protect these…and anyone who needed help. Paintings represent our history, our culture. When the war is over, I will return these paintings to the museums and other owners. Until then…protect them from harm."

Filled with relief, Ivy lowered the paper. "So, Amelia *was* planning to give them back."

Shelly inched closer and tucked her hand into her sister's. "I'm glad you were right, Ives."

"So am I," Ivy said. Even when she'd tried to be realistic, she'd still felt that Amelia had meant no harm.

Megan motioned to a place on the script. "This part is about the paintings and artists. We already know all this. Now, look at this."

Ivy began reading again.

"When the S.S. St. Louis was denied entry, I wept for my friends. So, I opened my home to anyone who could get here...sent money for travel... Artists, scientists, doctors, children. Illegal, perhaps, but I saved lives. All that matters..."

"That was an ill-fated ship," Megan said softly. "I saw a documentary about its 1939 crossing attempt. It was sobering."

Bennett cleared his throat. "Today, Amelia would be recognized for her efforts."

"That's what I'm thinking," Megan said, brightening. "I'll keep researching, but we might be able to find people—descendants, perhaps—that Amelia sheltered here."

"She bucked the system," Shelly said. "Have to respect that."

Megan pointed to the papers. "And look at this down here—this is the later footage. Probably after the war. Amelia had a mysterious smile on her face at first, as if this were a clever, inside joke. And then, she became confused and held up her hand to stop the filming. However, the camera operator didn't immediately cut off the camera. There wasn't much after that."

Ivy lifted the paper and continued to read.

"The theft of royal jewels…the trophies of war. I will return them with a little helper I call… Her name is… Oh dear, I think it is Alma. Or is it Mary? Maybe Anna… Anna, I think… Or no… Please cut. The lights are too hot. I can't remember… I can't…"

Ivy lowered the paper and glanced at Shelly and Poppy. "Anna was the doll that the jewelry was stitched into. Her name was stamped on the doll trunk. That must be what she meant." Ivy removed the reading glasses and handed them back to Gilda. "Amelia might have suffered a slight dementia episode. Probably what we would call Alzheimer's today."

"Amelia Erickson wasn't that old, not really," Megan said. "It might have been an early-onset form of the disease."

"But look what she accomplished," Ivy said, awestruck at the words on the page before her. "Amelia saved historical treasures and probably lives."

"We have to send this to Ari right away," Shelly said. "Amelia Erickson was a brilliant, gutsy woman. Megan, your documentary is going to bring her back to life and surprise a lot of people."

As everyone began chatting about the new details Megan had discovered, Ivy thought about this latest find. She'd now seen Amelia Erickson on film and read her words. Today, Ivy wore one of Amelia's most precious possessions—the modest ruby ring that had belonged to her mother.

More than ever, Amelia's determination inspired Ivy. She realized they were very much alike. Both were passionate about art, and both were widowed. After Amelia's husband died, she had embraced her freedom and forged a path guided by her conscience.

Much like the opportunity that now lay before Ivy.

Bennett kneaded her neck, and she smoothed her hand over his, still thinking.

"What a day this has been," Ivy said, feeling a sense of accomplishment over the tax and credit card bill payments, as well as the insights gained into Amelia Erickson.

"An excellent day," Shelly said. "And many more ahead."

Ivy felt a new aura of peace in the house. Whatever lingering vestiges of Amelia she'd sensed were now at rest. For her part, Ivy was grateful for the opportunity to steward the grand old house through the next era and whatever challenges that might bring.

As he so often did, Bennett gave Ivy's hand a little squeeze. She looked up at him, realizing she still had an important decision to make.

***

Later that evening, Ivy sat on the edge of the claw-foot tub, trailing her hand in the warm water. The party had been fun, but she was glad it had ended early. She was just stepping into the tub when a tap sounded at the door. Quickly, she slipped on her robe.

Bennett stood in the hallway with his hand on the door-jamb. "Turning in early? I'd hoped you might be up for a walk on the beach. I have something I want to talk to you about."

Ivy shook her head. "I'm taking a long bath and collapsing in bed." The roller coaster of emotions over the past weeks had left her exhausted.

"You've been going full throttle," Bennett said. "I understand, but—"

"I hope you do." She folded her arms and leaned against the other side of the door jamb. "But it's not just that. It's us," she said hesitantly.

Sunny had given Ivy her approval for her to date Bennett. While she was pleased that Sunny's attitude toward Bennett had improved, Ivy was a grown woman who didn't need her children's permission.

Taking her hand, Bennett cast a loving gaze toward her. "I like the idea of us."

"So do I, but..." Ivy was comfortable right where they were, even though they could forge ahead if she liked. Bennett had given every indication that he was willing. How could she explain what she felt when she hardly knew what that was herself?

Bennett looked up. "Seems like we've been at this doorway before. I respect you, Ivy, but I won't act like I'm not disappointed."

"I need...to think. What was it you wanted to tell me?"

Behind them, Gilda's door opened, and Pixie raced out,

with Gilda hurrying after him. "Wait for me, sweetikins," she called out.

Just beyond Gilda, Jamir bounded up the staircase to his room.

"Not much privacy tonight." Bennett turned back to her and put his hand on his hip. "I hadn't planned on telling you here, like this, but I got a call earlier today. My home is finished, and it's ready for me to move back in. The insurance company is cutting the final check for accommodations."

"Oh." She'd known this day was coming, but nevertheless, tonight this was sudden news.

He shifted on his feet. "I guess there's no reason for me to stay any longer?"

"Well. No." When had he been planning to tell her about the progress on his house? And now, he was checking out. *Just like that.* Had she merely been a convenient *friend?* She wrapped her robe tighter around her torso as if it could contain her emotions. "I suppose I'll miss you," she managed to say.

"Yeah?" Bennett stood staring at her, awkwardly, waiting for her to say more. When she didn't, he reached out and kissed her cheek.

"When you've made a decision," he said, his voice sounding oddly thick. "You know where I'll be."

Almost as an afterthought, Bennett slid his arm around her. While this little movement felt like a warm snuggle in a favorite quilt, it also awakened in her a desire for more. And yet, after all she'd been through, she finally had room to breathe. She was as free as the gulls that soared over the beach.

Growing light-headed, she pulled back from him, torn between her desire for freedom and her desire for him.

She pressed fingers to her temple, massaging a throbbing blood vessel. *What do I want?*

Chapter 28

AFTER GOING TO BED EARLY the night before, Ivy rose with the sun. She pushed back the drapes in her room and glanced from the window into the car court below, where a marine layer misted the property. Peering closer, she sucked in a breath.

Bennett was lifting his bags into the back of his SUV.

Their conversation from the night before flooded back to her.

Her phone buzzed with a text, and she saw that it was from Poppy, who was up early this morning to put out breakfast for guests. *Bennett checked out.* A string of sad face emojis followed.

Feeling a sudden sense of urgency, Ivy tried to open the window to call out to him, but the old wood frame jammed.

"Bennett," she called out, knocking on the glass. "Bennett!" But he couldn't hear her. She watched helplessly as he swung into the driver's side and slammed the door. The engine roared to life.

He was leaving without even saying goodbye.

She pressed her hands against the old wavy-pane glass. *But wasn't that why Bennett had wanted to go on a walk last night?* She spun around, chastising herself and unable to watch him leave.

Ivy smacked her forehead. It was her own fault for not talking to Bennett last night. The past couple of days, he'd been trying to talk to her, but she'd always been busy. She could have made time, she realized now. As much as she had grown to care for him, one question still loomed large in her mind.

What did she want? Of all the to-do lists she'd made in her life, she had never made a What-Ivy-Bay-Wants list.

And it was about time she did.

A thousand thoughts swirled through her mind. Ivy blew out a breath of exasperation. Now she needed that walk on the beach. Alone. To clear her head and take inventory. After splashing water on her face and pulling a loose turquoise sundress over her head, she hurried down the rear stairs to the kitchen.

She glanced outside the bank of windows to the empty

car court and frowned. He hadn't even stayed for coffee.

Poppy bustled into the kitchen with a tray. "You're going out early. Did you change the time for the beach walk?"

"Could you take that today?"

"Well, sure, but—"

"Thanks, love," Ivy said, intent on escaping before Poppy asked about Bennett. Snatching a pair of sandals by the back door, she charged outside toward the beach. A blanket of mist hung low in the sky, and she shivered against moisture in the air.

It was early, and the terrace and pool were empty. It was even too early for Shelly's yoga class. *Why couldn't Bennett have waited a little longer?*

Or, had he waited long enough? The thought gnawed at her. Then again, maybe she was the one who'd waited too long.

Once she hit the beach, Ivy dug her toes into the sand as thoughts raced through her mind. If she were honest with herself, this wasn't about Bennett or his departure.

This time, it was all about her. Who she had become and what she wanted now.

Jeremy's death had shattered the foundation of her life. Ivy had gone from being a comfortable housewife and mother to being cast adrift on a sea of uncertainty—in a new town with a new identity.

What did she want? She squinted against the ocean breeze. To start with, good relationships with her daughters and her family. At that thought, she nodded with satisfaction.

That goes on the What-Ivy-Bay-Wants list. Relationships between parents and offspring were bound to shift as children grew in maturity and self-reliance. With their father's death, this step had been thrust upon Misty and Sunny.

And on me, too.

The old Jeremy, the one she'd fallen for at a little coffee shop in Boston, the one whose deep brown eyes shone with quick intelligence and a fierce will to make changes in the world, would have been proud of her now. The stresses of life had worn him down—the responsibility to keep clients and bosses pleased, to provide for his family, to care for his parents before they passed away. She understood now how a girl like Paisley with short skirts and sparkly dreams could briefly make a man feel like that coffee-shop kid again with the excitement of life ahead. As a testosterone-laden man, Jeremy—or his ego—had made that decision. Not necessarily in a moment of weakness or boredom—but perhaps in a moment of unmanageable stress.

People sometimes made mistakes when they felt overburdened. Maybe they drank too much, slept with the wrong person, yelled at loved ones. Or screamed at people on social media.

A fan of cool sea spray misted her face, and she realized that mistakes were all part of being human. Jeremy hadn't been a saint, any more than she was. If she'd had better relationship skills, she might have diffused Sunny's anger and dealt with her grief much sooner.

Turning toward the ocean, Ivy released her images of Jeremy—of the deceitful husband who'd betrayed her, as well as the perfect husband she'd wanted to grow old with. Neither picture was accurate.

She didn't want perfect anyway.

Ahead of her, near the lifeguard station, Mitch was chatting with a lifeguard. "Morning, Ivy," he called out. Mitch wore a short summer wetsuit and looked like he'd already been surfing.

"Hi, Mitch," she replied without breaking stride. Friends were her treasure, too. In her new life ahead, she wanted moments to savor, opportunities to share, and friends to enjoy.

Check, check, and check.

Glancing back at the inn, Ivy smiled with satisfaction. She could have walked away from the grand old house, and yet, she had stayed and fought for it. It wasn't only about keeping a roof over her head, or creating an income, although that was certainly part of it.

From the moment she'd seen the house, she'd felt a magnetic draw to it. The house had challenged her, and she'd met those challenges. She'd learned to take action.

And as a result of her actions, how many people's lives had she impacted? She'd read about some of the families who'd lost their precious paintings during the war and who'd regained the valuable artwork. She loved hearing about their joy of rediscovery, of restitution. Often the artwork provided a much-needed financial boost.

Would any of that have been discovered under a developer's jaws of heavy machinery?

And then there was Shelly—her sister had found a healthy relationship with Mitch. Or Darla, who'd shed her crusty shell of self-protection and become a friend. Even Paisley, who now had a chance to start fresh.

Ivy paused on the shore, watching the sun break through the dense marine layer. She lifted her face to the warm rays.

From Las Brisas del Mar to its current incarnation as the Seabreeze Inn, the home had played a crucial part in blessing many lives. Amelia Erickson had started the story, and now it was Ivy's to continue. When she'd stepped on the plane from Boston that would bring her to Summer Beach, she'd been feeling sorry for herself and asking, *Why me?*

Ivy grinned to herself. Now she asked, *Why not me?*

What differences can I make? Lives were entwined in Summer Beach. She saw how Celia had fostered a love of music in young people. Nan and Arthur kept the past alive with their historical research and love of antiques. Megan and Josh would make contributions, too. She paused at the water's edge and spun around, making herself dizzy with possibilities. Some ideas would go on her list, some not.

Ivy thought about everyone she had met here in Summer Beach—though one person stood out.

And there was still an opening on her list.

But wait.

She paused, idly watching shorebirds skittering around her. After spending her adulthood serving her family, she now had freedom. Yet with freedom also came loneliness, despite the people surrounding her. What she missed, she realized, was the intimacy of a partner, of someone she could count on, laugh with. Someone with whom she could be herself and enjoy the moments of life, small and large.

Reflecting on that, Ivy walked through the surf, saltwater frothing around her ankles. Since arriving in Summer Beach, she *had* come to know herself better.

Glancing back, Ivy saw that her thoughts had carried her a long way from the inn. Ahead of her was the marina, where waves lapped against the boats. With her sandals in hand, she turned toward it.

Bennett's boat was near the end of the long walkway. *Could he be there?* An urgent need to see him rose in her, and she'd didn't stop to put on her sandals. Her bare feet slapped against the sun-bleached wooden slats. She trotted past a few people who were cleaning their boats or getting ready to take them out.

"Good morning, Ivy," Jen called out from the boat she and George were repairing.

"Going to be a gorgeous one," Ivy said, her spirits lifting like a full sail in the wind.

Jen stood up, surprised to see her. "Don't see you much here. Want to come aboard? Fresh pot of coffee."

"Can't stop, Jen. See you later."

As Ivy quickened her pace, the sun burst through the clouds. All around her, the palette of blues from sea to sky was an artist's delight, from azure to indigo, from iris to ultramarine. A surge of energy shot through her, propelling her toward the end of the walkway.

And Bennett's boat.

Was he there?

Just ahead, a motor turned over, rumbling. And then, as she drew closer, she saw him. With his hand on the throttle, Bennett eased his boat from its slip.

He hadn't seen her. Was she too late?

She hardly knew how to force out the words lodged in her throat, but she had a desperate need to try. In another few seconds, Bennett would be too far to reach.

"Bennett! Wait," she cried out. "Wait for me."

He eased off the throttle until the boat bobbed in the water. Surprise registered on his face. Tenting his hand, he gazed at her.

Waiting.

On impulse, she dropped her sandals, raised her hands overhead, and dove off the end of the walkway. A cocoon of icy cold water rushed around her, crystallizing her thoughts. She'd forgotten how bone-chilling the Pacific waters were. Gliding under the surface, she spied the hull of Bennett's boat beneath the lapping waves.

Surfacing, she flung her wet hair from her eyes. The time for treading water was over. With powerful strokes, she swam toward his vessel.

As soon as Bennett saw her swimming toward him, he cut the engine and rushed aft. Extending his hands to her, he helped pull her aboard. "Mighty impressive dive."

"When I know what I want, I dive right in." She flung her arms around him.

Without hesitation, he wrapped his arms around her soggy, dripping sundress and lifted her mass of wet hair to kiss her neck. "Do you? Last night you weren't so sure."

Arching her head back into the sun, Ivy reveled in the warmth of his kisses on her skin. "I do. Even if you're abandoning me for the comfort of your ridgetop home."

He chuckled. "Is that it?"

"No," she said softly, shivering slightly in his arms, more from excitement than from the air hitting her wet skin. "Well, maybe a little. Things will be different between us now." Gazing into his adoring eyes, she realized she'd been saving a spot for him on her list all along.

As Bennett pulled away, a smile curved his lips. "On the drive here, I got an emergency call from a client back east. They had a contract pending on a house here, but the deal fell through when the selling couple decided not to get a divorce after all. Good for them, bad for my clients. Now they need to rent a house right away so their children can start the school year in Summer Beach. They wanted to know if I know of any vacant houses."

Ivy's heart fluttered. "The apartment over the garage is

probably too small for them."

"Afraid so."

She looped her arms around his neck, enjoying the feeling of his now damp body against hers. "How can you help them, I wonder?"

Bennett grinned. "I wonder."

"Isn't there a vacant house on the ridge?"

"Might be." He leaned over, nuzzling her neck.

Ivy closed her eyes, her pulse quickening at the touch of his lips. "You could get a good rental price for your place."

"Bet I could." He lifted his head to meet her gaze. "Want to think about it for a while?"

She laughed, though more at herself. "Sometimes I overthink things."

"I love a woman who has a mind of her own."

Ivy teased his lips with her tongue. "I think you should help out your clients." Ivy raised her lips to his. Their relationship wasn't over. In fact, it was just beginning. And making the decision to go for it felt so right.

"You're sure about this?" he asked. "You know what this might mean."

Ivy ruffled his hair and nipped his ear. "I do, and you'd better."

"Wow. All righty then," Bennett said, chuckling.

"Why not check in today?" Ivy suggested. "Your bags are in your car. I'll even help you get settled. The last guest might have left the apartment in a mess. He was in such a hurry this morning."

Bennett grinned. "You were spying on me."

Feeling her face flush, Ivy tilted her chin in defiance. "Maybe I was. For all I knew you were skipping out on the bill."

He laughed and lifted her until her toes dangled above the deck. "I have another idea. My bags are onboard, and Kendra left a few clothes down below. I was heading to Catalina Island for a couple of days off. We can get whatever you need there." A smile played on his lips. "Want to join me and watch the sunset in Catalina Bay?"

"As long as there are many more sunsets to come," Ivy said, lowering her lips onto his eager mouth.

"Yes to that," he murmured in a husky voice, warming her in his embrace. "I've loved you for a long time, Ivy Bay."

And she'd loved him, too, she realized. Her high school surfer crush had deepened into a relationship she never wanted to end. As their bodies melded as one, Ivy knew, without reservation now, that Bennett was the one for her. She was lost in their kiss when she heard cheers and applause from the marina.

Bennett laughed. "I think that's for us."

She glanced back and saw Mitch and Jen and George waving. "Guess this won't be a secret much longer." She threw a hand up and joined them all in laughter.

"Welcome to Summer Beach," Bennett said, waving back at their friends. "Where life is better—and the sunsets never end."

And just to give Bennett a taste of what was ahead, Ivy cradled his face in her hands and kissed him with every drop of love in her heart.

The End

Note from Jan Moran

THANK YOU FOR READING *Seabreeze Sunset*, and I hope you enjoyed it. If you'd like to return to the shores of Summer Beach, then you'll want to read *The Coral Cottage*. Join these sisters as they each seek haven in the family beach house.

To hear about my new releases, please join my VIP Readers Club. Thank you very much for reading.

MORE TO EXPLORE

If you like historical novels set by the sea, you might like to read *The Chocolatier*. Set on the Italian coast of Amalfi, the saga follows a newly widowed chocolatier from San Francisco who discovers her husband's mysterious past. You'll be whisked away into a fascinating world. Between chocolate tastings and fabulous 1950s styles and music, this was one of my favorite books to research.

My next novel is *Hepburn's Necklace,* which is set in beautiful Lake Como, Italy. Find out what happens when a costume designer discovers a necklace that Audrey Hepburn gave her great-aunt—and the long-buried secret its discovery reveals.

And if you like reading contemporary series, you might enjoy my *Love California* collection of linked, standalone books, beginning with *Flawless.* Meet a group of devoted friends and their romantic interests, and join them on their adventures with a trip to Paris, France. My love of travel inspired these stories, so get your literary passport ready.

Books by Jan Moran

Contemporary
Summer Beach: The Coral Cottage Series
The Coral Cottage

Summer Beach: Seabreeze Inn Series
Seabreeze Inn
Seabreeze Summer
Seabreeze Sunset

The Love, California Series:
Flawless
Beauty Mark
Runway
Essence
Style
Sparkle

20th-Century Historical
Hepburn's Necklace
The Chocolatier
The Winemakers: A Novel of Wine and Secrets
Scent of Triumph: A Novel of Perfume and Passion

Nonfiction
Vintage Perfumes

About the Author

Jan Moran is a writer living in southern California. A few of her favorite things include a fine cup of coffee, dark chocolate, fresh flowers, laughter, and music that touches her soul. She loves to travel and her favorite places for inspiration are those rich with history and mystery and set against snowy mountains, palm-treed beaches, or sparkly city lights. Jan is originally from Austin, Texas, although she has lived in California near the beach for years.

Most of her books are available as audiobooks, and her historical fiction is widely translated into German, Italian, Polish, Dutch, Turkish, Russian, Bulgarian, Romanian, Portuguese, and Lithuanian, among other languages.

If you enjoyed this book, please consider leaving a brief review online for your fellow readers where you purchased this book, or on Goodreads. Thank you!

Made in the USA
Middletown, DE
16 May 2020